Nu...

As Nuroc rode to ... by memories of his last few moments ... nia. They had walked alone, hand in hand, in the palace courtyard as he had told her of his recent adventures, and they had spent those last few moments pledging their hearts to one another.

Nuroc knew the rapture could not last, not in the face of what lay before him. The air was dotted with the circling forms of hawks and vultures. A shift in the winds brought with it the carrion scent from the battlefields, where the dead had lain for more than a day.

There were traces of conflict everywhere. Nuroc came across the bodies of several men who had been cut down in their retreat and left to die.

Nuroc was so engrossed with the dead around him that he did not realize he was being watched until he was startled by a deep-throated growl sounding from atop a rise a few dozen feet behind him.

Five kildwolves stared at him through the tendrils of fog, their mouths hung open to expose flesh-rending jaws. Their preference was for freshly-slain meat, and the bodies littering the meadows were long past that state.

Nuroc would provide them with a fair meal—and he knew it . . .

Also by Ross Anton Coe:

WARRIOR OF VENGEANCE #1:

SORCERER'S BLOOD

#2

TRAILS OF PERIL

PINNACLE BOOKS  NEW YORK

This is a work of fiction. All the characters and events portrayed in this book are fictional, and any resemblance to real people or incidents is purely coincidental.

WARRIOR OF VENGEANCE #2: TRAILS OF PERIL

An original Pinnacle Books edition, published for the first time anywhere.

First printing, September 1982

ISBN: 0-523-41710-1

Cover illustration by Romas

Printed in the United States of America

PINNACLE BOOKS, INC.
1430 Broadway
New York, New York 10018

This book is dedicated to my wife, who cheers on the good and points out the bad. . . .

Foreword

> *"What is there to tell of Nuroc,*
> *hero of heroes, champion of Dorban?*
> *Give me hours and I would but light*
> *the wick of his wonder.*
> *Give me days and the candle*
> *of his glory would be no more*
> *than slightly burned. . . ."*
> *—Rambo, bard of Cothe*

Indeed, the task of chronicling the epic saga of Nuroc, servant-born shepherd who came to be the greatest figure of his age, is immeasurably difficult.

It is said that the orators of his time, attempting to confine his exploits to the framework of epic poems, went mad with frustration and took flight from their cities, pulling at their beards and wizened faces, never to be seen nor heard from again. Ancient scribes in the hire of kings and emperors, paid princely sums and treated to accommodations befitting the highest royalty, were known to renounce their commissions and crush their fingers in the wine press rather than attempt to do justice to the tales handed down to them in the time-honored oral tradition. There is even a school of thought that points to certain yellowing scrolls found during recent excavations near Athens and suggests that none other than Homer himself was reluctant to undertake the challenge of the Nuroc stories and opted instead to tackle the *Iliad* and *Odyssey*, works which borrow freely in parts from various episodes in Dorban history.

This being the case, it is only natural to wonder how or why an humble writer such as myself has dared to venture where so many before have failed. An initial incentive lay in the fact that few-to-none of the Nuroc adventures have seen the light of day in several millennia, which leaves me free from the burden of competition with more gifted souls whose accomplished prose would most certainly make my efforts seem woefully inadequate. There is also the realization that we live in a time when heroes of the traditional cloth are hard to find—in books, on film, or, more importantly, in real life. Faced with such a climate of nihilistic cynicism, one cannot resist the urge to step forth and tout a figure who embodies those traits we could all stand to practice with more diligence.

The final, and most compelling reason for launching this vast endeavor is a matter of medical urgency. Since my honeymoon sojourn in Europe three years ago, when I first stumbled upon the long-buried crypt containing the last remaining fragments of scroll, stone tablet, and other media upon which bits and pieces of the Nuroc saga had been written in a dozen forgotten languages, I have been plagued by incessant and recurring dreams, in which the scenes depicted by those undecipherable runes and hieroglyphics are played out in my mind with the vividness of some cinematic extravaganza. Many have been the times my wife has shaken me awake to ask why it was I had been writhing madly about in bed, clutching at the blankets and shouting, "Once I've rid myself of this crawler, you will taste the anger of my sword, Ghetite dog!"

A friend of mine, who dabbles in the occult, set forth the odd theory that my contact with the ancient artifacts (which crumbled to dust within days of being exposed to the polluted air of Athens) had somehow made me a medium through which long-silenced voices from the past sought to ensure that Nuroc would achieve his deserved immortality by way of the printed page, and that it was my chosen duty to see to their bidding. Naturally, I scoffed at this evaluation at first, but after endless months of consultations with so-called scientific specialists, I was still uncured and much the worse for wear from lack of sleep. Recalling my friend's counsel, I began to write my dreams out as best I remembered them. *Voilà!* I found quickly that those dreams that were committed to paper no longer intruded upon my sleep. Thus was borne into life the first saga of Nuroc, *Sorcerer's Blood*. It is my hope that there will come, some day in the none-too-distant future, that time when the dreams will end and I will have managed to relate the full story of Nuroc, intrepid warrior of Dorban.

Until then, this book you hold relates the second installment of that sprawling saga. Although the first offering provides a fuller understanding of Nuroc's origins, I have made every attempt possible to make *Trails of Peril* a self-contained whole, just as future chronicles will exist in their own right, independent of the surrounding history.

Of course, if you failed, for whatever reason, to read *Sorcerer's Blood*, you might be curious to find out how Nuroc came to save the world from imminent destruction just before the time *Trails of Peril* picks up the action. You might also wish to learn about gods who fly down from the skies during the lunar eclipse; about sorcerers who transfuse their blood into others through the recitation of chants and the use of ceremonial daggers, then vanish from sight by plummeting into stone altars that prove to be portals to another realm; about eelsharks, kildwolves, Iatse crawlers and other strange creatures that stand between Nuroc and his destiny; about flesh-peddlers who ply their trade in whoreships and travel from riverport to riverport, seeking young runaways to add to their offerings; about the risen dead who haunt the catacombs that reach beneath Cothe, the greatest city of Dorban, their minds enslaved by the archfiend Augage; about ointments, herbs, plants, and other necromantic paraphernalia used to weave the world in a web of sorcerous intrigue. . . .

But enough. That is another tale. Read it later if you will, but for now, it is time for this, the latest adventure.

Behold, another world. . . .

Ross Anton Coe
February 1982

TRAILS OF PERIL

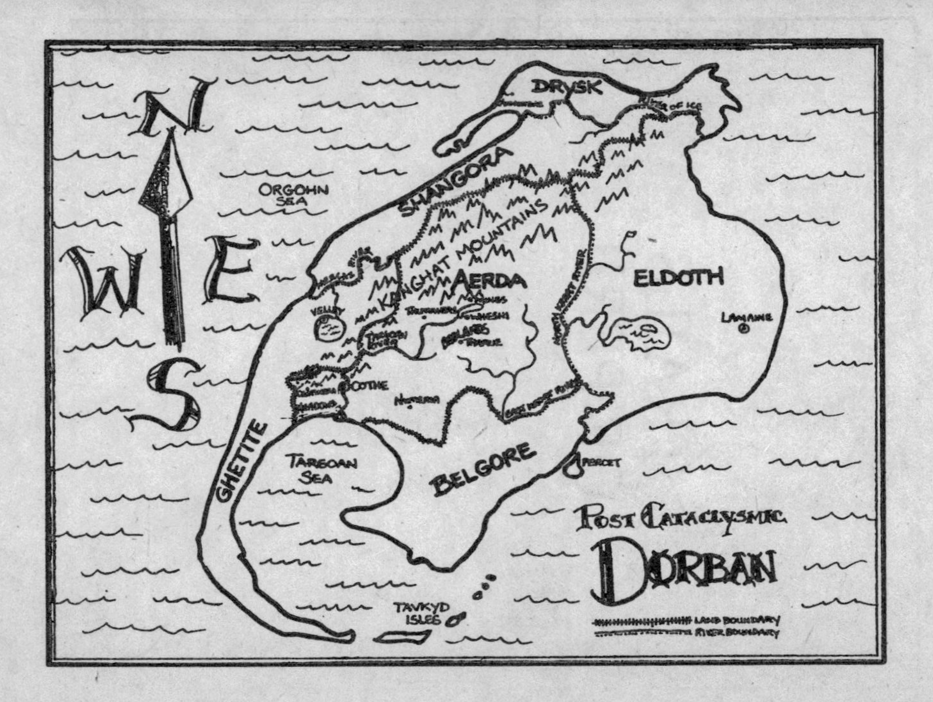
N
W
E
S
ORGOHN SEA
DRYSK
SHANGORA
KANGHAT MOUNTAINS
AERDA
ELDOTH
LAMAINE
NORTH KOBBY RIVER
COTHE
BELGORE
GHETITE
TARGOAN SEA
TAVKYD ISLES
POST CATACLYSMIC
DORBAN
LAND BOUNDARY
RIVER BOUNDARY

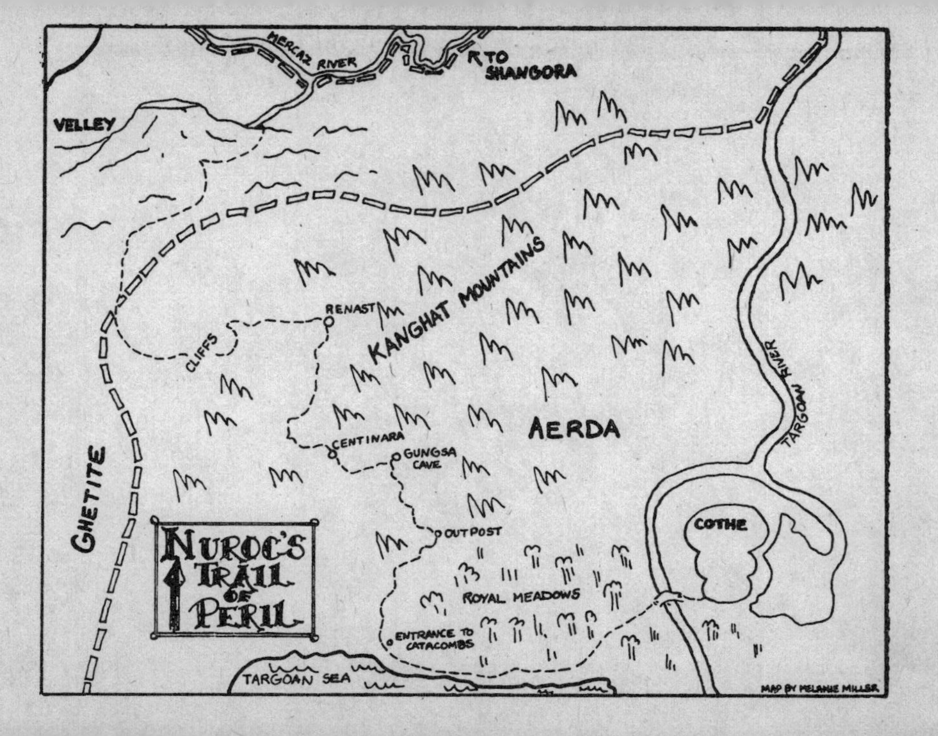

Nuroc's Trail of Peril
Mercaz River
To Shangora
Velley
Renast
Cliffs
Kanghat Mountains
Ghetite
Centinara
Gungsa Cave
Aerda
Targoan River
Cothe
Outpost
Royal Meadows
Entrance to Catacombs
Targoan Sea
Map by Melanie Miller

One

They came from the south. Under cover of the black moon, they forged a wake through the wavering grass of the coastline like a monolithic, drifting shadow, filling the air with the hoof-pummeling thunder of their advance. Ghetites and Shangorans they were, riding side-by-side, hands on reins and weapons, mouths closed tightly as they strained to see the way before them—the way to Cothe and their long-awaited clash with the assembled forces of Aerda, their sworn enemy.

What a battle it would be. Ghetite spies had calculated that the Aerdan capital was defended by no less than eight thousand troops, with more arriving every day. The Ghetite militia was only five thousand strong, so they had turned to Shangora, their neighbors to the north, for assistance. The Shangorans had bargained a stiff price for their part in an alliance, but at last a deal had been struck, and now four thousand of them rode with the Ghetites as they rounded the foothills of the Kanghat Mountains and started across the jagged terrain that led to the royal meadows and, ultimately, to Cothe.

In sheer numbers, Ghetites and Shangorans outnumbered those defending the enemy capital, but the Aerdans had the advantage of the formidable walls that surrounded Cothe. From behind the crenelated stone teeth of the battlements, the Aerdans could fire down upon the attackers without exposing themselves to whatever threat the nine thousand horsemen might present as they seethed about the walls.

There was, however, one factor that would offset this disadvantage and tip the scales in favor of the invaders. As the horsemen urged their steeds on toward the distant winking lights that marked their destination, they curled their sealed lips into confident smiles, looking up to the sky and seeing that no part of the new moon had yet pried its way through the ebon cover of night. The meaning was obvious. Augage, sorcerer-king of the

Ghetites, had succeeded in stealing inside the walls of Cothe and gained access to the long-forbidden obelisk, where he could invoke powerful chants from the hidden moon. Not only would he be able to call down and imprison the mightiest of all gods from the heavens, but Augage would also be able to raise the dead sorcerers of old that lay in crypts beneath the Aerdan capital. With this necromantic legion under his command, Augage was now undoubtedly heading through the underground catacombs toward the strategic opening that would bring them to the surface near the gates to the city. Taking the guards by surprise, Augage's risen horde would assume control of the gates and see that they were opened in time for the arriving horsemen to pour through and engage with the enemy. Whatever toll the riders could not then wreak upon the Aerdans, Augage would inflict with his wizardrous prowess. By dawn, Cothe would fly the flags of Shangora and Ghetite. It would be the first step in the eventual domination of the entire continent of Dorban.

The men in the saddle held dreams not only of conquest, but also of the spoils to be had as their reward for aiding in the victory. Commoners who had been born in squalid huts among the hill tribes before the coming of Augage now yearned for titles and position in the new order. They craved a chance to rule over not only their own lives but the lives of others as well. Augage had proclaimed that those who survived the defeat of the Aerdans would receive grants of land carved from the overthrown kingdom. It would be divided according to performance on the battlefield—the better the warrior, the redder his sword by battle's end, the larger the domain he would have to choose from once Aerda fell under rule of Augage. There might be only room for one king, but under that one king there could be many nobles.

As the Ghetites and Shangorans reached the flattened grasslands of the royal meadows, the number of campfires dotting the mountains that flanked either side of them grew more prevalent, betraying the flitting shadows of the posted enemy guard. The horsemen paid little heed to these Aerdans in the hills. Even when their clarions began to relay the call to battle back to Cothe, they rode on with single-minded intent. There could be no more than a few hundred of the enemy in the Kanghats, and they would not be so foolish as to pit their slim numbers against the mighty horsebound throng. The real fighting would be in Cothe itself. Of that the raiders were certain.

At the head of the formation, which now sent the royal sheep bleating in panic away from the pounding hooves, Molent of Shangora rode upon a coal-black mount. Shorter than his Ghetite counterparts, Molent's light skin was streaked with dark paint to match the deep brown of his woven jupon and boarskin shield. From head to toe, he, like the others, was dressed to blend with the darkness, save for a crown of gold worn over a form-fitting hood of meshed steel and a crimson insignia embroidered on his back. The coming battle was to be one where any advantage could prove crucial to the outcome, and it was the hope of the horsemen that by masking themselves against easy detection, they might keep the Aerdans from guessing the true size of their force.

Molent was king of Shangora, but he had agreed to accept a lesser title under Augage in exchange for an expansion of the territory he would hold dominion over as a prince in the new order. Molent was promised control of the mountainous regions of Aerda, which would provide him not so much an increase in subjects as access to the countless mines from which Aerda had long extracted ore for weapons, gems for jewelry, and sundry other resources with which he could strengthen his position. He would be second in power only to Augage himself. Of course, he speculated in his most private thoughts, should Augage suffer the misfortune of dying during the upcoming battle, it would be Molent who would emerge as the most powerful ruler in all of Dorban.

Molent was plotting in his mind a way to assure Augage's death when he was distracted by a sound coming from the direction of Cothe. It sounded at first like the blast of a war trumpet answering the clarions in the hills, but there was something to the strident peal that struck him as unnatural. He sat upright in the saddle and listened warily above the surrounding clamor of hooves on the grassy terrain. He heard the sound again, and an icy shiver rippled along his spine.

Beside him, General Wheas, head of the Ghetite force, likewise shuddered and turned to Molent as they continued to ride toward Cothe. Wheas was the larger man and the older of the two. His skin, like most Ghetites', was the color of olives. He also wore a headpiece of chain mail.

"I heard it, too," Wheas shouted above the drone of hooves. "Do you think it might be Dorban?"

"I've never heard this sound before, either. It could well be Dorban."

Wheas smiled widely. "It has to be! Augage has succeeded! He's captured the god from the sky and made it his slave! Our victory is assured!"

"Aye," Molent said, casting a swift glance over his shoulder at the thousands of shadowy riders that followed behind him. The sight gave him comfort. He had no great love of sorcery. As for himself, he preferred to use strength one could readily see, not the type that had to be conjured from thin air. Let Augage do his chanting and see that the gates to Cothe were opened, Molent figured. He and Wheas would lead the others in doing the rest. Then, once victory was at hand, he would see that both Augage and Wheas ended up on the wrong end of a sword. And when it was his kingdom he would no longer tolerate sorcery. He would command his territory by use of the military. It was the way he knew best, the way he could keep things in control.

The meadows stretched up a barely discernible incline until the cavalry reached a point providing them an unobstructed view of Cothe, now less than three miles away. The torch-lit battlements betrayed the interlocking ovals of the city walls. The fortress formed the outline of a skull, whose reflection glowed eerily on the adjacent waters of the harbor. Towering above the walls, rising higher than the highest palace spire, was the many-sided stone obelisk in the sorcerers' gardens. Light shone from within the uppermost portal of the obelisk. More than one of the horsemen let out a jubilant cry at the sight, knowing its import.

Then, before their disbelieving eyes, the walls of the distant obelisk wavered, and fell away like withered husks from an ear of corn. Where it had stood, the Ghetites and Shangorans saw a massive winged creature. A dozen times the size of any condor they had ever laid eyes upon, it hovered in the air above the gardens.

"Dorban!" the cry went up, echoing through the ranks with a fearsome urgency. Dorban, the condor-god, had come down from the heavens! Reins were pulled taut and deep-breathing steeds ground to a halt, straining at their bits. In a matter of seconds, the entire formation had ceased its rhythmic advance. Cries faded and the night air fell silent.

One last, piercing screech, unmuffled by stone walls, smote through the uncertain silence, followed by the dull flapping sound of wings as the great bird swept itself away from the city and toward the horsemen.

"Dorban comes to slay us!" one of the Shangorans wailed fearfully. "We have blasphemed the gods!"

"Silence!" Molent shouted, although he himself was racked with a sense of grim terror.

As the condor-god flew over the meadows and began to tilt its flight upward and away from the invading troops, Wheas pointed at the bird. "It's holding something! A man!"

Indeed, there was someone clutched in one of the giant condor's massive talons. As Dorban began to disappear into the inky blackness of the night sky overhead, it released the man, sending him plummeting toward the earth, where he landed with a sickening splash in a shallow marsh close to where Molent and Wheas sat upon their nervous mounts.

Molent gently slapped the rear flank of his steed with the flat of his sword to coax it in the direction of the fallen man. The knot in his stomach tightened. As his horse waded into the murky waters, the warrior saw part of a hideously contorted figure poking up through the surface. The man's robe was torn and stained, and the hood was off the pallid shaven head. The face, even in the darkness, bore a startling countenance that made Molent cringe.

"Augage," he whispered hoarsely, staring at the body. An angry bitterness crept into his voice as he stayed his horse. "Augage the almighty, the all-powerful, has failed."

Another of the horsemen broke the silence behind Molent, shouting, "Look! A new moon!"

Molent looked up and saw it, too. Like a sleepy eye, the razor-thin crescent shone against the surrounding black. Once darkened stars began to give off a dim light, revealing the constellations that adorned the sky. Around the moon, the star-studded outline of a condor came into view. Dorban had returned to its celestial throne, slave to no man, once more ruler of the heavens and the land that bore its name.

Up in the hills, horns were again held to lips and used to sound the renewed call to arms. Ghetites and Shangorans alike fidgeted in their saddles, looking to Wheas for a command to resume their ride on Cothe. The general, however, was reluctant to take action. What he had just witnessed had thrown grave doubts on his strategy for taking over the Aerdan capital. He looked over to the marshes, where the sorcerer had sunk farther into the dark waters.

"What should we do now, Molent?" he asked.

Molent did not answer. He was sniffing the air about him, his brow furrowed with consternation. There was something wrong, something that had nothing to do with the untimely demise of Augage.

Slipping out of the saddle, Molent stepped down into the murk of the swamp, still breathing suspiciously through his nose. He crouched over and ran his hand through the water.

"What is this?" he mumbled to himself, rubbing his fingertips together, feeling a slick, greasy film sticking to his skin. He held the fingers up to his nose, then jerked his hand away and shook the fingers violently before rubbing them on his jupon. Bounding back into the saddle, he turned his steed about and headed back to the others, roaring, "A trick is afoot! They've poured oil into the marsh! Ride, dogs! Make haste!"

But it was too late. Up in the hills on either side of them, hand-held torches were flung in long arcs down toward the meadow floor. Most of them were extinguished with the force of their landing, but several spread their fire to the oily waters of the marsh. Flames leapt upward from the water and raced the length of the marsh, forming a wavering belt that surrounded the entire meadow.

The riders struggled to control their mounts, but the beasts were spooked by the ring of fire that flickered about them like an unbroken wall of flame. Frightened, they neighed and bolted into one another, seeking escape. Several of the horsemen were thrown. They scrambled desperately to avoid the pell-mell crashing of frantic hooves. The less fortunate soon lay dead in the grass with crushed skulls and chests.

Although flames did catch onto the branches of some trees situated too close to the water's edge, most of the meadows were still green and vibrant from recent rains so the fire did not spread from the marshes onto the grass.

Swords readied, Molent and Wheas stared out at the encircling fire. Molent saw flames sweep over the carcass of Augage and begin to devour the sorcerer's robe. Black smoke curled up from the tips of the flames, further obscuring what lay beyond the meadows. Several of the horses ignored the rein-tugging pleas of their riders and lunged headlong into the fiery marshes. There were cries from the horsemen as they vanished into the red haze, and then their voices were abruptly stilled.

"The Aerdans are slaying them as they emerge through the fire," Wheas guessed aloud. He turned to those around him and shouted, "Dismount if you must, but stay on this side of the flames. We have to remain together! Let the blaze burn itself out and then we'll teach these Aerdans how to fight!"

Most of the horses were brought under control once they had overcome their initial fright. Those that continued to rail against their riders were let free and invariably galloped off through the curtain of fire, which burned on relentlessly.

Finally, above the shouts and whinnies, above the crackle of flames, there came the drum of hoofbeats sounding in unison, much like the echo of the cavalry's earlier advance on Cothe. This sound, however, came from the Aerdan capital, and grew louder by the second.

All eyes turned toward Cothe, and the invaders gripped their swords and spears tightly, ready to fight for their lives. The first sign of the Aerdans, however, did not come from the northern city, but from the hillsides on either side of the trapped cavalry. Arrows began to rain down from the mountains, striking randomly within the circle of flame, an alarming percentage imbedding themselves in enemy horses and riders. The dead fell silently. The wounded screamed. Then suddenly arrows ceased to fall upon them.

Surging forward, Aerdan horsemen poured through the flaring veil and split into two separate columns along either inside edge of the fire. "They're trying to surround us!" Molent shouted out. "Retreat! Quick, before they close us in!"

In unison, the raiders veered their horses about and headed through the bent grasses that marked the way by which they had ridden into ambush, the Aerdans racing alongside them. At the head of one Aerdan column rode General Palem, chief aide to King Pencroft. Behind him were the cavalry's elite riding groomed mounts gilded with light armor.

Nuroc led the other column, trailed by his young lover Myrania and the youthful recruits who had accompanied him on his arduous trek to Aerda only days before. Filling out the assaulting force were several thousand more armed horsemen, who continued to ride through the barrier of flame to surround the stunned invaders.

For months, the Ghetites and Shangorans had trained under the assumption that they would be fighting within the tight confines of the Aerdan capital. To find that the Aerdans were confronting them on horseback in the open meadows was as incredulous an occurrence as any they had so far witnessed on this fateful evening.

Nuroc felt both apprehension and excitement as he rode before his half of the six thousand Aerdans who had charged forth from Cothe, leaving the rest of their number to defend the capital. To his right, the marsh seethed with unnatural illumination, throwing off a heat he could feel through the sweat of his exertion. The Ghetite and Shangoran cavalry was coming to grips with the ambush on his left, and the sight of their swarming numbers staggered him. He had imagined that the Aerdans were overreacting with the number of troops Palem had dispatched into battle, but he now realized that, if anything, they were vastly outnumbered by the enemy.

His light hair flapped about his head in the breeze and, out the corner of his steely gray eyes, he could see Myrania driving her horse on to keep up with him. Her windblown face was radiant with maturing beauty, and in the scintillating depths of her cobalt eyes he saw both loving devotion and a free spirit entwined by the force of their love. In contrast to the winsome allure of her features and full figure, the sword clenched tightly in her hand gave her an aura of menace. She was like an angel of vengeance come to claim her due.

"Revenge!" she shouted out to Nuroc. "This spawn of Augage will pay dearly for what we have suffered!"

Nuroc's teeth were clenched and he could only nod his agreement before turning his attention back to the way before him. But fresh memories were stirred up by Myrania's cry, and he recalled with growing wrath the savage butchery of his family by a small band of Ghetites and Shangorans only days before. It was that act of treachery that had propelled him into the fantastic chain of events that now put him in the position to strike back against those he had come to loathe. He also remembered the soul-churning sight of Myrania's father bobbing lifelessly in the flood-filled caves along the coast the previous evening. That had been Augage's doing, but in Nuroc's and Myrania's minds Augage and his disciples were one and the same—avowed enemies marked for death.

The closest Ghetites and Shangorans were more than fifty yards away, but the distance was closing fast as the Aerdans followed either side of the curving wall of fire toward the coast and the spot through which the enemy would have to attempt its retreat. Between the adversaries, there were more than fourteen thousand weapons waved in the air threateningly, but the first blows had yet to occur. It almost seemed as if the assembled forces were mutually allied and putting on a demonstration of riding prowess for the benefit of the gods and goddesses outlined by the constellations overhead. Even the deities would have to be impressed by the thundering formations surrounded by the arena of burning marsh.

Soon Nuroc's force was heading straight toward that of Palem. Like the pincers of a crab, the two flanks of Aerdan horsemen had closed in around the invaders before they could ride free of the entrapment.

"Well done, youngster!" Palem shouted as the two flanks merged together and turned about to meet the oncoming Ghetites and Shangorans. The general even flashed a grin at his counterpart, as if to announce a cessation of the ill feelings he had held toward Nuroc ever since his arrival in Cothe the day before. Nuroc had no chance to reply, however, before the enemy was upon them, brandishing swords and pikes with a grim ferocity as they tried to hack their way toward escape or victory.

Shouting orders, King Molent and General Wheas backed their horses away from the thick of battle, placing as many of their subjects between them and the death-dealing Aerdans as possible. There was no order to the confrontation any longer, and there could be no tactics or strategy other than fending off whatever foe was closest at hand. Bathed in the flickering light cast by the blazing swamp, the forces clashed chaotically.

Nuroc had never fought from the saddle before, and he felt uncomfortable trying to wield his sword and keep his balance simultaneously. He managed as best he could, however, knowing that to leave his mount and attempt to fight on foot would mean certain death.

Jerking on the reins of his horse, he met the charge of his first aggressor. The advancing Shangoran rode into him broadside, but Nuroc was prepared for the collision and kept a firm hold on his saddle. Not so the Shangoran, who went wild-eyed with confusion as his horse butted into Nuroc's and threw him off-balance. Wrested from his saddle, he fell easy prey to the swipe of Nuroc's sword and slumped to the ground, his chest carved open. He spat blood twice and died. The dead man's steed kicked its front hooves in the air, just missing Nuroc, and raced off into the surrounding pandemonium.

His sword baptized in the blood of the enemy, Nuroc pulled his stallion about and cut down several more opponents as he fought his way back toward Myrania. The sorceress was in no position to defend herself with whispered chants or mere waves of the hand. Fortunately, she was no stranger to the sword and traded proficient blows with a feisty Ghetite near the edge of the marsh, where flames continued to dance like vibrant specters.

The Ghetite flashed his sword defiantly, but Myrania parried each assault with a sure grace that made Nuroc proud. Before he could reach her side, she dispatched the Ghetite by locking blades and moving him from his horse into the marsh. Flames immediately devoured his uniform, and he howled in agony as he tried to douse the flame by splashing even more of the burning water on himself. Soon he was entirely ablaze, silenced by the blistering heat. He slumped beneath the water and failed to surface again.

Myrania rode away from her vanquished foe and smirked at the look of worry stamped on Nuroc's face.

"Surprised to see I can defend myself?" she taunted as she brought her horse alongside Nuroc's.

"After all I've gone through to have you back at my side, I'm not about to see you felled by one of these curs," Nuroc replied evenly.

"In that case, let's see to it that we're rid of them once and for all." Myrania rode ahead of Nuroc and put her sword to use on the next assailant. Nuroc followed, leaning away from the spear thrust at him by a charging Shangoran. He slew the raider and quickly snatched up the dead man's shield, putting it to immediate use deflecting an ax blow from a Ghetite who tried to take him from behind.

"Coward!" Nuroc howled, turning in his saddle to face his latest foe. "Let's see how you fare face-to-face!"

The Ghetite managed to bring his ax around in time to block Nuroc's first swipe, but before he could move in offensively, Nuroc brought his sword around in a vicious blur. The blade bit deeply into the Ghetite's side, splintering ribs as it sought out the man's heart. Dropping his ax, the raider's eyes went blank and he slumped lifelessly over his horse.

The toll taken by Nuroc and Myrania was magnified by the other Aerdans, who lashed out at the enemy with vengeful zeal. Ghetites and Shangorans were dying as fast as their dreams of conquest. The combined shock of Augage's downfall and the fiery swiftness of the Aerdan ambush had shattered any strength of unity they might have mustered as their best defense. Their advantage in numbers quickly dwindled until the two sides were evenly matched.

Molent and Wheas were able to hold control over those troops acting as their buffer from the onslaught of the Aerdans, but the rest of the invaders were caught in the grips of hysteria. Concerned only with their own survival, they let their comrades fall beneath Aerdan blades as they spurred their chargers toward the edge of the battling masses, where they hoped to ride through the fire and escape in retreat. Few of them succeeded in this ploy. The majority of those who managed to ride beyond the fiery circle were instantly cut down by Aerdan archers descending from the hills.

The recruits fought well alongside their more seasoned comrades. Bordo, the boastful Thutcherian with a face of a child, slashed at the opposition with deadly accuracy. Tudier, Nuroc's short and wiry friend, licked at his thin moustache between strokes of his sword, concentrating fully on the life-and-death struggle before him, making each blow count. Caught up in the heart of the battle, he knew there would be no refuge were he to let his swordarm tire to the point where he could neither defend himself or maintain his hellish offensive. For each adversary he cut down, there were two more to take his place. Three thousand of the enemy had already fallen on the blood-drenched sward, and another two thousand had taken their chances on flight, but that still left four thousand raging Ghetites and Shangorans to contend with, and they were fueled by a hateful rage for their ambushers.

The discordant clamor of clashing swords resounded through the smoke-streaked air as the seconds stretched out into grueling minutes, which in turn bled into hours. Night surrendered to the gray tinge of dawn, and still the fighting continued. Kites and vultures began to fill the air above the battlefield, and four-legged predators crept forth from hiding, all lured by the promising scent of carrion hanging in the slight offshore breeze. The trampled meadows heard the moans of the dying and the curses of those still engaged with the enemy. Men stared through hazes of blood and sweat, shaking off the fatigue that crouched upon their shoulders, and whispered for them to relent in their fighting long enough to rest. Few heeded such calls, because any rest at this point was apt to prove permanent.

It was morning by the time the oil in the marshes had been

consumed and the rays of the sun began to pry through the dissipating smoke, revealing the bleak fruit of carnage. The dead were piled in layers, covering the grass like a grisly carpet of errant limbs and spattered gore. Blood covered everything as if it had rained down upon the battlefield. More than fourteen thousand men had met on this stretch of land hours before. Now only a few hundred were left among the living, far outnumbered by riderless horses that sought out an unsure footing between the bodies of the dead. The surviving Ghetities and Shangorans were outnumbered five to one by Aerdans, and once they realized as much the invaders threw down their weapons and held their hands outward in a gesture of surrender.

Chest heaving with exhaustion, Nuroc wiped sweat from his brow and staggered over to Myrania, who had slumped down to rest against the flanks of a slain horse. They were both streaked with cuts that trailed blood, and their tunics, tattered before the fighting had begun, now barely held together. Nuroc pulled off a woven surcoat from the body closest to him and handed it to Myrania as he helped her to her feet.

"Here," he gasped. "Are you all right?"

"I'm in one piece, I think," she answered wearily, slipping into the garb. "How about you?"

Nuroc nodded and embraced the woman. They kissed briefly, then walked side-by-side over the strewn casualties toward the edge of the battlefield, where the other surviving Aerdans were rounding up prisoners. Palem was overseeing the men with one of his arms wrapped in a makeshift dressing soaked through with blood. Another strip of clothing was bound tightly about his head.

"So," Palem commented at the sight of Nuroc and Myrania, "it would seem you two work well as a team."

"We're alive," Nuroc affirmed absently as his eyes roved over the faces of the survivors. His face clouded when he realized that only a handful of the recruits were among those still on their feet. Bordo was standing guard over prisoners, clutching a wadded piece of cloth over a wound on his swordarm.

"Good to see you, Nuroc," he offered with a weak smile.

"Where is Tudier?" Nuroc asked worriedly. "And the others?"

Bordo took a deep breath and shook his head. "I saw Roere and Fafhe die back near the marshes. I haven't seen the others."

Beside Nuroc, Myrania began to sway uncertainly on her feet.

Nuroc noticed and reached out, placing his arm around her and guiding her to the charred stump of an overturned tree.

"Rest here," Nuroc said. "I want to look for the others."

Nuroc joined a few other Aerdans and waded back through the battlefield to gather up the treatable wounded. It was a gruesome sight, and Nuroc felt a sickness in his heart at the magnitude of the slaughter. Future generations would bemoan the toll of this battle, wonder futilely how the course of Dorban would have changed had so many men not died in the prime of their lives. Aerda had been spared the threat of overthrow, but they had suffered an irreparable loss in the process.

Nuroc spotted the bodies of Roere and Fafhe, as well as those of other recruits from Thutchers. But he found no trace of Tudier, his closest friend among those with whom he had shared the first taste of battle, days before on the Targoan River. The short, spirited recruit was missing, as were more than a dozen of his companions.

Beyond the marshes, where the bodies were less prominent, the royal sheep bleated nervously. The Aerdan archers who had first spotted the Ghetites and Shangorans the previous night now milled about the edge of the battlefield, lending what help they could.

Nuroc came over to one of the archers and asked, "Did you see any men leave the battlefield?"

The archer nodded. "Of course. Ours and theirs alike. Hundreds of them. Ghetites and Shangorans whipping their horses as if they were possessed, heading back to their border. Our men rode after them as fast as they could. So did some of the recruits like yourself."

Nuroc felt a twinge of hope at this revelation. He turned his eyes toward the coast, seeing the myriad paths beaten in the grass. Yes, Tudier had to be among those who gave chase to the retreating foe. Tudier and the others. Soon they'd be back, leading a string of prisoners at swordpoint or waving the blades they'd reddened cutting down the enemy.

His spirits slightly risen, Nuroc helped another of the men carry a wounded soldier back to where Palem was pacing furiously before the captured soldiers.

"They got away, curse them!" he scowled bitterly, kicking up dirt.

"Who do you mean?" Nuroc said, glancing over at Myrania,

who stood shakily and offered him a feeble smile that did little to offset her ailing expression.

"Molent and Wheas!" Palem snapped angrily. "They're gone! Our one chance to snuff the enemy and we let Augage's top henchmen escape our clutches!"

"All the bodies haven't been checked yet," Nuroc said. "We still might find them among the dead."

"Hardly a chance of that," Palem brooded. "In this light the chain mail of their hoods would be shining like diamonds. I tell you, they're gone and you can be sure there will be hell to pay once King Pencroft learns of our failure."

Nuroc came over to Myrania and said, "You still look ill. Sit back down."

Myrania shook her head irritably. "I've just lost a little blood is all." Her voice weakened with each word she spoke, however, and Nuroc once again was forced to hold her up as she sagged to her knees.

The first of several ox-drawn carts was arriving at the battlefield to load the wounded for transport back to Cothe. Nuroc carried Myrania in his arms over to the cart. She draped her arms around his thick shoulders and rested her head against his firm neck. He could feel the intense heat on her brow.

"See to her first," Nuroc told Hoarth, the elderly man who was dabbing at the wounded with cloth strips soaked in scented ointments. Nuroc placed Myrania on the cart and laid her out. Her eyes were closed and she was breathing irregularly.

"What was that woman doing on the battlefield?" the old man said with a tone of annoyance.

"If you would have seen the way she handled herself you wouldn't speak so. She swings a sword as well as any man."

The medic looked Myrania over, squinting at wounds and gently stroking her bruised flesh. "She'll live, sure enough," he finally pronounced as he began cleaning off the deepest of the slash wounds across her lower leg. She groaned at the sting of the ointment, but did not open her eyes.

"Are you certain?" Nuroc asked nervously, watching his beloved.

"I'm not an oracle," Hoarth grumbled. "I only know that none of these wounds seem fatal. There are a few that will take some time in healing, but that's the worst of it. She's a lot better off than some of the others." He jerked his head to the back of the cart, where moaning soldiers displayed missing limbs or deep stab wounds.

"I appreciate your help," Nuroc offered.

"And I appreciate your concern," Hoarth replied. "If I had a woman this beautiful, I'd look out for her, too. Tell me, lad, is it true what they say about King Molent and General Wheas? Did they truly escape?"

"We still have men out in search of them," Nuroc said. "But Augage has been slain and Cothe has been spared from attack. That's the important thing."

The old man slowly shook his head as he finished dressing Myrania's wounds. "You don't understand, lad. The capital could have withstood attack without the loss of life and limb you see out there before you. We took the offensive because King Pencroft thought we could crush both Ghetite and Shangora at once. With Molent and Wheas loose, neither country can be deemed truly vanquished. We have won the battle, but I fear we must now suffer through a prolonged war. We've wasted the lives of many good men, gambling that it would all end here. Now, if you'll let me see to the others. . . ."

As the medic walked to the other end of the cart and began working on a soldier who had lost several fingers in the fighting, Nuroc stayed at Myrania's side, stroking her feverish brow and feeling a profound sadness. He saw Palem still fuming nearby and understood the general's chagrin. This was not the end of the conflict between Aerda and the alliance of the Ghetite and Shangora. It was only the beginning. . . .

Two

The throne room in Cothe was an opulent chamber, with the gleam of polished marble reflecting the glint of oil lamps. Vaulted ceilings reached into darkness, swallowing sounds and giving them back with an echoing din. Finely woven tapestries hung from the stone walls to buffer the chill. The hangings were large, two dozen feet high and twice as long across, depicting historical scenes that glorified highlights of the kingdom's first five years after the overthrow of Tàlmon-Khash's empire, which had once encompassed the entire continent. It was not surprising that the central figure in all the tapestries was King Pencroft, assuming a stoic grandeur in poses as warrior, statesman and ruler. Larger than life, he was depicted in the hangings as tall and forbidding, with ruggedly handsome features and clear, somber eyes.

The fleshly king who paced before his likeness was a less imposing figure. Beneath the scintillating crown and plush robe, Pencroft's countenance was bland and a visible paunch hung about his waist. Since assuming the throne of his self-created kingdom, he had turned his back largely on the rigors of physical training in favor of the political schemings required to maintain his position of power. While his physical appearance did not match the renderings made by his favored artisans, any foe who misjudged the shrewd mind lurking behind the king's slowly aging flesh would soon learn—usually at great expense—that he ruled by his wit and cunning rather than his appearance.

As Pencroft continued to stride in circles before his golden throne, General Palem stood by watching him, gauging the king's reaction to the news he had just imparted. Palem felt uneasy. He had never seen the king act in this matter. Pencroft was not a man to brood or mull over his thoughts. By nature, Aerda's king was the sort who seized upon his impulses and lived by their counsel. Some called him hard and unyielding; others saw the same traits and called him wise and committed. The man Palem watched seemed none of these. The news of the heavy casualties and the escape of Molent and Wheas had struck Pencroft deeply. His downcast eyes were clouded with doubt, sorrow, and even a trace of fear. It had been *his* decision to send the troops out from the security of Cothe's walls to engage with the enemy. He had thought the act would lessen the death toll and at the same time secure a more certain defeat of the enemy. Neither result had come to pass, and he would have to live with the consequences of that decision.

"What a hollow victory," he finally said, his voice empty. "Aerda is ruled by a fool."

Palem stepped forward and cleared his throat. "You had no way of knowing the outcome, your majesty. The plan was sound, the intention noble, the—"

"That means nothing now," Pencroft interrupted, forcing aside his feelings and concentrating on his duties as king. "What matters now is that we have lost almost half our entire military force in neutralizing the Ghetites and Shangorans. We have left our other borders inadequately defended and now we are short of men to guard against invasion from other quarters."

"But, your majesty, we are in alliance with both Eldoth and Belgore. They will surely make no move to take advantage of the situation."

Pencroft looked at Palem and snorted contemptuously. "Eldoth and Belgore have been tenuous allies at best, kept from moving against us only because of the strength of our militia. With that strength gone, what is to prevent them from moving to extend their boundaries across our undefended land?"

"Gratitude, perhaps," Palem suggested. "After all, the Ghetites and Shangorans posed a threat to them as well as us. By our sacrifice, we have all but eliminated the chance that Eldoth or Belgore might fall under domination of the sorcerous alliance."

As Palem spoke, the king strode away from his throne and made his way to the one wall in the swollen chamber that was not covered by a single tapestry. A series of windows carved out of the marble lined the wall, covered by velvet draperies that rustled slightly from an outside breeze. Pencroft tugged aside the curtains blanketing the largest of the windows and squinted as the light of day poured into the chamber. The warmth of the rays felt good and he tilted his head upward, smiling slightly at the welcome sensation.

Palem warily followed the king to the window and tied the curtains in place so that they remained open. He waited for a response, but when Pencroft continued to stand with his eyes closed the general realized the king was lost in thought. Pencroft's eyes slowly opened and he continued to stare out the window, the smile widening on his face.

"What is it, your majesty?" Palem finally asked.

"Take a look down below and tell me what you see," Pencroft said calmly.

Palem frowned and glanced out the opening. The throne room was on the third level of the palace, which was situated adjacent to the twenty-foot high wall separating the sorcerers' gardens from the rest of the city. Declared forbidden grounds since the sorcerers fled to Ghetite five years before in the wake of the Great Cataclysm, the gardens were overgrown with untended flora, save for one quadrant that was studded with dolmens and stone markers showing where the people of Cothe had taken to burying their dead the past few years. A crew could be seen there now, tending to the burial of casualties from the bloodbath in the meadows earlier that morning. The sound of spades biting into the rich soil carried all the way to where Palem and the king stood. In the center of the gardens, where the sorcerer-kings of old had once held power over all of Dorban, the splintered fragments of the fallen obelisk lay in a ruinous heap, spilling over the edge of the island that had served as its foundation and into the turgid waters of the moat that set the former ruling seat aside from the rest of the gardens. Beyond the far walls surrounding the gardens, Palem could see the edge of the harbor and the rolling foothills that gave way to the Kanghat Mountains. It was, all in all, an awesome sight.

"I see the reminders of days when sorcerers sat on the throne in Cothe," Palem said uncertainly. "I am afraid I miss your point, your majesty."

Pencroft turned to his general and said, "Five years ago, while I was far from Cothe doing duty along the River Kroat, there was revolt here at the capital. The townspeople were joined by stragglers who had survived the cataclysm in storming these gardens. You remember that time, I trust."

General Palem nodded his head. "I was there, your majesty. I helped instigate the revolt. You know as much. It was one of the reasons you put me in so high a position when you came into power."

Pencroft went on as if Palem had not spoken. "You were there and you were also among those who gained entry to the obelisk and confronted Talmon-Khash before he drove you off with his last act of necromancy and sealed off the tower so that no one could enter."

"Yes, but—"

"Then you know of the wealth that was kept in the obelisk," Pencroft continued patiently.

At last Palem began to understand, and a faint smile began to play upon his features as well. "What a fortune it was," he said, recalling the discovery. "Jewels, precious stones, statues and figurines . . . there were pieces of the like I've never laid eyes upon before. And no wonder. No doubt much of the wealth goes back a hundred . . . nay, a thousand generations."

Pencroft turned away from the window and fell back to his pacing. With one hand he stroked at the thin strip of beard framing his once-square jaw. Gone was the remorse in his eyes, replaced by the sparkle of vitality that belied his racing thoughts.

"The riches of the obelisk are known throughout the land," he said excitedly. "King Onfeons of Belgore and Yute of Eldoth would both pay any price for a share of that fortune."

"Even allegiance," Palem said with a grin.

"Exactly!" Pencroft said excitedly. "If I agree to share the spoils of the obelisk with them, they will most certainly agree to honor our existing borders. Not only that, but I may be able to earn their assistance in tracking down Molent and Wheas and whatever scrap of followers they might try to put together in hopes of salvaging their dreams of domination."

Pencroft climbed the few steps to the dais containing his throne and sat down, relishing once again the power inherent in his position. He had come up with a plan for making the best of his position. The cost had been high, but in the end it would prove worth it. He was positive of it.

General Palem, however, suffered an instant and disturbing change in temperamant. He backtracked to the window and glanced back down at the ruins of the obelisk, his face growing dark.

"What is it, Palem?" Pencroft called out from the throne.

Palem turned around and faced the king, saying, "The obelisk has fallen when it was thought to be indestructible. I can see no trace of the treasure beneath the rubble. What if it is no longer there?"

"Impossible!" the king shouted.

"What if Dorban destroyed the treasure the same way he destroyed the obelisk?"

Pencroft rose from the throne and hastened back to the window. He pointed at the ruins and said, "Look how the slabs of broken stone lie on one another. The foundation is completely covered, so of course you cannot see any jewels. That does not mean they aren't there."

"It also doesn't mean they are," Palem said, stiffening at his brashness.

"They are there . . . because they have to be!" the king uttered. "They have to be! Go and prepare a crew to begin excavation immediately."

Palem saluted and started off. His bootheels sounded loudly on the marble floor as he headed for the arched doorway at the far end of the room, where two sentries stood at motionless attention in their ornate uniforms.

"Wait!" Pencroft called out from the window. Palem stopped and looked back at the king. "Before you begin that task, see that messengers are dispatched immediately to both Eldoth and Belgore. Have them take word of the battle, but do not have them say how many of our men were lost. Make sure Onfeons and Yute know that an equal share of the loot from the obelisk will be theirs provided they personally come to claim their portions. That way I will have them within my reach should their armies choose to strike against our borders."

Palem saluted again, beaming his approval. "It shall be done. An excellent plan, your majesty."

Once the general was gone, King Pencroft returned to his throne and sat, pleased with himself. If he schemed correctly, there would soon come the day when he and the kings of Eldoth and Belgore would be dividing not only the wealth of the sorcerer-kings, but their land as well.

Three

Only a narrow shaft of daylight penetrated the subterranean gloom of the stonewalled chamber where Nuroc dozed on a straw-lined cot, wearing the issued woolen tunic that designated his status as a member of the Aerdan militia. Like the other survivors of the battle, he had been fed and treated for his wounds before being taken to the underground area directly beneath the coliseum. In the welcome silent darkness, they had all quickly succumbed to the racking fatigue that had dogged them since the waning hours of the battle. Few cared that their beds lay in stalls normally set aside for the lodging of horses used in chariot races. Many of those steeds had been pressed into service during the clash in the meadows; those that had not died in battle were corraled in the stables by the harbor for the time being.

A light beam reached down through an airshaft connecting the chamber with the open air of the coliseum, and with the passage of time it slanted across the packed dirt of the floor and up the side of the cot, finally falling on Nuroc's face and waking him.

He tried at first to turn over and fall asleep again, but it was too late. He was kept up not only by the dull pain of his many superficial wounds and the strain of every muscle in his body, but also by the raucous chorus of snores emanating from the other stalls surrounding him. With a groan, he finally sat up in the cot and rubbed the sleep from his eyes.

Across from him, Bordo lay in a limp sprawl on his cot, breathing loudly through his half-opened mouth. As he stood up, stretched, and began to walk down the wide aisle separating the two rows of stalls, Nuroc saw that the others were equally oblivious to the world around them. More shafts of light beamed down on the stalls, providing the only light in the area. Nuroc could barely make out the features of his fellow soldiers, but he could see enough of them to realize that Myrania was not among their numbers.

Worry began to taunt him, and he made his way out of the underground stables and into the adjacent tunnel, where a guard stood leaning against the wall with a bored expression on his face. Nuroc didn't recognize him, but he still asked, "I'm looking for Myrania. Where is she?"

The guard smirked lightly as he regarded Nuroc. "She? There's no women to be had down here, soldier. The officers up above might have gotten their hands on a few wenches for sport, but I don't think that you'll be—"

"She was on the battlefield this morning while you were probably down here cleaning the stables," Nuroc said hotly, taking a step toward the guard and eyeing him narrowly. "Now where is she?"

The guard put his hand to the hilt of his sword and returned Nuroc a scowl of his own. "You'd be wise to treat those who outrank you with a better show of respect, recruit. And don't reach for your sword or I'll slice your hand off before you can blink."

Nuroc saw the fierce malice in the other man's gaze and decided not to test the guard's threat. He took a step back instead, saying, "Forgive my temper. It's been a long few days for me."

"For you and all the rest of us, soldier," the guard said coolly, keeping his hand on his sword. His expression softened some, however, and he added, "If this woman you seek was truly among our warriors, she might be among the wounded being treated up above in the medical tents. I shouldn't let you pass because of your insolence, but since you are new, I will make an exception this once." He moved to one side and gestured Nuroc through the passage.

"My thanks," Nuroc muttered, holding his temper in check as he walked by the soldier, who chuckled lightly to himself with self-amusement at his show of rank. Nuroc realized there were certain things about being a soldier that would take some getting used to.

The tunnel he proceeded down was lit by oil lamps, which filled the air with a pungent, uncomfortable smell and blackened the walls with the taint of smoke. He passed an opening and looked in at a large chamber filled with unused chariots, lined in careful, dusty formation, awaiting the return of summer afternoons when they would be put to use again in the entertaining races held for the pleasure of the masses. During the twelve years Nuroc had lived in the sorcerers' gardens, as son to the servants of Talmon-Khash, he had often heard the gatherings in the coliseum and longed to witness the games, but because of his position he had never been allowed to attend. Later, during his years of refuge in the northern hamlet of Wheshi, he had had the opportunity to participate in sporting games at the tournament field outside of town, but the scale of those events was undoubtedly overshadowed by the spectacles held in the arena of Cothe. Perhaps, once order had been fully restored and the evacuated masses had returned to the city, he would have his chance to view a chariot race and share in the enthusiasm of the other spectators.

Nuroc soon came to a fork in the tunnel. More sunlight poured down the shaft to his left, and he was about to head that way when he was distracted by a sound coming from the other direction. It was a guttural snort, akin to that made by the wild beasts he had encountered in the Kanghat Mountains near his most recent home. Intrigued, he proceeded down the right corridor until a series of barred cells containing a variety of magnificent, deadly beasts came into view. The animals were placed in the cells in twos, according to species. Nuroc recognized the wildebeests from his trip down the Targoan River several days before, and felt a renewed sense of relief that the fierce gnus with their lethally spiked horns had not come within striking range of his ship. There were also pairs of Shangoran lions, hill tigers, and the largest wild boars he had ever laid eyes on.

There was a moment's silence as the beasts turned their eyes on Nuroc, whose hand reflexively fell on the pommel of his sword. The tigers were the first to move, lunging forward against the bars that confined them. Kept from reaching their prey, the beasts snarled loudly and stabbed through the bars with their claw-lined paws. The other animals reacted with similar aggression, and Nuroc backed away from the sight with his blood racing and his nerves tensed. When his back brushed up against something blocking his way in the tunnel, he leapt to one side and jerked out his blade.

"Whoah, now, lad," wheezed an old man in a ragged smock as he staggered away from the edge of Nuroc's sword. "I've just come to see who roused my beasts. Don't be skewering me for their supper now."

Nuroc recovered his wits and sheathed the sword. "You gave me a start, old man."

"You're lucky I didn't give you more than that," the old man answered irritably. "Since you and your men have taken over this place, my beasts haven't been out of their cages once. They're in a foul mood and you've only helped them along."

"I meant no harm," Nuroc said, watching on as the man carried two wooden pails over to the cage, where the trapped animals continued to beat and rail at the bars holding them in captivity. The man set down the buckets and began taking out strips of raw meat and bound stalks of ripe green wiirhal and tossing them into the cages. The beasts turned their attention to the food, ceasing their fierce growling as they scrambled for the meat and began tearing at it and the greens with their powerful jaws.

"Those are the beasts you pit against criminals in the arena on festival days," Nuroc guessed, watching the hill tigers bat their chunks of meat across the cell, then race each other to pounce on the food, snapping at it with their yellow fangs. Nuroc saw the ravaged meat and shuddered, thinking of the fate of those set in the arena to face such tigers, armed only with a knife and shield.

"That they are," the old man said, throwing the last of the meat to the boars. "Executioners. That's what my beasts are. They bring death as surely as the hooded axman at the chopping block."

"But I've heard of men who have successfully stood up to the beasts," Nuroc said.

The keeper stood back next to Nuroc but continued to look at his animals with a look of intense pride, saying, "My beasts spare only those whom the king requests be spared. Still, few have slain my beasts in the arena. Five years I've tended to the beasts—ever since they were taken from the sorcerers' gardens—

and some of those same beasts are still alive. Look yonder at the larger of the hill tigers. It was a cub when I found it in the gardens. Now it is full-grown and has executed five dozen men in the past two years without suffering so much as a scratch at the hands of a fighter in the arena."

Nuroc observed the magnificent feline. It easily weighed as much as any two men and snapped at its supper of raw meat with teeth the size of fingers. The rich brown stripes encircling its enormous body almost blended in with the tawny hue of its fur.

"I must go," Nuroc said, turning away from the old man.

"I hear tell that there will be a grand celebration in the coliseum once the citizens of Cothe have all returned to the city," the keeper rambled on, unaware that Nuroc was leaving his company. "Any uncooperative prisoners among the Ghetites and Shangorans will face my beasts in the arena. That will be a sight indeed. . . ."

As the old man kept up his soliloquy and stared at his deadly menagerie, Nuroc stole away and rushed down the other leg of the tunnel, which veered and tilted upward, eventually leading to the arena inside the coliseum.

"By the gods," Nuroc muttered in awe at the sight. The sun stretched his shadow far across the dirt of the arena floor, which betrayed the recent presence of soldiers who had used the area for training drills. It was silent within the rounded walls of the stadium, and Nuroc's mind seemed to prance with rampant imagination. As he slowly strode across the center of the arena, Nuroc looked around at the endless rows of stone benches rising up to the rim of the structure. He felt an ominous, haunting presence in the air about him. It was as if the unseen eyes of twelve thousand slain warriors were staring down at him from the empty seats, demanding an explanation from him as to why he had managed to survive the conflict that had just claimed them.

"I defied death in the meadows because I was the better warrior," Nuroc cried out impulsively before realizing the folly of his outburst. His words echoed off the empty stands and came back at him mockingly.

No sooner had his echoing words faded in the still air than they were replaced by a faint roar sounding from behind him. The roar repeated and grew louder, filling the arena. Stunned, Nuroc wheeled about.

"It can't be!"

Lumbering into the arena with a confident gait was none other than the hill tiger Nuroc had been told about only minutes before. The great cat raised small clouds of dust from the ground as it cleared the tunnel and started into the arena. Suddenly the beast stopped and trained its eyes on Nuroc.

Nuroc stayed as still as he could, yet he slowly reached to his side and slipped his fingers around the hilt of his sword. He had nothing to pass for a shield. He longed to call out for the old trainer to call off this elaborate prank, but he feared that such a cry would only confirm his fear that no prank was afoot and bring the beast charging forward with the thought of rendering him into lifeless flesh.

The tiger held its position as well, turning its head to one side and giving off a threatening growl. Nuroc carefully looked around him for the closest cover and realized that he was more than a hundred feet from the nearest barrier. There was no chance for him to outrun the tiger to safety. His only choice was to fight or die.

The tiger fell silent and turned away from Nuroc. To Nuroc's amazement, the beast began to bound along the hardened dirt track that ran around the edge of the arena. Pulling his sword out, Nuroc watched the tiger slowly build up its speed in long, graceful strides. Just as Nuroc was beginning to wonder if he might be spared a confrontation after all, the mighty predator abruptly veered its course and began charging straight for Nuroc.

Bending to a slight crouch, Nuroc stared at the oncoming beast, trying to judge the rhythm of its lope. When he felt that the tiger was going to make its leap at him Nuroc lunged to one side and lashed out blindly with his sword.

The blade glanced off the tiger, barely wounding it. The beast was carried past Nuroc on the sheer force of its momentum. Howling with rage, it landed on the dirt and immediately spun about to face its attacker. Blood shone on the animal's shoulder, but the cut seemed to have had little effect on the tiger's strength or determination to slay Nuroc.

Nuroc quickly assessed his situation and knew that he would tire before the beast would. He could not hope to escape death by merely avoiding the beast's charges and slapping back with his sword. His only advantage lay in outwitting the cat. He did so by taking his sword and assuming the offensive, rushing forward before the tiger could coil its powerful legs into position to leap. Off-balance, the tiger swiped awkwardly at Nuroc with its front paw. Nuroc ducked the blow and barreled into the four-legged carnivore. The beast snapped its jaws at Nuroc's face but missed its mark and soon began to wail from the agony inflicted by the sword Nuroc buried between its chest and shoulder.

"Die!" Nuroc screamed at the beast, leaning his weight and full strength into the sword. The tiger refused to remain still, however, and managed to pull free from Nuroc's grip. The sword stayed buried in its torso, leaving Nuroc unarmed as he fought back his fear and watched the tiger shriek in pain and pace in the dirt before him. Finally, the animal's legs weakened and it sagged to the ground. Its cries took on a piteous tone, and Nuroc could see the beast's agony. It was dying in the dirt, too weak to move, although it continued to clack its jaws at the air and keep its massive head turned toward Nuroc.

"I had no choice," Nuroc declared to the dying animal. "If I hadn't slain you, you'd have done the same to me. All I can do for you now is help end your pain."

Stepping cautiously forward, Nuroc extended one hand toward the hilt of his sword. The great cat snapped at it feebly, but made no other sign of movement. Nuroc drew in a deep breath, then stepped forward and swiftly grabbed the weapon, turning the blade and twisting it farther into the tiger's chest until the point severed its heart. Life fell from the eyes of the beast and it fell limp in the dirt, blood spewing out around the blade.

Nuroc looked down at the slain hill tiger in wonder. Never again would it slay men and women for the enjoyment of onlookers. Its own death came without an audience, save for he who had dealt the mortal wound. Nuroc had succeeded where so many had failed. He had not only survived the attack of the most feared of the arena killers, but he had also slain it.

There was little time for him to dwell on the significance of his private victory. Back in the tunnels he heard the ragings of the other beasts, mingling with the cries of men.

"What treachery is this?" Nuroc cried out, yanking free his sword from the dead tiger and racing back across the arena. The sounds coming from the underground reaches built to a swift crescendo, then just as swiftly trailed off into relative silence.

Apprehensive, Nuroc stalked the darkened stretch of tunnel leading to the animals' keep, expecting to encounter the hill tiger's companion or another of the beasts. He could not fathom the trainer's motives for loosing one of his prize tigers on him, but he wasn't about to fall prey to another attack.

As he rounded the turn leading to the cages, Nuroc stopped in his tracks. Before him, the old man lay face down in a pool of blood before the row of opened cages, now empty of their deadly occupants.

Confused, Nuroc crouched over the body and slowly turned it over, expecting to find the slash marks of a hill tiger or Shangoran lion. Instead, he saw that the trainer had been cut down by a sword wound to the side. He was dead, but the blood streaming from the wound was still warm.

"That's him!" a voice cried out.

Startled, Nuroc looked up to see the barracks guard pointing at him, his eyes blazing with accusation. Beside him were a dozen Aerdan archers carrying loaded crossbows.

"Yes!" the guard gasped to the archers. "He's the one who last walked the tunnel! He's the one responsible for this!"

Nuroc slowly stood up and backed away from the body of the trainer. "What are you talking about?" he demanded. "I myself was almost slain by one of these murderous beasts—"

"Silence!" one of the archers called out, raising his crossbow and pointing it at Nuroc's chest. "Drop your sword."

"But, there has been a mistake here. I am not—"

"Do as I say or die!" the archer snapped.

Nuroc let his sword fall to the ground as the other archers quickly came up to him. Two of them took Nuroc's wrists and twisted his arms behind his back as they shoved him along.

"There had better be an explanation for this," Nuroc said threateningly, casting a hateful glance at the guard, who was grinning wolfishly at him.

"Well put," Seth, the head archer, said coldly, prodding Nuroc around the next bend in the tunnel toward the converted stables. "You'd be wise to give it, too." Reaching the archway separating the tunnel from the barracks, Seth pushed Nuroc harshly inside. "Explain *this*!"

Nuroc fell to the ground and quickly rose to his knees. He looked around him with grim amazement. The stalls, which had minutes before been a scene of peaceful slumber, were now caught in a tableau of carnage. Men and beasts alike lay dead on the bloodied ground. The men bore the wounds of fangs and claws; the animals were pierced with arrows. Wounded soldiers stood in the background, their eyes still wide with shock. Bordo was among the dead.

Seth shook Nuroc forcefully and spat, "You let the beasts loose upon our sleeping men. Why?"

Nuroc looked up and saw the tip of a loaded quarrel pointing inches from his face. Above that, Seth looked down at him with eyes brimming with wrath and self-righteousness.

Four

Nuroc was hauled away to another section of the underground chambers and tossed into a small cell that reeked of animal excrement. No light entered the enclosure save that which edged in around the Seth's face as he looked through a slit in the door. Nuroc felt nauseous from the foul odor, but since he had landed on his hands and knees in the dungheap, he could not remove himself from the smell, nor the smell from him.

"By what right do you do this?" Nuroc shouted angrily at the man peering in at him.

"I will ask the questions!" Seth replied calmly.

Nuroc flung the residue of excrement that had clung to his hands toward the face in the door. "Here's your answer, dog!"

Seth withdrew from the slit and Nuroc charged the door, striking it full-force with his shoulder. The door held firm but a sharp jolt of pain shot through his shoulder. Cursing, he backed away. The dung sucked at his feet every time he lifted them from the slime that layered the floor.

The slot in the door was closed and Nuroc found himself in total darkness and silence. He could tell that the walls were close by on all sides of him. Reaching out, however, he could not touch anything but the still, fetid air that assailed his nostrils.

"What place is this?" he called out. His voice boomed in the cramped quarters, but was not answered.

Several minutes passed. It seemed to Nuroc that the air was thinning around him. His lungs and throat were beginning to ache from attempting to breathe solely through his mouth to avoid the stench, which seeped up his nose anyway, making him feel more ill by the moment.

Then there was a sound above his head. He looked up and saw a panel slide away from a grillwork of iron bars. He expected to see another face stare down at him and resume the taunting, but all he could make out was a funneling of chiseled walls reaching up from the grating. Far above he heard a brushing sound, followed by the dull tumbling. Soon he could see a fresh heap of excrement sliding down the slanted walls above the grating. He quickly backed away as the waste slapped disgustingly against the bars and showered down into the pit, missing him by inches. Some bits of the waste stuck to the bars, only to be knocked loose when the panel slid back across the ceiling of the cell, returning Nuroc to darkness. The odor grew fouler about him.

"I had nothing to do with the animals being set free!" Nuroc shouted out. "Look in the arena, damn you! The hill tiger that lies dead there almost claimed me!"

The slat in the door opened once more, and Seth spoke without showing his face. "You are beneath the cages of those animals. You're fortunate the waste pits were emptied only recently or you would be up to your waist in it. Of course, if you choose not to cooperate, that may come to be your fate in time."

"I've told you the truth, curse your hide!" Nuroc snapped. "Now let me out of this sewer pit and we'll settle our score like men!"

"Who are you?" Seth persisted, ignoring Nuroc's retort. "What did you hope to gain through your act of perfidy?"

"I tell you, I committed no such act!" Nuroc shouted, his voice rising to hold pace with his temper. "I am Nuroc. I was son to a miner in the hamlet of Wheshi. The Ghetites and Shangorans slew my family, so I came to Cothe to seek my revenge. I avenged their deaths many times over on the battlefield, and now I'm rewarded by being flung into a dungpit by some fool who taunts me from behind a locked door. Spineless swine! Let me out of here—"

"I am Lieutenant Seth," the other man roared back. "I could just as well have slain you as saved your miserable skin. You'll rot in here for all I care if you don't change your story to fit the facts. You're a spy for the enemy, sent here to slay our men as best you can, right? Answer me or I'll have more dung dumped down on you, cur!"

Nuroc looked up again, judging the distance to the barely visible grating overhead. Gritting his teeth, he crouched down, tensing his legs as he called out, "Do as you wish! The smell can get no worse in here."

Seth laughed, "We shall see about that, devil soldier."

The slat in the door was closed once more, and soon after the overhead panel slid across the barred grating. Nuroc sprang upward, reaching his arms out before him. His fingers closed around the bars and he hung in the air above the soiled floor. He quickly swang back and forth several times, then, just as more excrement was tumbling down toward him, he let go of the bars. Carried forward by his momentum, he kicked out with both his feet at the top of the door. As he had hoped, the bolt was drawn across the lower part of the door and gave him no resistance. The half-rotted wood gave way and Nuroc burst through with a splintering crash.

Seth fell back from the doorway, caught completely by surprise. Before he could bring up his crossbow, Nuroc landed and shoved the lieutentant to the ground. The crossbow fell to one side, and Nuroc kicked it away before Seth could get his hands on it. The officer turned to Nuroc, his eyes wild with fear. Nuroc clutched up a broken slat from the battered door and held it like a club as he moved closer to Seth.

"Now it's your turn," Nuroc said, reaching behind him and lifting the bolt from what was left of the door. Opening it, he continued, "Get in, on your knees!"

Seth hesitated, a broken man. For too long his authority had gone unchallenged, and now, in the face of aggression, he backed down like a dog. When Nuroc swept the length of wood to within inches of his head, Seth cried out, "I'll go!"

The lieutenant cast a furtive glance over his shoulder, but none of his men were in the corridor outside the room to come to his aid. Hobbling forward on his knees, he passed Nuroc and crept to the threshold of the pit, then stopped.

Nuroc pivoted and placed his foot between the man's shoulder blades. Before Seth could react, Nuroc straightened his leg and sent the lieutenant sprawling headfirst into the wretched mire. He then slammed the door and threw the bolt. The upper portion of the door was missing now, and Nuroc stared over the gap at Seth.

"It suits you better than me, Lieutenant."

Nuroc turned away and headed for the corridor, pausing long enough to pick up Seth's crossbow. The officer howled a steady stream of dark oaths as he rose to his feet and came back to the door.

"You'll die for this, Nuroc!"

There was another door separating the area from the main

tunnel. Nuroc stopped in the second doorway and looked back at Seth, who was reaching out through the splintered door of the sewer pit, trying to work free the bolt.

"I've had enough of your threats," Nuroc said, stepping out into the tunnel and slamming the second door shut. This one was made of newer sturdier wood, with an even thicker bolt to hold it closed. Seth was soon pounding at the door from inside the sewer chamber and unleashing a newly inspired volley of oaths and curses.

Nuroc turned and walked down the corridor, on his guard and well aware that to the others in the tunnel he would be considered an escaped prisoner, marked for death on sight.

Five

The sound of steady dripping led Nuroc through the bleakly lit tunnels to a massive underground cistern holding water for the many needs of the coliseum. Made of hammered sheets of metal bound in place by brass bands, the rounded tank was wedged tightly into its own chamber. There were several spigots extending out from its base, and Nuroc positioned himself under one and opened it, rinsing himself off with a steady stream of cool water. The putrid odor from his ordeal still clung to his nostrils, but he suspected the worse of the scent had been washed down the drains at his feet.

As he was about to leave the chamber in hopes of finding a means of drying himself against the subterranean chill, he heard voices coming his way from the tunnel behind him. There was no mistaking the vengeful outbursts of Lieutenant Seth.

"Two of you check the cisterns while we go through the chariot room. He has to be here somewhere. Apprehend him, but don't harm him. That pleasure is to be mine alone!"

Nuroc quickly looked about him. The cistern chamber, like all the other underground rooms, was carved from the bedrock beneath the coliseum. Four stone walls stared back at him. The only way out on foot was through the tunnels, where he could hear the approach of armed guards.

Desperate, Nuroc looked up at the sides of the cistern, which rose into the inky blackness that shrouded the ceiling. The space between the stone walls and the metal siding was no more than the width between Nuroc's shoulders. Still, there was enough room for him to throw himself up into the narrow crevice and grab hold of the nearest brass band. Groaning, he lifted himself higher until his foot could rest upon one of the spigots and give him a chance to reach up to the next band. With the same motion, he worked his way around the side of the cistern, so that by the time the two soldiers charged into the chamber, he was more than twelve feet up and halfway behind the container, well-hidden in shadow.

Nuroc was able to press his back against the stone wall, otherwise his grip on the narrow bands would not have been good enough to support himself. Holding his breath and his position, Nuroc rolled his eyes downward, but could only see the shifting shadows of the men who sought him.

"He's not here," one of the men said.

"Not unless he's squirmed around the sides," the other replied. "We'd best check to make certain."

Nuroc cringed, silently shifting in place until he had one hand free to grab at his sword. He strained for a better view of the floor and soon saw one of the soldiers moving beneath him. The man's crossbow was held out before him, his face tense as he peered into the darkened recess behind the cistern.

His companion called out, "No one on this side."

"Nor here," the soldier answered back, turning away and walking off without raising his gaze the few feet it would have taken for him to have spotted Nuroc straining in the shadows, ready to drop to the floor and risk his sword against crossbows.

The sound of footsteps retreated to silence. Nuroc exhaled with relief and prepared to descend from his precarious perch when he was startled by a sudden splash from within the cistern.

"What the . . ."

The splash was followed by the distant creak of rope straining against a windlass, and Nuroc realized that someone above was reeling up a bucket of water to the surface of the coliseum. Inching his way farther up the side of the cistern, Nuroc reached the upper lip just as a large bucket was rising through the rounded opening in the wooden platform. Through the opening, Nuroc could see a pair of soldiers tilt the bucket to pour the water into smaller containers. They then let the pail drop back into the cistern's hold, trailing the length of rope behind it.

Water splashed out against the walls of the cistern, sprinkling Nuroc slightly.

Nuroc quickly assessed his situation. By climbing back down to the underground chambers, he would still have to make his way through the tunnels and past Seth's archers. His best hope was to reach the surface as quickly as possible, before word of his imprisonment and escape had reached the other soldiers. Perhaps he would have time to track down General Palem or another officer from the battle in the meadows to vouch for his loyalty.

The cistern was fed by four stone conduits bringing in both rainwater and overflow from the harbor at times when the water level there rose high enough to reach the aqueducts. One of the conduits was a few feet away from Nuroc, so he made his way along the rim of the cistern until he could get a firm hold on the carved stone, which extended out a yard above the waterline.

Nuroc checked to see if there was a way out along the conduit, but found there was less than a foot of clearance where the stone channel passed through the wooden platform. The conduit was also lined with a slick layer of green moss that would have given him poor footing at best were he to try climbing up the pitched incline.

Reaching out, he found that he was able to grasp the rope that stretched down from the windlass. Remembering the size of the large bucket, Nuroc guessed that when it was filled with water it probably weighed as much as he. Accordingly, he hoped the rope would support him as well. He tugged on it several times to make sure it had been let down as far as possible, then swung free of the conduit and began to climb the rope, hand over hand. The wooden platform was twenty feet up, and Nuroc's muscles began to ache before he had cleared half the distance. Still he pushed on, gasping deep breaths, hearing the swish of the rope cutting through the surface of the water below him.

When he finally reached the opening, Nuroc paused, gritting his teeth as he strained to lift his head above his hands to look out at the area above the cistern. To his relief, he found that the well was situated between the mess tent and the coliseum wall, where no one was about. He could hear the grumbling of the cooks in the nearby tent and see their outlines through the gently swaying walls.

Nuroc pulled himself up the last length of rope until he was able to swing his feet onto the wooden slats of the platform.

Then, rubbing his chafed palms together, he stole from the well and circled around the back of the mess tent.

Between the walls of the coliseum and the fortifications that surrounded the entire city was a wide avenue that was normally left clear for the thousands of people who flocked to the stadium. Now, though, scattered tents were pitched in the dirt at irregular intervals, serving as quarters for the bulk of the massive force that had been summoned to Cothe over the past month. Work crews were in the process of tearing down some of the tents, a harsh reminder of the staggering losses suffered during the clash with the enemy. Other soldiers mingled about, filling the moments before the call to mess.

Most of the men Nuroc saw were among the troops who had stayed behind to defend the capital the previous night, and none of their faces seemed familiar. He walked among them, trying to appear in no great hurry as he scanned the makeshift housing for the one that might look like the quarters used by Palem and the other officers.

The largest was located halfway around the coliseum, and when Nuroc saw two soldiers carry the limp form of a fatally-wounded comrade out through the side entrance, he assumed it was where the casualties of both the battle and the attack of the arena beasts were being treated for their wounds. At once his thoughts turned to Myrania and he walked directly to the tent.

Inside, the physician Hoarth was leaning over a wounded soldier who writhed in silent agony on a rickety cot. Two attendants held the victim down as Hoarth took careful hold of a broken arrow imbedded in the man's side. With his free hand, the physician clutched a strip of cloth soaked with herbal juices and pressed it next to the wound.

"I have to take out this arrow or you're going to die," Hoarth informed the grimacing soldier on the cot. "You may die anyway, but perhaps the gods will smile on you. It is long past the time they started to."

"You give me little hope," the wounded soldier moaned through his swollen lips. His face was waxen, and the color of his flesh was like that of weathered ivory. Life crouched pitifully in the corner of his eyes, half-hidden behind the delirious stare the fallen Aerdan cast up toward the physician. Standing behind Hoarth, Nuroc found himself looking into the victim's eyes.

"Neandro!" Nuroc cried out, recognizing the man as one of the recruits from Thutchers, the one who had played the lute and sung romantic ballads by the campfire on their way to Cothe days before.

The glimmer of recognition crept into Neandro's eyes. As he opened his mouth to speak, the wounded youth suddenly jerked in place. His eyes closed and his teeth clenched, straining out an unintelligible gasp as he struggled fiercely against the hold of the two attendants. Hoarth pulled out the arrow, then placed the treated cloth over the wound and pressed, but to no avail. The cloth turned red with spurting blood. Neandro stiffened and his eyes fell open, void of life. His final jolt was his last. He slumped laxly on the couch and the attendants pulled their hands away from him.

Hoarth shook his head and stepped back from the body, holding the fragment of arrow that dripped Neandro's blood onto the dirt floor. "Another one," he said sadly. "For each man I've saved today, two have died in my hands."

One of the attendants told Hoarth, "Without your aid, no doubt all the wounded would die."

Nuroc watched numbly as the attendants lifted Neandro and carried him out of the tent. Hoarth saw Nuroc for the first time and said somberly, "If you've come to check on the woman, I must tell you there have been complications."

"Myrania?" Nuroc said, startled. "She's in danger?"

Hoarth nodded silently and gestured across the tent. Nuroc saw Myrania lying on a cot in the back corner, not moving. Hoarth told him, "The wound on her leg has become infected with the same poison that would have slain your friend had I left the arrow in his side."

"No!" Nuroc said with agony. He turned away from the physician and moved past the other wounded men to Myrania's side. His heart sank at the sight of her. Like Neandro, her skin was drained of blood and sickly textured. Her wounded leg was covered with a clear, glistening ointment, through which Nuroc could see the advanced state of the festering infection.

"Myrania," he whispered gently, leaning over and kissing her brow. She was feverish, damp with perspiration.

Her eyes slowly opened, taking Nuroc in. She struggled to swallow, but was too weak to speak.

Coming up behind Nuroc, Hoarth said, "It seems blades and arrows used by the Ghetites and Shangorans were dipped in some sort of poison. Every man in here who suffered a cut that broke the skin is battling the same infection. I treat it as best I can, but without knowing the source of the poison, I can only guess at the ways to counter it."

"Augage's doing, no doubt," Nuroc said, anger creeping into his voice. "Still, there must be an antidote. . . ."

"I've tried all that I know, and nothing works," Hoarth said. "If I wait too long with Myrania, the poison will kill her by this time tomorrow, I am certain."

"If you wait too long for what?"

Hoarth took a deep breath and licked his lips. He tried to avoid Nuroc's gaze, but in the end decided that he had no choice but to be blunt. "If I cut off the leg and can stop the flow of blood, there's a chance the infection hasn't spread to the rest of her body. I may be able—"

"Never!" Nuroc said hoarsely, reaching out and wrapping his fists around the physician's blood-flecked tunic. Without changing the sad, resigned expression on his face, Hoarth looked down at Nuroc's hands until the younger man released his grip.

"I understand your feelings," Hoarth said simply. "I only tell you because I think you should know the situation fully."

They were both interrupted by a pained, rasping whisper from the couch beside them. It was Myrania. They looked at her. She had raised her head slightly, and was pointing with trembling fingers at her dry, cracked lips.

"W-w-w-water."

"Myrania!" Nuroc blurted out with sudden, hopeful joy.

Hoarth reached over for a wooden ladle set in a pail of fresh water. He scooped up the water and carried the ladle over to Myrania. She reached out for it, but he shook his head and assured her, "I can keep it steady for you. Now drink."

Myrania slowly moved her lips, taking in the welcome liquid. It seemed to have an almost immediate effect on her. A spark more of life came to her eyes. She swallowed hard and cleared her throat, then reached up and gently pushed away the empty ladle in Hoarth's hand, telling him, "I want to speak to Nuroc—alone."

Hoarth nodded. "But not for long. You will need all the strength you can manage."

As Hoarth walked away to tend to other victims, Myrania turned her eyes to Nuroc. "Come close," she said.

Nuroc crouched down beside her. "I love you, Myrania."

"I love you, Nuroc." Her voice was strained and labored. She spoke slowly, gathering in her breath before every few words. "Next to the obelisk . . . bushes . . . find the one with yellow blossoms . . . red-veined leaves . . . makes a paste . . . stops poison. . . ."

"The neotolan bush?" Nuroc asked. "Is that the one?"

She took his hand and squeezed it weakly. "It is the only chance. . . . Don't look at me so. . . . I will be better if . . . you must go. . . . Bring neotolan. . . . Now."

"Myrania. . . ."

"Now!" Myrania eased back onto the cot and let go of Nuroc's hand. She swallowed again and her face twisted with the pain. She closed her eyes and the expression softened. Soon she was breathing shallowly, drifting off with the fire of her fever.

"Hold on," Nuroc whispered to her. "Hold on to life until I return."

Hoarth headed back toward Myrania's cot and opened his mouth to speak, but Nuroc hurried past him and out the tent. He was well aware of the neotolan bush, cultivated on the grounds directly surrounding the obelisk. He had often watered and pruned such plants during his years in Cothe. The memory gave him little cause for hope, though, for he recalled that the neotolan was one of the most sensitive plants in all the gardens, requiring diligent care in order to thrive to the point where its healing blossoms could be used in the creation of medicinal salves that could perform miraculous cures. Since the gardens had been declared off limits by edict of Pencroft for more than five years, the chances that he might find a single neotolan bush in bloom seemed despairingly slim. And yet, there was no other way.

Six

There were only two gateways in the outer walls surrounding the coliseum. One led from the city to the open farmland worked by the peasants of Cothe. The other provided passage between the stadium and the city itself. To reach the sorcerers' gardens, Nuroc had to pass through the city, so it was to the latter gateway that he strode with firm intent.

A handful of soldiers were standing guard before the iron

portcullis that had been lowered in the gate's archway, barring entry to the city. Half of the men assumed their vigil with a semblance of attentiveness, but the others were occupied with playing a game of knucklebones against a wall that separated the city from the coliseum. Those doing their duty stepped forward to intercept Nuroc as he made his way toward the gate.

"Hold there, soldier," the tallest of the guards called out. Like his compatriots, he carried a broad-bladed spear and wore a half-sword slung from his waist. He did not hold his weapon as if he intended to use it, but there could be no doubting he would if the need arose.

"I must go to the sorcerers' gardens," Nuroc said emphatically.

The head guard shook his head. The two men behind him crossed their spears to form an additional barricade before the portcullis. "The king's orders are that none are to leave the coliseum until the citizens have all returned to the city," the head guard informed Nuroc in a deep, forceful voice. "Too many men have fallen to the temptation of thieving from untended shops and the homes of the rich."

"My business is in the gardens, not the city," Nuroc insisted.

"But you cannot reach one without passing through the other. Besides, even if we let you pass there would be more guards posted before the gates to the gardens, which are also off limits."

"But I must get through."

One of the men behind the head guard smirked. Under his breath he muttered, "The dead get through, if you're that desperate. Of course, there's little for them to do—"

"Enough!" the head guard snarled over his shoulder at the two subordinates. As he turned his attention back to Nuroc, the metallic clang of a distant triangle chimed in the air.

"There's the call to mess," the head guard told Nuroc. "You'd do best to forget your outing to the gardens and rush to the line. Only the first served have a chance for edible rations. Trust me."

Nuroc realized that he would not be able to reason his way past the guards without divulging his intentions. He doubted they would believe him and feared they might suspect his knowledge of the gardens and detain him until Lieutenant Seth showed up. Crestfallen, he left the gates and trudged back toward the encampment.

The avenue was alive with hungry soldiers. They seemed to pour out from the tents and merge into a crowd gathering near the distant mess tent. Nuroc fell in with a group of men, straining his mind to come up with a plan he could use to get past the guards. So caught up was he in his thoughts that he almost failed to see Lieutenant Seth emerging from the underground ramp leading up from beneath the coliseum. When he spotted his pursuer, the officer was already making his way through the crowd, less than twenty feet away from him.

Nuroc crouched over slightly and weaved through the clot of other men to the far edge of their procession and away from Seth. When he stopped to look, he saw the lieutenant scanning the faces of the men who passed him. He'd changed his uniform and carried a broadsword now, with his crossbow slung over his shoulder.

Nuroc broke away from the crowd and took refuge behind the nearest tent. He knelt and pretended to be adjusting his sandals so that those around him would not disturb him and draw attention his way. He watched Seth warily. When the lieutenant let the last of the men pass him and then crossed the walkway toward one of the tents, Nuroc stood quickly and made his way to the nearest rampway leading up into the coliseum. Glancing around to make sure he was not being watched, he headed up the ramp and was soon out of view of those outside the coliseum.

The stadium was still vacant, save for the five men who labored to remove the slain hill tiger from the center of the arena. Nuroc took cover behind a stone pillar and stared out at the operation, marveling at the size of the beast he had slain. It seemed impossible that he had survived the onslaught of so large a creature. He found himself wondering if perhaps he still carried some trace of the blood of the old sorcerer-king Talmon-Khash, which would supposedly keep him clear of harm's way so long as he remained true to his destiny, however unclear it seemed to be with each passing moment.

The setting sun cast a curving shadow across the arena and into the stands where Nuroc hid. He felt the chill carried on the wind blowing across the stadium from the harbor. Rubbing his arms to stay warm in the shadows, Nuroc contemplated the pool of blood left in the dirt after the lion had been dragged away. He still could not figure out the meaning behind the attack on him and the others. Who had killed the trainer and let the beasts loose? Was there a traitor in their midst after all?

"I thought I saw you run in here," Seth called out suddenly from behind Nuroc.

Nuroc spun about, then ducked to one side as an arrow thudded into the wooden bench before him. As Seth withdrew another staff from his quiver and nocked it in the crossbow, three more soldiers rushed up beside him, carrying longbows and arrows that were more accurate at far distances than Seth's weapon.

Nuroc sprang into action, fleeing up the rows of benches that formed the stands. He veered his path to and fro to provide an erratic target as more arrows crashed into the stone seats around him.

"Try just to wound him so I can finish him off with my sword!" Seth called out to his men. "But if you have to, kill him! Don't let him escape me again!"

Nuroc's legs pumped furiously as he propelled himself farther up the slope of the stadium. Finally he reached the uppermost row of seats and found himself staring over the back wall of the coliseum at the city. From where he stood, there was a gap of more than twenty feet between the rim of the coliseum and the turrets rising over the gateway he had failed to gain passage through minutes before.

Seth's men continued their pursuit up the aisles. One of them stopped long enough to loose another arrow, but it hissed past Nuroc's head and splintered against the stone of the coliseum wall.

After gauging the distance he had to clear, Nuroc broke into a run along the top walkway. Three steps led up to the rim of the coliseum, and once he cleared them, Nuroc crouched and pushed off, flinging himself across the chasm between the two towering walls.

A wooden pole rose from the turret over the gateway to the city, flying the snapping banner that bore the shield insignia of Aerda. Nuroc's jump brought him crashing into the pole. With a sharp crack it gave under the stress of his weight. The impact was enough to break Nuroc's fall onto the stone walkway atop the parapets. He rolled gingerly with his landing and came to his feet, bleeding from several fresh scrapes but otherwise uninjured.

Although the turret was unattended, there were guards pacing the parapets to either side of Nuroc. They both gaped at him with outrage and incredulity. Not about to wait for a reaction, Nuroc sidestepped a volley of arrows from the guards atop the coliseum and scrambled over the edge of the wall facing the city, dropping into space.

The city's livestock was quartered in this corner of Cothe, and Nuroc was able to direct his fall into the bulging mound of loose hay heaped next to the livery stables. The goats and pigs in the nearby pens let out boisterous protests at the intrusion. Chickens squawked and dragged themselves across the dirt, flapping their stubby wings in a futile attempt at flight.

Nuroc burrowed down into the hay, hiding himself from view of those along the parapets above him. The haystack nestled against the side wall of the stables, and Nuroc was able to slip into the structure without exposing his position. Only then did he pause to catch his breath.

The sun had fallen fast during Nuroc's flight, and the darkening shadows gave him further cover. Leaving the stables, he quickly made his way along back alleys and abandoned side streets that brought him closer to the heart of the city. How it had changed in the years since his childhood, he thought as he padded noiselessly across the flagstone pavement. Most of the shops and buildings were new, erected in place of those structures burned to the ground during the riots of the Great Cataclysm. The newer edifices were smaller but sturdier than their predecessors. Brick and stone had replaced wood and thatch as the primary building materials. But beyond mere appearances, there was also a different feeling to the capital. The sea mist rolling in from the harbor hung in the air, forming halos around the few crackling torches that lit the deserted streets. There was an aura of unrealtiy to the surroundings. Nuroc felt as if he had stumbled into some intricate maze contrived by a madman. Doorways and open windows yawned wide and dark like the maws of silent beasts. Streets reached out relentlessly in all directions, carving up the rows of shops and domiciles that marked this as the workers' side of town. The domed roofs and proud spires that adorned the homes of the wealthy rose in the distance, across the widened boulevard that divided the city according to class. Encompassing everything were the formidable walls of the city, where the posted sentries could be seen pacing between evenly-spaced crenelations with pikes and halberds held high. Looking back to the section of battlements he had bounded over to enter the city, Nuroc saw that the guards had fallen back to their normal duties, but he suspected that word had been passed around and that men were already roving these same streets in search of him.

Nuroc was halfway across the city before he encountered any of the citizenry. Ducking into the blackness of a doorway, he peered out at the market square, where a huge bonfire blazed in a dugout pit, throwing light on a group of blank-faced women and confused children gathered nearby on stone benches. Large baskets filled with personal belongings rested on the dirt beside the women. Nuroc guessed these were among the first of the townsfolk to have returned from the forced evacuation of Cothe ordered by King Pencroft in anticipation of the ill-fated invasion.

Farther away from the fire, almost beyond range of its fluttering glow, men stood around casks of wine and a keg of ale they had rolled out from one of the meadhalls serving the square. Most of the men held tankards and conversed amongst themselves in somber tones. They all wore clothing of traders and craftsmen; simple tunics of coarse, sturdy wool and vests made from the hides of goats.

The snorting of an ox team sounded over Nuroc's shoulder and he pressed himself farther into the shadow of the doorway. Down the main street from the direction of the coliseum came a work crew guiding a wooden-wheeled cart filled with the latest of the day's mortalities, destined for burial in the sorcerers' gardens. Armed soldiers marched in formation at each corner of the cart, while a pair of gravediggers sat on a bench hammered across its top. One held reins and a long leather whip. Two teams of oxen pulled the death cart past the market square as the citizens fell silent and watched them gloomily. As with everyone else, the people of Cothe could not find cause for joyous ecstasy in their tentative victory over Ghetite and Shangora.

Nuroc took advantage of the distraction to sneak around the market square and into the wealthier part of the city. Here the buildings were larger and the streets wider. Marble columns and tiled frescoes took the place of drab stone surfaces on the outside of homes and buildings. Oil lamps lit not only the streets, but also a few of the homes, outlining silhouettes of lush gardens and ornamental sculptures placed about the more lavish estates. Nuroc recognized the rounded shell that formed the roof over the private baths, and the temple for public worship rising up next to the mansion used by visiting dignitaries from foreign countries. The newly built palace reared in the corner of the city, marked by a cluster of rigid spires and open colonnades woven in rampant ivy and bougainvillaea. The gateway to the gardens lay near the palace, and it was in that direction that Nuroc headed.

The streets near the palace were far from vacant, though.

Nuroc's progress was impeded severely by the presence of wealthy merchants and land-owners who gathered in small groups at the edges of their estates to exchange rumors and gossip regarding the future of their city and all of Aerda in the aftermath of the battle. There were troops about as well, contrary to what Nuroc had been told at the gates earlier. Members of the king's guard, they were on watch against the intrusion of petty thieves and vandals. Nuroc stole close to one group of soldiers and learned what he had feared, that they were also searching the city for him.

Slipping away, Nuroc tried to make his way to the garden gates without encountering other soldiers, but each block closer to his destination he found more men with their weapons out, diligently seeking him out in every niche and cranny. They were methodically closing in on him, and soon he was trapped in a shop entryway with guardsmen making their way toward him from both sides of the street.

Nuroc discovered the shop was vacant and stole inside. Enough light poured in through the unshielded windows for him to see his way. A flight of steps reached up to the second floor. Suddenly he heard soldiers searching through the buildings on either side of him, and rushed up the stairs to the blackness of the upper chambers. Inching his way along the darkened hall, Nuroc crept into one of the rooms and moved cautiously to the nearest window, where wooden shutters had been drawn shut. Peering through slats in the shutters, he saw that the roof next door was almost flat. He waited, figuring that once the men came into this shop, he could leap out the window and land on the other roof and earn another chance at fulfilling his mission.

He was about to unhitch the shutters when he heard a quiet shuffling sound. The hairs on his neck rose with fear.

He was not alone in the room.

He could hear slight breathing in the far corner of the room, beyond reach of the light that filtered in through the shutters.

Pretending he still thought he was alone, Nuroc stayed near the window, but shifted slightly until his fingers were on his sword and ready to yank it from his scabbard. He listened hard and waited.

Soon he heard light footsteps, and the breathing sounded closer every second.

In one fluid motion, Nuroc pushed away from the window and jerked out his sword, stabbing it in the direction of the noise.

There was a choked groan as the blade found flesh. Nuroc drove his sword farther into the figure before him. The man dropped to his knees and issued a second, louder cry that carried to the streets.

In the faint light that seeped into the chamber, Nuroc saw that his victim was a grizzle-faced beggar in torn clothes and bare feet. In the dead man's hand was a rusty dagger. His other fingers were wrapped tightly around an urn made of hammered gold and inlaid gems.

"A thief," Nuroc muttered. "A petty thief."

Downstairs, Nuroc heard both groups of guardsmen congregating near the front doorway.

"Surround the building!" a soldier called out. The command was followed by the urgent footsteps of others sounding down the alleyways.

"Seth," Nuroc whispered to himself. "Curse him!"

Sheathing his sword, Nuroc pulled open the shutters and climbed out the window onto a ledge encircling the building. Seeing several men look up at him, he quickly leapt across the alleyway to the roof of the adjacent building. Springing back to his feet, he broke into a run across the roof and managed a second leap to a mound of dirt piled next to the foundation of a new shop being built at the end of the block.

He had gained enough distance on the pursuing guards to strike out unseen across the street and into the strip of bush-lined parkway bordering the wall between the city and the sorcerers' gardens. The hedge was shoulder-high and thick enough to conceal Nuroc as he bent low and made his way toward the gates.

Even before he reached his destination, Nuroc became aware of a flurry of activity taking place near the archway. Staying close to the hedge, he looked out and saw two groups gathered on the city side of the open gates. Only a few yards away from him, the burial cart was stopped. Its crew stood by to watch the arrival of the two horse-drawn carriages heaped high with bountiful treasure that shone in the surrounding torchlight. Three mounted soldiers rode beside either carriage, and a dozen more men in the garb of the royal guard walked alongside the treasure. King Pencroft and General Palem rode at the head of this stirring procession, occasionally looking back at the first share of spoils that had been lifted from the ruins of the obelisk, as if to make certain it hadn't vanished upon leaving the former realm of the sorcerers.

"Will you look at that," one of the gravediggers murmured from atop his cart.

HIs partner replied, "I'd take the smallest bauble from that catch and live free for a month, I'll wager."

"No chance of that. We'd do best to turn our heads. The guards look as if they'd slay us for merely looking at the loot."

"Aye."

Once the royal procession had passed clear of the archway, the rider of the burial cart took his reins and urged the ox team back into motion. Slowly the large wooden wheels turned and the cart began to roll toward the opening. The four guards stepped back into position at all corners of the cart. On either side of the gates, two soldiers stood at attention but let their eyes rove back to the grim cargo heaped under a sheet of canvas.

"Wait!" Seth called out from down the street as he and his men rushed up to the cart.

"What is it?" one of the gravediggers called out over his shoulder, making no effort to hide his irritation. "We're behind schedule as it is."

"We're looking for an escaped spy," Seth told the burial party. "We know he came this way."

Even as Seth spoke, his men drifted into the parkway area, swords drawn, and began searching the shrubs with fast precision.

"I hope you find him," the man with the reins said, cracking his whip over the heads of the oxen. "If you do, we'll be glad to see that his body gets a traitor's burial."

"And what is a traitor's burial?" Seth asked.

The two men riding the ox cart looked at one another and shared a knowing chuckle. The one without the reins told Seth, "A spy works for two sides. He is buried in two pieces."

Seth's men emerged from the gardens, shaking their heads at their leader.

"Keep looking!" the lieutenant shouted angrily. "I want him found! Check every building and bush if you must. I will go to the palace and make certain he hasn't slipped in there. The gods help us if he gets near the king!"

Seth's men divided up once again into separate groups and fanned out, leaving the burial procession to go on its way through the gateway to the sorcerers' gardens. No one noticed a slight motion beneath the canvas draping the bodies of the dead.

Seven

Once through the gates, the burial party lit torches against the darkness that lay over the sorcerers' gardens, then proceeded along the narrow, winding trail that forged through the lush foliage.

From his place of concealment among the dead bodies, Nuroc was hard-pressed to remain still and silent. The cold touch of dead flesh and the rousing stench of putrefaction assailed his senses with even more aversion than he'd been subjected to in the sewer pit. He felt grateful, at least, that in the darkness beneath the canvas he could not make out the faces of those he lay among. To find himself staring into the lifeless eyes of Bordo or Neandro or another of the recruits he had come to know as friends would have unnerved him more. He tried to ignore the distasteful means by which he had entered the gardens and concentrate on a way to escape the cart unnoticed. Outside the blanketing canvas, he could hear men on all sides, grumbling their way to the burial grounds.

"Some fate we share, men. We come to the gardens to toss dead men into the ground, while the king and his chosen few leave with a fortune in gems and stones."

"You can bet that if I were among the chosen, I'd have a bauble or two slipped into my pockets on the way out."

"Ha, and I will bet you that all the men are searched before they leave the gardens to make certain they haven't been bitten by the bug of greed. Trust me, those who labor for the king fare no better than us, and we do not have his majesty standing by to lord over our every move."

There were mumbles of approval to this, and one of the gravediggers chortled to his companion, "Well put, friend. If the king were watching us, we would have to bury the dead one to a grave instead of three. We would have no time to sneak off into the brush for a nip or two from the wineskin."

"And we would not be able to play cubes in the dirt, either," one of the guards put in.

The rider sniggered, "What we need besides wine and cubes are a few wenches to roll with us in the dirt."

"You may have your chance yet," the second rider said. "You saw that tart lying back in the medic's tent with the leg wound. I'll wager you she's dead by this time tomorrow. You can ravish her then to your heart's content, and she won't say a word about your foul breath and the size of your lovestick."

The other men chuckled and sneered at the insult as the ox team led the cart up the slight incline leading to the burial grounds.

An arm suddenly shot out from beneath the canvas and clutched at the collar of the joking gravedigger. Both he and the others jolted with fear and surprise as Nuroc emerged from cover and closed both hands around the throat of the man who had made sport of Myrania's condition.

"I should slay you for that," Nuroc said harshly.

The digger's eyes widened in a look of terror as he gasped for breath. He could not respond, and the others were equally smitten with horror.

"The dead live!" one of the guards finally sputtered, his face turning white at the sight of Nuroc looming over the trembling gravedigger. He clutched tightly at his torch, as if he hoped it would help ward off any attack by Nuroc. His sword remained in its sheath, as did the weapons of the other men.

Nuroc let go of the gravedigger's neck and slowly turned his gaze from man to man, doing his best to look the part of a lost soul returned to life by some act of unspeakable necromancy. To a man, they all backed off and looked away from his glances, caught up in their primordial awe. When Nuroc stepped from the cart and strode purposefully into the darkness beyond reach of their torches, none dared pursue him. It was only after he was gone from sight that the uneasy silence was broken by one of the soldiers.

"It's a curse from the sorcerers! They are taking revenge for the looting of the obelisk, be sure of it."

The man Nuroc had confronted swallowed several times as he rubbed his neck. His voice wavered as he spoke. "I have seen enough! I'm not about to pay the toll for the king's blasphemy." Still shaking, he stumbled to the ground. "I say we leave the gardens before more of the corpses come to life."

"Aye," several of the others hastily agreed.

Working swiftly, the guards unyoked the oxen and led them away from the cart, all the while keeping wary eyes on the unmoving mound of bodies under the canvas. They started back the way they had come, leaving the cart untended.

Nuroc watched them from behind one of the tablelike dolmen on the burial mound. Once he could no longer see the torchlights of the burial crew, he stepped out from cover, carrying his sword.

To be alone among the dead filled Nuroc with his own sense of dread. When he took a step forward and felt his foot sink into the soft dirt of a fresh grave, he jumped back, startled. After his pulse returned to normal, he cautiously made his way through the clot of markers and up to the highest point of the burial mound. From there he could see over the encircling belt of shrubbery and take in the entire gardens. There was little to see. Most of the area was lost in darkness, betraying only vague shadows of trees and brush. However, in the center of the gardens, smoke rose from a dozen torches set in place around the ruins of the obelisk. Another work crew was busy prying at the rubble for another haul of treasure. Besides the workers, a handful of royal guardsmen paced along the outer edge of the moat, watching over the proceedings.

From his vantage point, Nuroc felt the tuggings of despair, but shook them off. Myrania would die unless he succeeded. Her fate was in his hands. He looked up to the waxing moon and muttered a quiet chant to the constellation Dorban, barely visible in the twinkling stars, then headed down the slope of the burial mound and into the adjacent brush.

Although the fires from the riots after the Great Cataclysm and the subsequent neglect of the gardens had radically changed the topography, Nuroc was still able to remember his way through the half-hidden paths obscured by unchecked growth. This was the place of his youth, where he had played innocently amidst the conjurings of novice sorcerers. Many were the times he had stolen through the brush, just as he did now, and taken refuge behind trees or boulders to watch an apprentice mage practice at coaxing smoke from stones or reciting a chant that would make the birds of the garden speak in the voices of men. It had been a world of wonder for him then, in the early years of his youth. It was the passing of time that had caused his enchantment with sorcery to be replaced with a yearning to partake in the life to be found outside the walls of Cothe. For several years he had served as shepherd for the royal flocks that roved the meadows now red with the blood of fallen warriors. Then, after the Great Cataclysm, his family had been forced to flee the persecution of sorcerers and those who held any shred of loyalty to the old ways. It was in Wheshi that they had settled, in Wheshi were Nuroc had labored in the mines until the coming of the black moon had set into motion the events that now found him back in the gardens he had once called home. This was far from being home for him now, however, he realized. He made his way toward the obelisk with the utmost care, aware that discovery of his presence could well end in his death and, indirectly, that of his beloved.

To lessen his chances of being seen, Nuroc circled in toward his objective, staying clear of the wider paths he knew the workers had taken to reach the obelisk. Hunched over, he trod through knee-high grasses and past bristling shrubs tipped with spiteful thorns. Anxiously, he hoped that he might stumble across the bush Myrania had described to him, thus saving him the dangers of approaching the obelisk and hastening his return to her. But he did not slow his progress on this chance happening, for he knew that those plants grown on the small island around the obelisk were nurtured in imported soil, that they could not flourish in the native earth of Cothe.

He was almost within sight of the obelisk when he suddenly stopped, hearing a strange sound on the ground before him. Instantly on his guard, he drew his sword and held it out before him, squinting into the darkness. The sound continued, and he could finally see a litter of piglet boars whimpering and squirming in the cavity beneath an overturned tree only a few feet away. Their soft squeals sounded more pleading than frightened, and Nuroc lowered his sword, glancing around him, his senses alert.

As he had anticipated, he soon heard a rustling in the nearby brush and slowly turned to face it. In the clearing through which he had just come, a full-grown boar appeared, moonlight showing on its ivory tusks and in its small, angry eyes. The beast was staring at Nuroc, snorting contemptuously through its flared nostrils.

For several seconds, Nuroc and the boar remained still, each regarding the other. Nuroc knew that his only hope of avoiding an attack by the beast was in its realizing that he hadn't disturbed the litter, and yet he stood between the beast and its offspring.

"Easy," Nuroc whispered, firming his grip on his sword as he slowly moved to one side. "I mean no harm."

The boar snorted and shook its massive head. In size the beast was twice Nuroc's weight, with tusks the length of daggers and every bit as lethal. It pawed at the dirt with its front hooves and Nuroc braced himself for the boar's lunge. To his surprise, however, the beast only moved over to the fallen tree, then turned so that it was facing Nuroc once again. Moments later, more noise sounded in the brush as the boar's mate emerged. The second boar was slightly smaller and without tusks. It paused to train its eyes on Nuroc, then continued past him into the crevice beneath the tree. Once she had settled down, the piglets nuzzled against her, seeking out the nourishment of her teats.

Behind Nuroc was an embankment that pitched upward into a grove of fruit trees. With the utmost care, Nuroc backed up the slope, keeping his eyes on the male boar, who continued to stand guard over its family. It was not until he was up amongst the trees and within reach of their lower limbs that Nuroc began to consider himself safe from attack. If the boar pursued him now, he would have sufficient time to climb the nearest tree. He had no desire to battle such a beast under any circumstances, much less in the crowded darkness of the gardens.

When he had advanced halfway through the grove without hearing the boar follow after him, he felt free to pick up his pace and concentrate on his mission. Tired and hungry, he pulled a piece of ripened fruit free from a low-hanging branch. Sinking his teeth into the pulpy flesh, he moaned pleasurably at the sweet, familiar taste, which revived more memories of his childhood.

As he neared the edge of the grove, Nuroc could see once again the lights of the crew working near the obelisk. Voices carried through the still air, along with the strain of activity amidst the ruins. Nuroc paused behind the row of trees marking the grove's border and stared out.

The moat surrounding the former home of the sorcerers was less than a dozen yards away. Between Nuroc and the edge of the moat stood a grim-faced guard, his head cocked as if he had just heard a noise behind him.

Nuroc's pulse raced anew.

Eight

On the main floor of the palace there was a small, windowless room that normally saw service as planning chamber for the military. One wall was filled with a map of the continent Dorban, showing the borders of its many kingdoms. The map was made of taut leather stretched over a thick layer of crushed bark, which allowed Pencroft and his advisors to mark off areas with pin markers made from filed bone and sharpened talons. Along the borders of Aerda, which embraced no less than four surrounding kingdoms and a coastal stretch of the Targoan Sea, there were a number of markers designating the placement of troops to defend the country's boundaries. More numerous than the markers, however, were the visible pinholes showing where battalions had been withdrawn from the borders to aid in the recent defense of the capital. It would be some time before the king would be able to fill those holes with new markers—to man his borders with new troops. It was only fitting, then, that the king would choose this chamber as the place to store the treasure by which he hoped to secure the continued alliance with the kingdoms of Belgore and Eldoth. With the wealth taken from the obelisk, he would attempt to buy the peace normally enforced by manpower.

Only two lamps threw light on the chamber, but the myriad polished surfaces of the plundered fortune amplified that light, filling the room with an eerie radiance. King Pencroft and General Palem stood together before the stored loot, drinking in its stunning beauty.

"This room will be filled by this time tomorrow," Pencroft mused. "When Onfeons and Yute set their eyes on what we've gathered, they will surely agree to our terms for dividing the fortune."

"I agree, your majesty," Palem said, picking up a ruby the size of his fist and admiring its fiery sheen. "Although there is always the chance that they might decide these spoils would be better split only two ways instead of three. In fact, I would not put it past either king to covet the entire prize for himself. We could be buying ourselves more war instead of peace."

"Greed," the king contemplated. "It does have a way of assuming rule over the minds of most men. We will have to watch our allies closely for the first signs of treachery, and hope such signs never appear. This is a fragile time for Aerda and all of Dorban. If events come to pass as we anticipate, the future will hold nothing but promise."

"And if they don't . . . ?"

King Pencroft took a jeweled saber from atop the nearest heap of treasure and held it aloft so that the lamps on either side filled it with their light. "If they don't," he said gravely, "the land will drown in the blood of conflict, as surely as it drowned in the flood of cataclysm."

Neither man spoke for some time after that. Together, they looked across the room at the map depicting the continent, wondering how it would look a year, five years from now. Would Ghetite and Shangora come under rule of Aerda and its allies? Or would that alliance be shattered and all boundaries fall into question? History stood at the crossroads of a new era, and both Pencroft and Palem knew that their actions would determine the fate to come.

"You look tired," Pencroft told his general. "You should retire for the evening. Tomorrow we must assemble what is left of our troops and decide where they might serve us best."

Palem nodded, then left the chamber. The king stayed behind a few minutes longer, going from item to item of treasure, marveling at the skill that had gone into the making of some pieces. Many had been made by techniques long-forgotten by contemporary artisans. All bore a quality that set them apart from anything to be found elsewhere in the palace. His favorite of the pieces was a tiara of banded gold with a strange, luminescent stone fastened to the raised filigree of the headpiece. Pencroft took the crown and stared into the gemstone. It was faceted and sparkled in the lamplight, but, beneath the brilliant exterior, Pencroft could see a small speck seemingly imbedded in the heart of the stone. Holding the tiara closer and shielding the stone from the glare of the lamps, he gazed closer at the speck.

"By the gods!" Pencroft hissed excitedly. "I don't believe it!"

The king secreted the tiara in the folds of his surcoat and left the chamber. Outside the doorway, four soldiers stood at rigid attention, armed with pikes.

"No one is to enter this chamber, under penalty of death," the king told them. "Is that clear?"

In unison, the four men nodded their affirmation. Pencroft walked away from them and started down the large corridor that ran the length of the main floor. Pillars of polished granite rose at regularly spaced intervals along the hall, supporting the tiled mosaic of the ceiling, which depicted the Tree of Favo. According to legend, it was the fruit of this tree that had nurtured the gods when they lived on earth, ensuring their immortality. Although no tree similar to the Favo now existed on Dorban, it was believed that the gods had left behind several of the seeds when they had flown from the earth to take up their residence in the celestial heavens. The legend persisted that the seeds were somehow protected so that, if the need arose, the gods could send down their offspring to grow new trees and partake of the fruit to gain their immortality.

As he started up the flight of steps leading to the second level of the palace, Pencroft stopped, seeing Lieutenant Seth emerge from the chamber nearest to the staircase, sword in hand and a foul expression on his face.

"What are you doing, Lieutenant?" the king demanded.

Seth stood at attention and said, "Your majesty, I sent a messenger to tell you of the situation. You were not notified?"

"I was in conference with General Palem and gave orders not to be disturbed," Pencroft said. "What is the matter?"

Seth told him briefly of the incident below the coliseum and of Nuroc's escape. Pencroft's face darkened at the revelation. "Continue with your search." he said. "When you find this infidel, I wish to have a word with him before his execution."

"Of course, your majesty," Seth intoned. "Should I report to General Palem now that—"

"No, leave him be for the evening," Pencroft interrupted. "He has concerns of his own that take precedence. As you were, Lieutenant."

As Seth fell back to his search, Pencroft proceeded to the second level and made his way down a corridor as lavishly designed and decorated as those downstairs.

Several of Seth's men were in the hall, in the midst of their searching the chambers of the royal family.

"No trace of him yet?" the king asked one of the men.

"None at all, your highness."

"I trust a guard has been placed on the queen."

"Yes, your highness. Men are posted before the doors to the sculptor's studio, where she is sitting for Connec."

"Ah, of course." Pencroft bade the men to carry on and strode down the corridor and around to where four members of the royal guard stood vigil before a gilded silver door. At the sight of the king, two of the men stepped to one side while the other two opened the door to allow Pencroft into the studio.

It was a large chamber of scenoak beams and stone walls, warm from the fire blazing and crackling in a hearth near where the sculptor Connec was hammering his chisel at a slab of stone between glances at Queen Leindal, who sat in a wooden chair facing him. Elsewhere, the room was filled with massive blocks of granite and marble in various stages of transformation into lifelike figures. In the wavering light of the fireplace, the sculptures almost seemed to be breathing.

"Husband!" Leindal called out with a smile, changing her position slightly in the chair. Connec, hunchbacked and middle-aged, sighed with resignation and turned away from his work to greet the king with a stately bow.

"Good evening, your majesty," he said in a thin, broken voice.

Pencroft came over to the block of marble Connec was working on and stroked his chin thoughtfully as he inspected the sculpture. It was just beginning to take shape, and there was only the faintest suggestion of detail carved out of the stone, but already Pencroft could see the likeness of his loved one emerging.

"I see another masterpiece in the making, Connec," he told the sculptor sincerely.

"I thank you for the compliment. I try my best."

"You are the best without trying, Connec," Queen Leindal said, rising from her chair and walking to her husband's embrace. Her beauty was well-preserved, with her soft, gentle features framed by a lush head of coal-black hair. She wore a plain, thick robe of wool that served well in keeping out the chill that lay in the shadows, and her fingers were filled with rings of many designs. Pencroft held her close and they kissed lightly.

"I think that will be all for this evening," the sculptor told Leindal as he cleaned off his tools. "You have sat long enough for me today."

"I enjoyed it," the queen said. "It gave my mind a chance to wander long enough to dwell on things besides this dreadful warring."

Connec nodded and walked across the studio to a basin. Splashing water on his face and arms, he rinsed off the stone dust from his work.

"Was the excavation a success?" the queen asked Pencroft.

He reached into his robe and pulled out the tiara. Flashing a smile, he held it out to her. "Of all the goods we unearthed, this was the most beautiful and I knew it was meant for you."

"How wonderful," Leindal whispered warmly, holding the crown to the light of the fireplace and gazing at the jewel mounted amidst the filigree. "I've never seen a gem like this before. Do you know what it is?"

Pencroft moved closer to his wife and tilted the tiara so that the light showed through the crystal. "See that small fleck in the center of the stone?"

"Why, yes. How curious! It doesn't look like a flaw. . . ."

"It's not a flaw, Leindal," Pencroft told her softly. "It's a seed."

"A what?"

"From the Favo tree," the king went on. "I'm almost certain of it. Do you realize the implications?"

"Of course," she said after a moment of stunned quiet.

"We must never tell of this, however. In the wrong hands, I can see only evil coming from it. Better that such powers are not tampered with by mortals. My thought was that you would wear it knowing that it represents the love I have for you, which is immortal."

"Oh, Pencroft." The queen's eyes were misty with joy. She kissed her husband again, then stood back and placed the tiara on her head. "There! I shall wear it proudly, because my love is also undying."

As they embraced once more, Connec cleared his throat to remind them he was still in the room. They parted, smiling shyly at one another before Pencroft turned to the sculptor. "I have a proposal for you, Connec."

"You have only to say the word. . . ." the sculptor said, rejoining them.

"I will take my leave," the queen said to her husband. "I wish to see how this present looks with my finest gowns. I will join you for late dinner and you will find me irresistible!"

"I already do," Pencroft said with a wink.

"We shall see. . . ." Smiling coquettishly, she blew her husband a kiss and nodded a farewell to the sculptor. "Good evening, Connec. I will be by in the morning for another sitting."

"I look forward to it," Connec said with a bow. "Good evening."

Pencroft watched her leave the room, still feeling a warmth of profound joy. Leindal gave him so much pleasure. He could not conceive of enduring the duties of his reign without her presence to provide him with an outlet for those more tender and vulnerable traits he was forced to hide from his subjects.

Wiping his hands with a strip of cloth, Connec said, "What is your proposal, your highness?"

Pencroft turned and walked among the sculptor's various projects. Besides the bust of Leindal, there were sculptures of soldiers, statesmen and beasts. There was even a life-sized rendering of the king himself, on the verge of completion. Stopping before the figure of an armed warrior, Pencroft said, "When I came to power, I had the large frieze over the main gates to the city torn down because it depicted the practice of sorcerers."

"I remember the occasion well," Connec commented. He hesitated a moment, then added, "You know that I opposed your action. A work of art as well done as that frieze deserved to be left standing for all to see, regardless of its content. There are few works in all the land to match the awesome splendor of that piece."

Pencroft looked Connec in the eye and said, "What I had in mind was for you to replace that frieze with one of your own, depicting our victory over the Ghetites and Shangorans. I want a work that will be the talk of Dorban and an inspiration to all who pass through the gates of Cothe!"

Connec's eyes lit up and he was mute with excitement.

"I see that you are interested," Pencroft said. "I want to pay tribute to those who gave their lives, and a monument to our country's courageous defense of its capital in the face—"

Pencroft's words were cut short by a chilling scream issued from across the hall. It was a high-pitched cry, filled with pure terror, raising the king's flesh with trepidation.

"Leindal!" he gasped. His hand went to the belt wrapped around his surcoat and he pulled forth a dagger as he charged past Connec. In long strides he cleared the room and burst into the hallway. The royal guardsmen fell in beside him as he rushed to the queen's chamber and threw aside the doors. The soldiers charged in first, pikes lowered.

The queen was nowhere to be seen. Lying dead in the center of the room were two royal chambermaids, their throats slit and bleeding on the woven carpet.

"What deviltry is this?" Pencroft roared at the sight, looking around him wildly for a trace of his beloved or the assailants. The guards spread out immediately and began to search the room, pulling aside satin draperies and probing their blades into closets and veiled niches. The chamber was large, filled with stuffed divans, ornate furnishings and elaborate artworks, some of them created by Connec himself. Every space, every object was hastily inspected, but no clues were yielded as to the fate of the queen or the identity of her abductors. The precious tiara was missing as well.

"They have to be here!" the king raged as he angrily shoved aside the divan closest to him. "We would have seen anyone who tried to leave by way of the corridor."

But the search proved fruitless. One by one, the soldiers exhausted any possibilities of a hiding place and shook their heads grimly at one another. With desperation, the king advanced to the lone window in the chamber, which looked out over the sorcerers' gardens. He could see the men still laboring at the obelisk, but glancing straight down he saw that the sheer walls of the palace dropped almost eighty feet to the flagstone pave of the courtyard. Soldiers milled about the courtyard, glancing up at the king with looks of consternation.

"Did anyone leave or enter by way of this window?" the king shouted down. He was answered by shaking heads and a few cries of "No, sire."

"Madness," Pencroft muttered, backing away from the window and facing those who stood in the chamber with him. "This is madness."

Nine

Crouched at the base of the closest fruit tree, Nuroc remained motionless, although his muscles and nerves were poised on the brink of action. He watched the guard who stood between him and his objective, ever vigilant, turning to point his crossbow in the direction of every sound that cracked the silence of his post. Nuroc had been frozen in position for minutes on end, and his body was beginning to cramp from the tension of his unnatural pose. Still he dared not move.

Past the guard, he could see clearly the crumbled remnants of the obelisk. Great stone slabs lay across one another, covering the foundation of the former temple. As one crew of workers continued to extract the last portion of treasure to be uncovered by the first phase of the excavation, others were preparing to clear another part of the ruins. Two short, agile servants scrambled nimbly over the piled slabs. About their waists each carried lengths of thick rope woven from the sturdiest fibers to be found in all of Aerda, the sort normally used for mooring large ships in the harbor. Carefully, the young men sought out the best footing on the tilting slabs, realizing that despite the great size of the stones, any one of them might give way under their added weight and come sliding down on the other work crew.

When they came to the largest of the stone shards, which jutted out defiantly from a handful of other slabs weighing several tons apiece, the servants set to work. Tying loops into position at the tip of the largest slab, they began their cautious descent, feeding out the twin lines of rope connected to the stone. When they were back on solid ground, the servants signaled to their fellow workers, who gathered up their last handful of plunder and carried it across the drawbridge spanning the moat. There, the gems and jewels were added to the growing collection filling a second carriage.

The servants fed out the last of their lines as they came to the team of twelve oxen hitched on the far side of the moat, facing away from the obelisk. Tight knots were tied to the yoke connecting the last pair of oxen, then the servants stepped to one side as the oxmaster flexed his leather whip and cracked it over the heads of the beasts. Bellowing futile protests, the oxen edged forward, straining at their yokes. The twin lines reaching to the ruins quickly tautened, then held firm as the stone slab they were connected to refused to yield to the tug of the beasts.

"Harder!" the oxmaster howled, using his whip for emphasis. The oxen responded with more rebellious grunts and leaned their broad shoulders forward against the resistance of the great stone.

Nuroc's eyes were riveted on the ruins of the obelisk. He saw that almost the entire garden area on the island was buried under the slagheap that the men were trying to clear. His chances of securing a branch of the desired bush, much less finding one, were slim, if not negligible. His timing would have to be perfect, as would his coordination and speed. He tried to will away the cramping in his legs as he trained his gaze on the single piece of broken wall rising from the heap of other fragments.

Finally, the slab began to move. Cheering filled the gardens and the soldiers paced excitedly along the edge of the moat. Nuroc took advantage of the noise to spring forward from cover. With long strides he rushed toward the distracted guard. Failing to hear Nuroc's approach above the din, it was too late for him to defend himself. As the guard was turning around, Nuroc took a broad swipe at his head with the butt of his sword-hilt. His knees buckled and he slumped noiselessly to the ground, unconscious.

Nuroc looked over to the island to make sure he hadn't been spotted. Everyone else had their eyes on the obelisk, where the wavering slab began to give off a foreboding crunch as it shifted position under the pull of the oxen. The noise grew louder, until finally the slab tumbled over. Dislodged, the stone also sent the surrounding fragments free of their resting places. Like an avalanche of stone, the entire section of ruins shifted and rumbled down the slope of the island into the moat.

Loose dust rose in an instant cloud about the foundation, and Nuroc took advantage of the temporary obscurement to charge down the knoll and around to the side of the moat, where no guards had been posted. Without hesitating, he dropped over the edge and landed on the pieces of fallen stone that rose above the waterline. Trusting his judgment, he bounded from stone to stone until he reached the island, then clambered up onto solid ground. He had dropped his sword while crossing the moat so that he could better balance himself, and now he was unarmed, protected only by the thin cloud of raised dust that also hampered his vision.

Unable to see the position of the work crews and soldiers, Nuroc circled around the edge of the island to the spot that had just been cleared. The slabs of broken wall had fallen in such a way that another large portion of the obelisk's ground floor lay exposed. Even through the choking dust Nuroc could see the wealth that had been uncovered. Gold, silver, and an array of jewels shone from between the stone shards. But treasure was the last thing on Nuroc's mind. Blinking to keep the fine dust from settling in his eyes, he looked for signs of plant life growing through the rubble.

"Look!" someone cried out from across the moat. "There's a soldier trying to steal some of the plunder!"

"Stop!" another shouted.

"After him!" a third commanded.

"Slay him on sight."

Nuroc ignored their cries when he had waved away the dust with his hand. He'd succeeded! He spotted sprigs of green sticking out from beneath the large slab that was still connected to the two ropes. Nuroc inspected the leaves and blossoms with exultation. He had to touch the plant to make sure it was real.

"Neotolan!" he whispered, jerking at the branch until it snapped free in his hand. But before he could look around for more, an arrow slammed into the stone a few inches away from him. The arrow shattered and Nuroc felt the sting of shrapnel on his arm like the burn of a hot coal. He wadded the branch into a ball and stuffed it into the pocket of his jupon, then scrambled back over the jagged terrain of broken stone to the area behind the obelisk. More arrows whistled past him and clattered off the stone. He could feel blood seeping from the wound on his arm but ignored it.

A second time he descended into the moat and bounded across the exposed slabs back toward the main gardens. His sword was still laying where he'd dropped it, but when he bounded onto the stone, it tilted to one side and the weapon slipped off into the black waters of the moat only seconds before he could close his hands around the hilt. An arrow whistling past his shoulder kept him from trying to grope through water for the sword. The soldiers were rushing toward him, and it was all he could do to scramble to land and bolt into the foliage. More arrows sped into the thickets after him.

Branches and thorns lashed out at him as he propelled himself through the overgrowth, trying to widen the distance between himself and his pursuers. He could hear them thrashing their way down his well-marked trail. He wished he could come across one of the pathways, where he might stand a chance of throwing them off his track. In the darkness that lay beyond the torchlight of the obelisk he felt he could elude the soldiers indefinitely, if only he could gain a few seconds on them.

Nuroc finally broke through to a clearing and saw a dirt trail winding through the shrubbery only a few dozen feet away. Breaking into a full run, he dashed across the clearing, his lungs laboring to keep pace with his momentum.

He was almost to the path when his foot came down hard on a hollowing in the ground. The next thing he knew the earth had swallowed him. Everything went black, and he let out a cry of anguish as his fall ended on contact with the firmly-packed dirt of an underground walkway. He'd fallen through a rotted trapdoor leading to the catacombs.

It was only by virtue of his quick reflexes Nuroc was able to land in the tunnel without breaking bones or knocking himself out. Still, a sharp pain ran up his leg from a turned ankle, and he wheezed painfully a few seconds to regain the air that had been knocked out of him.

Leaning against the cold dirt of the tunnel wall, he looked up and saw the night sky showing through the gaping hole that had claimed him. He knew that it would not take long for the soldiers to discover his route of escape and take up the pursuit.

He peered down the tunnel in both directions, getting his bearings and determining which route would take him back toward the city. Once he heard the approaching shouts of the armed posse, he decided on a course and took it, favoring his wounded ankle as he headed off into the black maw of darkness, where the air was thin and cold.

He made his way with one hand in constant contact with the walls of the tunnel so that he could judge the bends and turns. The darkness was more of a curse than a blessing, especially when he heard the soldiers enter the tunnel and immediately strike fire to a pair of torches. With their way lit, they would quickly gain ground on him, who was slowed by both the darkness and his limping gait.

It had been only one night ago that Nuroc and Myrania had traversed the catacombs beneath the obelisk, but nothing about this particular stretch struck him as familiar. He began to fear that he might have stumbled onto one of the several arms of the subterranean tunnels that served only as a resting place for parted sorcerers and dead-ended in a shrine. Several times already his fingers had brushed alongside crypts set in carved niches, where the kings of old lay in their final rest. Each time he had recoiled involuntarily at the touch and felt a dizzy fear chill his blood, remembering how the dead sorcerers had come to life the night before and almost succeeded in helping Augage overthrow the city. He and Myrania had battled futilely against the risen dead, and he held no desire to pit himself against them again, especially in his condition.

The echoing advance of his pursuers pushed him on down the dark shaft until he began to see a faint light shining from the direction in which he was headed. He slowed his pace a moment, fearing that another group of soldiers had somehow found a second entrance to the catacombs and were about to close him in. If he were caught between two groups of armed men with orders to slay him on sight, Nuroc doubted that he would live to see the world above again.

Nuroc was about to stop running and save his strength for a final standoff when he turned the next bend in the tunnel and realized that the light before him came, not from the torches of more soldiers, but from glowing crystals imbedded in the ceiling of the tunnel. Amazed, he went on once more. The pain in his ankle was subsiding somewhat, but he was hesitant to put his full weight on it yet. He moved through a section of catacombs bathed in the eerie greenish radiance emanating from the roughly faceted, semi-clear crystals. Nuroc had never laid eyes on stones with such properties before, but he was not in a position to fully appreciate the sight. To him, they served as a light that allowed him a chance to move faster through the catacombs; nothing more.

The tunnel gradually widened until the crystal glow showed the walls to be more than fifteen feet apart. The distance from ceiling to floor was almost the same, and Nuroc's footsteps sounded increasingly louder in the vaster space. He figured that he had, by now, fled far enough that he was somewhere beneath the city instead of the gardens. If he could come to another trap door similar to the one he had fallen through, he might be able to surface in a darkened part of the town and steal his way back to the coliseum to Myrania in time to save her. Unfortunately, though, the tunnel seemed to stretch on unbroken as far as he could see. Not only was there no sign of a ceiling niche or an alcove in the walls, but the entire passageway was void of anything but chiseled stone and shining crystals. No crypts, no torches, no old weapons he might snatch up for his defense against the troops who continued to make known their pursuit with shouts and footsteps.

As he came toward the next turn, Nuroc smelled a familiar scent fouling the way before him. Once he recognized the odor, he abruptly halted and fell silent. Of all the smells he had been subjected to the past few days, none was more persistent or more fear-instilling than the smell that now hung in the thin air around him.

"A crawler!" he surmised with a pang of terror.

Stepping warily to the bend of the next turn and peering around the corner, he saw that which he hoped he would not see—an Iatse Crawler, thirty feet of crawling, segmented horror, a centipedelike beast whose massive head was bisected by vertical jaws layered with razor-sharp teeth. In girth, the beast filled out almost the entire space of the tunnel it lay in. Large, rounded eyes rested on either side of the powerful mouth. It was when he saw those eyes that Nuroc's initial shock was tempered by the faintest flicker of hope.

Nuroc also noticed that the beast wasn't moving. It seemed far from likely that the crawler, with one of the most highly-developed senses of smell of all creatures, would not have been alerted to Nuroc's presence by the streaks of fresh blood that flowed from his few wounds and scrapes.

Stepping fully around the corner, Nuroc approached the crawler, trusting his instincts but still prepared to take action if the beast came to life. As he came closer to the monster, he noticed a sword buried to the hilt in the folds of vulnerable flesh lying just below the crawler's horn-spiked neck. A darkened ooze bubbled slowly from the wound and spilled into a puddle in the dirt.

"Dead," Nuroc whispered with relief.

He had little time to contemplate the sight before him. The clamor of footsteps and the clanging of swords were sounding closer. They were almost upon him now. Looking back at the slain crawler, he knew there was too little room for him to squeeze by and continue his flight before he would be overtaken.

He was trapped.

Ten

"He can't be much farther ahead of us!" one of the guards cried out, leading the handful of men that charged down the crystalline corridor of the underground catacombs.

"You've said as much since we first took up the chase," the man behind him snarled between breaths. "I say to hell with him. Let's catch our wind and see if we can't pry a few of those gems from the walls."

Another babbled, "There will be time for that after we've slain this thief. I haven't come this far to let him escape our clutches!"

"Aye," a fourth piped in, all the while adding his measured step to the trampling of feet that echoed down the tunnels before and behind them. On they pressed, swords in hand, anger in their hearts, eyes peering through the greenlit gloom at the tracks Nuroc had left in the dirt.

As they were approaching the next turn, a resounding scream raked along the walls. It was a cry of tortured agony, piercing each man's soul with primitive apprehension. One by one, they slowed their headlong rush and unslung the shields strapped across their backs. Several gagged on the vile reek wafting in the passageway.

Rounding the corner, they dropped back in terror. The Iatse crawler blocking the tunnel was shaking its massive head as it closed its deadly jaws around Nuroc's struggling frame. Nuroc wailed again, this time with even more pain in his voice. His limbs were bathed in blood.

"Babyl and Dorban!" one of the men cried out, "By all the gods, I've never seen a crawler that size!"

Another sheathed his sword in favor of his crossbow. He started to load the weapon when one of his companions reached over and shoved the bow aside, hissing, "Don't be a fool!

Provoke the beast and it will come after us as well. Let it have the thief! Let's get out of here!"

The others were already heeding the advice. With a speed surpassing that by which they had arrived at the scene of the crawler's frenzy, the soldiers beat a hasty retreat back the way they had come.

It was only after the din of their footsteps no longer sounded near the crawler that its head ceased its spasmodic churning. With a groan of displeasure, Nuroc held the head up by the roof of the beast's mouth and moved clear of the countless fangs, then heaved the crawler away from him. The limp head bounded off the wall and landed on the ground with a sick crunch. Overcome by the unendurable stench of the crawler's jaws, Nuroc dropped to his knees and retched violently, as if to purge himself of the inhaled putrefaction.

Weakened but thankful to be alive, Nuroc wiped off the smeared blood from his surface wounds and muttered to the dead beast, "My thanks to you. You played your part as well as I."

Standing, Nuroc withdrew the sword from the crawler's neck and stared curiously at the weapon. From what he had seen on the battlefield the previous night, he knew the design of the sword to be Shangoran. The insight puzzled him further as to the true identity of the monster's slayer. Once he made his way past the beast, he found another clue in the set of footprints that marked the dirt floor of the tunnel. From the size, they looked to be those of two men. Nuroc thought at once that perhaps some of the resurrected sorcerers of old had clung to life even after the defeat of Augage, but that possibility did not explain the presence of a Shangoran sword. Shangora was a kingdom no older than Aerda, and in the five years of its existence, he doubted that any of its subjects had gained access to the catacombs before the return of Augage several nights ago.

He followed the tracks by the light of the scattered crystals that continued to line the walls of the tunnel. Soon he came to a fork in the passageway. Down the narrower of the offshoots, the men's footprints went in both directions. A third set of tracks followed in only one direction, coming back from the offshoot to the fork. The third pair of feet were bare and only half the size of the booted prints on either side of them.

"A woman," Nuroc whispered.

He considered the two directions before him. The three who made the tracks had last traveled the larger of the tunnels. Much as he was curious to discover who they were, he was more concerned about reaching the surface and Myrania's side without further delay. He headed down the narrower shaft, noticing at once that the way sloped gradually upward. He lengthened his stride in anticipation, and even smiled as he thought of the expression he would see on Myrania's face once he had returned with the bush and word of the feats he had accomplished on her behalf.

The tunnel steadily rose to an end at the base of a stone staircase that reached upward into darkness at a precipitous angle. Nuroc quietly started up the steps, leaving behind the glimmer of the glowstones and entering what seemed to be a cold black void. When the steps ended, he found himself in a cramped passage, barely wide enough for him to walk without turning sideways. The tight space only brightened Nuroc's spirits, though, because he suspected he was making his way along a secret walkway built into the walls of some building within the city. He had only to reach the exit and make sure that his departure went unnoticed and he would be but a few minutes away from the medic's tent. Of course, he would have to sneak past a few men to reach his destination, but after the obstacles he had so far surmounted, dodging sentinels seemed akin to child's play.

Nuroc did not have far to go down the cramped passageway before he saw light seeping in through a small hole in the wall before him. He moved silently to the opening and peered through it. To his astonishment, he found himself staring into the chambers of Queen Leindal. The bodies of the two attendants had been removed, as had the woven rug they had bled to death upon. There was a man in the room whose back was turned to Nuroc. Across the chamber, a young, voluptuous servant girl stood smiling at the man and, without her knowing, at Nuroc.

"I've seen the way you look at me," the woman was saying to the man as her fingers toyed with the strings of her silken kirtle. She stood before the rising flames of the hearth, and the full contours of her body shone in silhouette through the thin material of her garb. "I think you would like to see more. Much more."

The man in the room did not reply, other than to slip into an ornate chair and stretch his legs out on a leather-and-jaunwood hassock. The woman chuckled slightly, then took the strings and gently pulled them until the knot gave way and the kirtle came apart in the front, baring her ample cleavage and the creamy whiteness of her stomach.

"You've looked everywhere for the queen but here," she teased, reaching inside the scanty shift and stroking her breasts. "Perhaps you should complete your search."

The man laughed lowly, "My queen is missing and I sit here being seduced by a servant. Have I no shame?"

Nuroc reflexively pulled away from the peephole at the sound of the man's voice. It was Lieutenant Seth!

"Those with shame miss out on the best of life's pleasures," the servant cooed, swaying over to the queen's bed and settling onto the plush coverlet draped across it. She pulled the comforter up before her and held it in place with one hand as she slipped out of her kirtle, all the while keeping her eyes on the lieutenant. "Come," she whispered dreamily, pushing the tip of her tongue along her upper lip. "I need more than the fire of the hearth to keep me warm."

Seth rose from his chair and began to approach the woman as he untied the drawstrings of his surcoat.

"Very well," he told her. "I will show you the way an officer makes love."

"I would rather you showed me something new," the woman said coyly. "In return, there are a few things I will teach you as well."

From his place of concealment, Nuroc watched the seduction uneasily. Of all the places to emerge from the catacombs, he had chosen the royal palace and a doorway that would lead him into the hands of the man who had first sent him fleeing from the coliseum hours ago.

There was a chance he could enter the chamber and rush past Seth before the lieutenant could react. But how would he fare once he found himself in the main corridors of the palace with a general alarm sounded and royal guardsmen all about? No, there would have to be another way. Nuroc reasoned that the hidden walkway he was in probably ran all through the palace. Rather than make his break now, he decided it would be wiser to move on until he came to an opening that led to an unoccupied chamber, or, preferably, to the outside.

He took a step away from the peephole, stretching his hand

out before him to feel his way along the wall. His fingers fell upon a lever sticking out from the inner wall, and before he could pull them away, there was a loud click and an entire section of the wall and floor swung about on a pivot. Suddenly Nuroc found himself inside the queen's chamber, his back turned to the room as he faced the wall concealing his abandoned hiding place.

"By the beard of Aerda's ghost!" Seth exclaimed, whirling about to face his intruder. "You!"

Nuroc turned from the wall, realizing what had just happened. He saw Seth's hand go to his scabbard and come out with a gleaming saber. Trapped, Nuroc had no choice but to raise the Shangoran blade and prepare to defend himself. In the background, the naked servant sat on the bed, watching the impending conflict with wide-eyed fascination.

"I knew you had to be behind this," Seth taunted as he circled about the room, holding his saber before him and inching his way closer to Nuroc. "Where's the queen? What have you done with her?"

"You are mistaken, as usual," Nuroc answered, matching the lieutenant's moves and staying out of the saber's range. "Put down your blade and let me explain."

"I have no interest in your lies, Shangoran dog!" Seth snapped his wrist and his saber whipped through the air at a sharp angle. Nuroc turned his own blade to one side and caught the blow, filling the room with the clang of metal. He pushed the saber away and followed with a swipe of his own, missing Seth's face by inches.

"I give you one more chance," Nuroc warned. "Sheathe your sword and apologize and perhaps we can shake hands as friends before the night is through."

Seth gathered phlegm in the back of his throat and spat at Nuroc, hitting him on the shoulder. "There's your apology, vermin! Now taste the price one pays for insulting me!"

In a sudden burst of fury, Seth fell on Nuroc with an unflagging series of cuts and stabs. His blade was a blur of constant motion, which would have left most opponents bleeding and dismembered. Nuroc, however, proved to be a swordsman of equal skill, parrying Seth's every thrust and countering with his own deft slashes. After this initial exchange, both men had suffered only rips in their tunics. Neither man fought in place, and the chamber furnishings paid a sad toll as Seth and Nuroc veered to and fro, kicking aside chairs and planters or grabbing up a vase or carving to shield a blow. Seth pressed on with a manic grin stamped across his features. Nuroc's face bore a scowl of concentration.

"The queen," Seth seethed between his clenched teeth. "Where is she?"

"I don't know!" Nuroc spat. "If she was abducted, it was by the men who own this sword."

"That would be you, Shangoran."

"Enough," Nuroc countered. "Who are you to question one's loyalty, when you try to bed a servant in the queen's own chamber?"

"I'll do more than *try* to bed her once I've finished you," Seth boasted. "I handle my other sword as well as this one." He flicked the saber at Nuroc's face, nicking his chin.

They fought beside the heat of the fireplace. Nuroc's back was to the hearth, and when Seth leaned into him with a savage stab, the younger man's backstep sent him sprawling over a bound stack of logs. Nuroc's sword fell from his hand as he braced himself to keep from striking his head against the hearth. As it was, he landed flat on his back, less than a foot away from the glowing embers of the fire.

Seth moved in and lashed out with his saber again. Nuroc rolled away from the blow, but the blade tore through the folds of his tunic and drew more blood from a light slice on his shoulder. Nuroc saw the fireplace poker resting in the fire and clutched at its handle, burning his palm with conducted heat. Mindless of the pain, he bounded to his feet, ducking another swipe by Seth and bringing the glowing tip of the heated poker around in a hissing arc that ended when the tip bit into the side of Seth's face. The force of the blow snapped the lieutenant's head to one side. For a second he stared at Nuroc dumbfounded, then the look on his face gave way to the blank stare of death. Dropping his saber, Seth keeled over. The smell of seared flesh and hair stung Nuroc's nostrils. He looked down at the trace of gore on the tip of the poker and tossed it back into the fire.

Nuroc stared past Seth's body to the queen's bed, where the servant girl watched him with a trace of fear crowding out her entranced expression. She held the coverlet closer to her. Neither of them spoke.

There was a commotion outside the chamber, and as they both looked to the doorway, in charged five members of the royal guard. Three of them carried crossbows, all raised so that Nuroc found himself facing the tips of three arrows. The ranking officer saw Seth's body and the dishevelled state of the room, then leveled his gaze at Nuroc and the servant girl.

"What has happened here?" he demanded.

The woman pointed at Nuroc and cried out, "He's the one behind the queen's disappearance! He returned through a secret panel in the wall and was about to rape me when Seth came in to defend me. You came just in time to save—"

"She lies!" Nuroc said. "Look at her, lying there unclothed. Check her clothes to see if they've been ripped from her. See if she bears any marks of manhandling and—"

"Still your tongue!" the officer shouted at Nuroc.

The woman coaxed tears into her downcast eyes and moaned pitifully, "He held a sword to me and forced me to undress. Look at the sword! It is the weapon of a Shangoran!"

The officer looked at the floor and frowned, seeing the blade Nuroc had lost in the fighting.

"She still lies," Nuroc insisted. "I can explain everything."

"Save your breath," the officer commanded. "Let the king hear your fables before you are put to death!"

Eleven

"I know you."

The king's first words smote Nuroc with despair. He was standing before Pencroft in the throne room, and the king had spoken after staring at him a few moments. When Nuroc did not respond, the king rose from his throne and stepped down to his prisoner's level, eyeing him closer.

"Yes, yes," the king went on. "You were the son of Talmon-Khash's private servants in the days before the cataclysm. You also worked as a shepherd for the royal flock. Am I right?"

Nuroc took a deep breath. There was no point in holding back the truth any longer. He would be fortunate to survive the night as it was. Members of the royal guard stood on either side of the throne with their crossbows aimed at his heart, looking as if they hoped he might make a move toward the king and force their hand.

"I am Nuroc, son of Stromthroad and Thouris, as you say. But you are wrong to believe that everyone who once swore allegiance to the rule of sorcerers is now an ally of Ghetite and Shangora. There is not a soul alive in this land over the age of five who was not once a follower of Talmon-Khash, yourself included. You were one of his generals, after all."

"Blasphemy!" one of the guards cried out. "Let me cut him down, your majesty, lest he insult you again!"

Pencroft turned to the man who had spoken, his eyes narrow with irritation. "I did not seek your counsel, soldier," he said coldly.

Rebuffed, the soldier fell silent, but continued to glare at Nuroc with hateful eyes.

"What has been your life these past five years?" Pencroft asked Nuroc calmly.

"I fled Cothe with my parents to the mining town of Wheshi," Nuroc confessed. "There we lived as loyal citizens of Aerda. I worked in the mines with my father, although my wish was to join the military. Stromthroad forbade it, though, fearing that you would recognize me and have me put to death as you have others who served under Talmon-Khash in the sorcerers' gardens."

The king stroked his beard as he regarded Nuroc. "Knowing this, why is it you risked the fate that has caught up with you?"

"Before Talmon-Khash invoked the Oath of Dissolvement and vanished into the altar of Dorban, he performed a ritual by which he joined his blood with that of myself and my parents. It was to be within our power to summon Talmon-Khash back to the world of the living should the need for his presence arise. When Augage was preparing for his second attempt at imprisoning the condor-god and taking over all of Dorban, he knew that we had to be slain so that we could not bring Talmon-Khash back to thwart his plans. A band of Ghetites and Shangorans slew my family with the coming of the black moon, and it was only by a stroke of good fortune that I did not fall to the same fate. I set out immediately for Cothe to do what I could to stop Augage, and I succeeded by reviving Talmon-Khash in the form of the condor-god. Had I not acted as I did, the obelisk you have looted today would still be standing, and Augage would be within it, ruling this entire continent by virtue of his enslavement of the condor-god."

Pencroft waved his arms in the air and walked away from Nuroc, saying, "Enough, enough! All this talk of oaths and gods has my head spinning." He stepped up onto the dais and sat back in the massive throne that all but dwarfed him in its ornate grandeur. He seemed troubled by Nuroc's story. At last he clasped his fingers together and said, "If what you say is true, then how is it—"

"It is true!" Nuroc insisted.

"Very well," Pencroft said drily. "Then why is it that in the course of a few hours, you have been found in the underground barracks under suspicious circumstances following the massacre of unsuspecting Aerdan soldiers? Then later you are found in the chambers of the missing queen, having killed the same man who apprehended you in the first place. And with a Shangoran sword at your side, no less. All the evidence points to you being an agent of the enemy. How am I to believe your wild tales? Is there someone who can vouch for anything you have said? Curse you, my wife is—"

"I will vouch for him," a voice boomed out from the entrance to the throne room.

All eyes turned to General Palem, who strode forward to join the king and the others. He was out of uniform, wearing a plain leather jerkin and the look of one just roused from bed.

"What are you saying?" Pencroft asked his chief aide with a questioning look.

Palem answered firmly, "I too had my suspicions about this lad when I first encountered him, but once I saw him on the battlefield my doubts vanished in the wind. He took up the sword against Ghetite and Shangoran alike and fought with the zeal of any three of my best men. I know as well that he had some hand in the destruction of the obelisk and the defeat of Augage. That is enough proof of his loyalty for me."

King Pencroft weighed his general's words with a brooding silence. He finally looked at Nuroc and asked, "You know nothing of the queen's disappearance?"

Nuroc shook his head. "The first I heard of it was when I stumbled into the chamber where Seth was about to bed the servant girl. He accused me of being a spy, just as he had in the coliseum. I tried to explain both times, but he would not listen. He meant to slay me. I had no choice but to defend myself."

"You still haven't told me why you were in the palace in the first place."

Nuroc quickly explained the plight of Myrania and his daring quest to secure the antidote for her poisoning. At the mention of the neotolan, he reached to the pocket of his tunic. "Gone!" he cried, turning the pocket outward, revealing only a partial leaf. "The branch is gone! I must have lost it. I need to bring it to Myrania or she will die, as will the others wounded in the battle!"

"Where do you think you might have lost it?" General Palem asked.

"It could be anywhere between the obelisk and the queen's chamber," Nuroc lamented dismally. He looked to Palem. "There's no time to retrace my tracks. We have to return to the gardens and find another of the bushes!"

The king held out his hand and shook his head. "Not so fast. Palem, you know the branch he seeks. Take a few men to the obelisk and look for the bush it came from—and check with Captain Naprope on the progress of the excavation. As for you, Nuroc, I will have to think more on your situation before I decide what is to be done with you. Palem speaks highly of you, but in light of what has happened today and this evening, I have no choice but to be wary. For the time being, you will have to be detained under guard. I will forego the dungeons and grant you the stay in one of the lower rooms here at the palace. You understand my need for caution, do you not?"

"Of course," Nuroc said bleakly, bracing to keep his temper under control. "But what of Myrania?"

"I will have her brought here as well," the king said. "You say that she is a sorceress?"

"I said that she was dying," Nuroc answered testily. "If you must know, she is daughter to the sorcerer Inkemisa, who lived a life in exile among the shoreline cliffs facing the Targoan Sea. It was he who first discerned that Augage was the bringer of the Great Cataclysm; he who sent Myrania and others to find me in hopes that Talmon-Khash could be revived in time to prevent another catastrophe. Inkemisa died for his concern, just as his daughter will unless the cure for her poisoning is prepared!"

"For one who claims allegiance to Aerda, you have a strange way of showing deference to its king," Pencroft said coolly.

"He is distraught, your majesty," Palem intervened. "Have

him placed in custody for the night if you wish." He turned to Nuroc, adding, "I believe you. Trust me, I will find this bush you seek if I have to turn over every stone slab in the gardens. After seeing so many of my men die on the battlefield, I long for the chance to see that the wounded live."

General Palem saluted the king, then departed from the throne room. Pencroft watched him leave, then looked at Nuroc and said, "You owe him your live, you realize."

"And Myrania's too, I hope," Nuroc said lowly.

Twelve

His wounds covered with salves and dressing under a newly issued tunic, Nuroc sat alone in a storage room adjacent to the palace kitchens. Blank walls shone dully in the moonlight that filtered in through the single, head-sized opening to the outside. Sacks of grain were lined along a shelf against one wall, and a wooden table stood empty against another. Two flimsy cots stuffed with fresh hay lay in the center of the room.

He was not sure how long he had been sitting there. It seemed like hours, but when he stood up and looked outside to measure the moon's march across the night sky, he realized how little time had passed. He went back to pacing, following the circle of tracks he'd already made in the dirt that lined the floor. He reached into one of the grain sacks and withdrew a handful of millet, biting into one of the hard grains before spitting it out and letting the feed sift back through his fingers. He wished the time would move as swiftly.

At last there was a sound at the door. The outside bolt was drawn and the door creaked open. Two guards made their way into the room, carrying Myrania on a stretcher between them. She looked on the verge of death. General Palem strode into the room behind them. His face was grave.

"You could not find the neotolan?" Nuroc asked.

"The work crew at the obelisk had started a fire to warm them through the night," Palem said. "To keep the blaze going they fed it brush on the island. I fear that the bush you took your branch from was already set to flame."

"No!" Nuroc moaned.

"Perhaps when another section is cleared away more of the bushes will show up," the general said hopefully. "I also ordered the men who pursued you into the catacombs to retrace their steps through the tunnel to see if they could find the sprig. They did not see it. Right now they are combing the gardens by torchlight to see if you lost it in the overgrowth. They cannot look too closely, however, for fear of igniting the brush. In the morning, perhaps they will be able to—"

"Look at her!" Nuroc said, pointing to where the two soldiers had transferred Myrania onto one of the cots. "In the morning she will be dead!"

"I am doing all that can be done, Nuroc," Palem said gently. "I also have to follow the other tracks leading to the tunnels from the queen's chamber. Leindal's disappearance must be my first priority. You have to understand that."

Nuroc moved away from the general and slumped down onto the edge of the cot next to Myrania. He stared down at her sallow face and noted the shallowness of her breathing, feeling a hopeless anger build in his chest. He held his lover's hand to his cheek and laid his lips to her wrist, feeling her faint pulse.

"If we find anything, I will bring it to you immediately," Palem promised. His men walked out of the room and he followed, pausing momentarily in the doorway to look back at Nuroc and Myrania. The sight filled him with remorse. Finally he turned away, cursing the fates beneath his breath as he closed the door on them and threw the bolt shut.

Alone with Myrania, Nuroc gently ran his fingers through her hair, clearing it away from her glistening forehead. The fever still raged within her, burning up what little strength she had left. The wound on her leg showed further signs of the poison's toll as well. The discoloration had spread out across the whole lower leg, and the fresh application of clear ointment only served to highlight the infection.

"Don't die," he pleaded. "You're all I have left, Myrania. Don't die, please."

Her eyelids fluttered and opened slightly. Nuroc leaned over and looked into her eyes. There was no focus in her gaze, however, and the lids slowly closed again.

Tears of grief began to well in Nuroc's eyes as he pulled away from Myrania. He was so overcome with his misery that at first he did not hear the whisper coming from the small window behind him.

"Psssst. Are you in there?" a soft voice hissed a second time.

"What?" Nuroc mumbled, startled by the interruption. He glanced around the room, then rose from his cot and crept to the window and peered out.

The servant woman who had betrayed him in the queen's chamber stood outside the palace, looking up at the opening. She wore a full cloak and looked around her constantly to make sure no one had seen her.

"I had to see you," she whispered to Nuroc.

"Why? You've done enough," Nuroc told her harshly. "Or do you wish to taunt me?"

"No, no," the woman said. "You must forgive me. I had to say what I did or I might have faced death for making love with an officer. It is forbidden for one of my station to—"

"None of that matters now," Nuroc interrupted. "I understand your plight. Take my forgiveness and leave. I want to be alone with my loved one before she dies."

"As you wish," the woman said, reaching into the folds of her cloak. "But first let me give you this."

She held forth the missing sprig of neotolan.

"Can it be?" Nuroc gasped, doubting his eyes.

"You dropped it during your duel with Seth," the woman said. "I was about to toss it into the hearth, but I thought there had to be a reason for your carrying it."

"Yes!" Nuroc said excitedly, grasping the branch and clinging to it with new-found hope. "Thank you! You have no idea what good you have done!"

The woman smiled, then turned her head as she heard a voice bellow out in the darkness, "Who goes there by the window?"

"I'm glad I came," the servant whispered to Nuroc, pulling the cloak's hood over her head before rushing off into the shadows. Nuroc pulled the sprig inside the building as a guard rushed up to the window.

"There was someone here," he growled angrily. "Who?"

"I cannot say for certain," Nuroc told him. "Only that it was a man. He cursed me and then ran off that way." He pointed out the window in the direction away from where the servant had fled.

"If he cursed you, well enough," the guard said. "I do the same, Shangoran!"

Nuroc had no time for the guard's folly. He turned from the window and hurried to Myrania's side. He crushed the branch into a swollen ball and rolled it back and forth between his palms until it began to soften into a ragged pulp. Then, gently prying Myrania's brittle lips apart, he squeezed the mixture until a few drops of greenish ooze fell into her mouth.

Nuroc bent over and kissed her lips, then moved down and held the mashed sprig over the festering wound. More of the strange-colored juice trailed down onto Myrania's leg and soaked through the glistening ointment. Nuroc placed the pulp over the wound and quickly bound it into place with strips torn from the stretcher.

"It can't be too late," he muttered aloud. "Take hold, take hold!"

Myrania lay motionless on the cot, showing no reaction to the treatment. If anything, her pulse weakened and her breaths became fewer and farther between. What little color there was to her skin faded and she took on a grim pallor.

"This can't be!" Nuroc agonized. "What have I done? Have I poisoned you further?"

Torn with frustration, Nuroc fled from Myrania's side and beat at the stone walls with his fists. "It's not fair!" he roared. "She belongs with the living. She belongs with me!" He continued to vent his anger with his fists and more epithets until the rage passed, leaving a void that filled with sadness and resignation. He sank to his knees and stared at the wall, taking deep breaths to fill his exhausted lungs. He rubbed at his throbbing knuckles and stared at the bruises that had already begun to form. As his breathing tapered off to normal, he leaned forward and pressed his head against the cold stone wall. He felt empty.

Then the hairs along his scalp tingled with shock. He listened harder, and heard it again. He was not the only one in the chamber breathing.

"Myrania!"

Jumping to his feet, Nuroc sprang to the cot and stared in wonder at the transformation that had come over Myrania. The color had seeped back into her face. Her chest rose and sank in time to her steady breathing. The discoloration of her leg was rapidly receding before his eyes, as was the swelling.

Nuroc knelt beside the cot and felt Myrania's forehead. The fever had broken as well. She opened her eyes and looked up at

Nuroc. He felt ecstasy in her look of recognition. She licked at her cracked lips and murmured weakly, "Where are we? What has—"

Nuroc placed a finger over her lips. "Save your strength, Myrania. You are going to be well. That's all you need to know for now."

Myrania raised a hand and placed it over Nuroc's. "You succeeded." She smiled. "I knew you would."

Nuroc held her hand tightly. The tears he had held back now came forth, filled with joy instead of sorrow.

Thirteen

Dawn was breaking when Nuroc was awakened by the sound of the opening door. He jolted upright on the cot, pulling away the hand he had draped across Myrania's chest. She was sleeping soundly, looking much as she had before the onset of the poisoning that had almost claimed her.

King Pencroft and General Palem walked into the small chamber and nodded their greetings to Nuroc.

"Good news. We have found two whole bushes of the type you seek under . . ." Palem fell silent as he and the king looked down upon Myrania. "The woman is cured!" he exclaimed.

"As will be the other troops if you treat them promptly with the pulp of the neotolan," Nuroc said.

"I don't understand," Pencroft stated. "How did you come upon the bush in here?"

Nuroc told him about the visit made by the servant who had earlier accused him.

"It's a comfort to learn she's done some good," Pencroft grumbled. "I've had men searching for her all night to answer a few questions about her doings in the queen's chamber."

Palem said, "It should seem she has righted any wrong she may have committed."

Pencroft was not convinced. "Had she not been there practicing her wiles on Seth, he would not have been slain."

"He was no credit to the Shield of Aerda," Nuroc protested.

"I regret that I had to slay him, but I do not think the militia will be hard-pressed to replace him with a better man."

"Such as yourself, perhaps," the king said.

Nuroc regarded the two other men with suspicion. "I think I misunderstood you, your highness."

Pencroft shook his head. "Not so. Our findings during the night have confirmed most of what you have told us, and I no longer am inclined to disbelieve the rest. Further, I have spoken to some of the other soldiers who survived the battle yesterday, and they all echo Palem's praise for your handling of weapons and example of leadership. I wish to name you Seth's replacement as lieutenant."

Nuroc was stupefied. There had been moments during the night when he had feared that Myrania's recovery was in vain because Pencroft would sentence them both to be executed in the morning as sorcerers and enemies of Aerda. Now, instead of facing the axman's blade, he was being offered the position of officer in Aerda's militia, the fulfillment of a long-standing dream.

"Well," Palem said, interrupting Nuroc's thoughts. Nuroc saw that the general was trying to contain a prideful smile. "Do you choose to insult the king by refusing his offer?"

"No," Nuroc said, rising to his feet and standing at attention before both Palem and Pencroft. "I will be glad to serve."

"Good," Pencroft replied. Noticing Myrania beginning to stir on the cot behind them, he continued, "Let us leave the woman to her rest. There is still much we have to discuss."

Nuroc nodded, although he had to restrain himself from a desire to shake her awake with his joyous news. He contented himself with a kiss on her cheek and followed the two older men from the chamber.

The kitchen areas were alive with the smells of breakfast cooking and thick soups stewing in preparation for lunch. A large slab of ham turned slowly on a spit set over the rounded fire pit in the back corner. At the king's signal, the round-bellied chef sliced off strips of the pink, sizzling meat and placed them on wooden plates, alongside heels of fresh bread and quartered pieces of fresh fruit.

"I trust that you are hungry," Pencroft mentioned to Nuroc.

Nuroc's watering lips were answer enough. He watched on expectantly as the chef ladled off rich cups of goat's milk and set them next to the plates. Servants who had been standing by idly now moved in and picked up the trays that the meals were set upon and carried them from the kitchen to an outside terrace overlooking the city. The three men stepped out and took seats before the hand-hewn table stretching half the length of the terrace.

The servants left and Pencroft gestured for Nuroc to begin eating. Nuroc went first to the milk, slaking his thirst and waiting to see how it was that kings and generals partook of their food. To his surprise, they ate the same as any man, taking the food in their hands and tearing at both meat and bread with their teeth, then swallowing a portion of milk to help the food go down.

As he began to eat, Nuroc looked past the other two and stared out at the city that lay before him. It looked less foreboding than it had the night before, and far more beautiful. Colors that had been muted by the dark of night now flashed brilliantly on the lavish buildings that girded the palace. Gold leaf blazed under the morning sun and polished stone sparkled vibrantly. The dazzle all but blocked any view of the less affluent parts of the city. Only the fortifications seemed to rise in somber bleakness against the horizon.

Palem broke the lapse of silence, speaking between bites of ham. "We followed the tracks in the catacombs that had been left by the men who abducted Queen Leindal. It seems that before they found their way to the palace, they rose up through a secret entrance beneath the coliseum and—"

"They're the ones who loosed the wild beasts!" Nuroc interjected.

"Exactly," Palem confirmed. "There was a hidden doorway that connected with the feed bins. They must have emerged there and taken the keeper of the beasts by surprise. Or, more likely, it was the keeper who came upon them first, forcing their hand."

Nuroc closed his eyes a moment, remembering the sight of the old man with the stab wounds he had found before the opened cages. "Who is responsible for all this villainy? Did you find that out?"

"Villainy indeed," Palem said. "These acts were committed by men who fled the battlefield yesterday and entered the mouth of a tunnel through which the sorcerers had fled from Cothe five years ago."

"I know the place!" Nuroc interjected. "I saw the sorcerers

myself that night as they rode from the tunnel and across the meadows toward the coast. Whoever found that entrance must have been told where to find it by Augage or one of the other sorcerers. It had to be someone trusted."

Pencroft and Palem exchanged glances. The king forced a grin, telling the general, "You are right about this lad, Palem. He has a quick mind. He will make a fine officer."

Palem nodded and reached beneath the table to the pocket of his surcoat. Nuroc heard a metallic jangle, then Palem set something on the table before him. "We found it near the body of the crawler," the general said. "Do you recognize it?"

Nuroc saw a partial headdress of chain mail, stained with blood. There was a jagged line where the woven mesh had been ripped with a force that had pried the links apart. "You told me only two soldiers were wearing such headgear during the battle," Nuroc said, fingering the fine mesh. "King Molent of Shangora and General Wheas of Ghetite."

"There you have it," Palem said with finality.

"They kidnapped the queen?" Nuroc said.

Pencroft nodded gravely. "No doubt if they would have emerged at my chamber here in the palace, they would have slain me and laid claim to the throne. As it is, I fear they may ask as much by way of ransom, provided they haven't slain my wife already." At the last words, Pencroft's voice trailed off and Nuroc noticed for the first time the pronounced worry that strained the king's features.

The general broke in to distract the king from his anxiety. "My suspicion is that Molent lost his headpiece to the crawler—it might have bitten his head off if he hadn't been wearing it. As it turned out, though, the wounds he suffered could not have been too serious, since there was no blood along the tunnels but yours. From the looks of the footprints, it appears both men left the catacombs in full stride, with the queen dragged along between them. We could see her tracks as far as the place where the tunnel surfaces near the battlefield, so we suspect she was kept alive at least that far. Out on open ground, there were too many other tracks for us to determine which way they headed, but it's likely they mounted horses and headed back toward their border."

With the situation laid out before them, the men finished their meals in an uneasy silence, each one lost in thought, affected differently by the news.

"What is to be done?" Nuroc finally asked.

"We will take three courses," Pencroft said, then paused a moment as the servants drifted out onto the terrace long enough to retrieve the emptied plates and cups. The king resumed, "I have no choice but to remain here and await word of their terms for ransom, provided that is their objective. I am also expecting the arrival of King Onfeons of Belgore and Yute of Eldoth with regards to matters of state. It is my hope that the three of us can unite in convincing Molent and Wheas that they have only to lose by not returning Queen Leindal unharmed and surrendering on our terms."

General Palem added, "For my part, I go from here to the coliseum, where I will assemble a full force from the best of our men, then ride out from Cothe and head for Ghetite's border. Molent and Wheas must be made to know that their treachery will not be tolerated and that, alliance or not, return of the queen or not, we will have their surrender or their heads!" Palem bit off the final words, and Nuroc cringed slightly at the general's vehemence. He looked at Palem and saw in the older man the same thirst for vengeance he had felt himself when he had first set out for Cothe to lend his hand in battle against the forces of Augage.

"That leaves our third course," the king said, once again in control of his emotions. He turned to Nuroc and stared into the young man's eyes. "You."

Nuroc leaned back in his seat, uncomprehending. "Me?" he finally managed to utter. "I don't see how . . ."

"There are certain situations that can be better handled by one man than an entire regiment," the king said softly but firmly. When he saw that Nuroc still did not understand, he resumed, "In seeking out the medicinal shrub in the sorcerers' gardens, in escaping Seth's imprisonment and eluding recapture, in the feats of heroism you performed on the battlegrounds—in all these acts you have proven yourself to be a warrior of the likes that poets and minstrels cannot match with their wildest imaginations. It is as if there were some guiding force behind you, something that has little to do with the incantations of sorcerers or any other form of necromancy I know of. You are special. After careful consideration, I must say that there is no other soul in all of Aerda I would entrust with the mission I am asking of you."

Nuroc felt lightheaded from both the praise and the implications of the king's words. Taking a deep breath to gain control of his trembling throat, he said, "I will help in any way I can, your majesty."

"Good," Pencroft said. "Good. What I am asking is that you leave Cothe on your own and set out for Ghetite. Seek the trail of Molent and Wheas and try to save the queen from their clutches. They are sure to be on their guard against a large force like that of Palem's, but they cannot be expecting one man to try to thwart their plans alone. We will do what we can on our part, but in the end I suspect that the fate of Queen Leindal may rest in your hands."

There was a prolonged silence as Nuroc absorbed the magnitude of his mission. Both Palem and Pencroft looked to the younger man, awaiting his reply. Nuroc's face was a mask, devoid of emotion, until at least he bared his teeth in a confident grin.

"For this you only promote me to lieutenant?" he said with a straight face.

All at once, the three men broke out in a show of hearty laughter. They slapped their sides with the force of their mirth, and the sound of their outburst echoed out into the courtyard, drawing concerned stares from those about the palace. In the laughter, the men found a wondrous relief from the tension that had built up inside of them. They continued on until tears came to their eyes and their sides began to ache. Once the moment had passed, they fell solemn again, well aware that it would be some time before they would have cause to wallow in delight again.

Fourteen

The gates of the city opened and a single horseman rode from Cothe, striking out on the beaten trail that reached to the Targoan Sea. Dust rose from the trampling hooves that sounded rhythmically in the day's tranquility. Fields of green, flecked with the widely-colored bloom of spring, rolled away from either side of the trail. The midday sun filled the air with warmth and coaxed sweet smells from the blossoms that waved in the gentle breeze. Nuroc was on his way.

The beauty around him sustained the memories of his last few moments with Myrania before he had taken to the saddle. Weak but recovered, she had held him close, smelling fresh from the royal baths, and covered his face with gentle kisses from her soft, healed lips. They had walked alone, hand in hand, in the palace courtyard as he had told her of his recent adventures and his pending mission for the king. Her pride had been obvious, her concern less so. But he had sensed the worry she tried to hold back and had assured her that he would return to Cothe soon enough, with the queen at his side. Out of consideration, the king had given Nuroc and Myrania the use of a private chamber for their final embraces, and they had spent those last few moments lying together on a plush divan, making gentle love and pledging their hearts to one another.

And so, as he urged his steed along the trail until the city was left behind, Nuroc took in the grandeur of his surroundings and felt at one with them. He slowed his pace, trying to prolong the feeling. There was a part of him that longed for serenity and a simple life, not unlike that he had so despised in Wheshi, before he had tasted the true meaning of battle and the sort of life that was, in the end, a dance with Death, danced to the strings of fate.

He knew the rapture could not last, not in the face of what lay before him. The first sign of what was to be came in the distant sky, where clouds could be seen rolling in from the coast, and where the air was dotted with circling forms of hawks and vultures. Next came a shift in the winds, bringing with it the carrion scent from the battlefields, where the dead had lain for more than a day.

His lone presence on the road ended as he started up the first rise and came upon an oxcart carrying bodies from the bloodied marshland. Eight beasts were hitched up to the cart. It was forty feet long, ten feet wide and filled completely with Aerdan corpses bearing the ravages of fatal wounds and the onset of decay. Stiff limbs poked through its walls and bobbed slightly from the bounding of the wooden wheels over the uneven pave. He gave a start, thinking one of the bodies was that of his friend Tudier. It proved not to be the case, but the sighting made him worry anew about the fate of his fellow recruits, who had yet to be heard from. What had happened to them?

Nuroc halted his stallion on one side of the road and watched the cart pass. The sorcerers' gardens would be filled with the buried dead by the time it was all over, he thought. It seemed grimly fitting that the fatalities would be put to rest there. Even King Pencroft had seen the irony and declared that a memorial to those slain would be erected upon the site of the fallen obelisk, in addition to the frieze Connec would create to place over the main entrance to the city. No more would the far edge of Cothe be known as the sorcerers' gardens. By the king's proclamation, it would now be called the Garden of Courage.

From atop the rise, Nuroc could see the battlefield. Thousands still lay on the beaten sward, waiting to be loaded into one of the several other carts present on the road that ran along the meadows and marshlands. More workers moved among the dead, lifting bodies or scaring off predators drawn to the promise of dead flesh. The blood had turned dark on the grass and ground. A rolling fog trailed beneath the clouds and began to spill out over the scene like a misty shroud.

In the face of this dreary tableau, Nuroc's mood swiftly darkened. He snapped the reins and sent his horse galloping down the road away from the carnage. He averted his eyes from the war site and held his breath until he had ridden to where the offshore wind washed away the charnel scent with the briny smell of the sea.

He had been equipped with provisions before setting out, and he paused on the road long enough to don a boarskin coat to block the stinging chill in the air. As the fog grew thicker, the air colder, his horse refused to move faster than a canter when he resumed his ride. It was just as well, as the way before him seemed to be constantly on the verge of ending in a misty wall less than a spear's throw away. He also had to peer along the side of the road for the marker Palem had left to indicate the spot where he would have to leave the road in order to seek out the tunnel opening through which Molent and Wheas had fled with the queen.

At last he spotted the marker, three spears driven into the dirt shoulder with strips of cloth snapping robustly in the wind from the blunt end of each shaft. Nuroc dismounted and led the horse down the gentle pitch of the shoulder and across the ruptured earth that still bore the scars of the cataclysm. Raw, wet soil was smeared by the trodden hooves of the enemy's cavalry. Small plants and shrubs had been uprooted and crushed into the mud by the charging advance of the Ghetites and Shangorans. Nuroc found it hard to believe that, years before, sheep had grazed on this same terrain under his watchful eye. The land had changed as much as he had.

Other markers similar to the first led Nuroc and his steed eventually to the clump of boulders set around the mouth of the tunnel. It indeed was the spot from which Nuroc had seen Augage and his traitorous followers make their escape from Cothe on the eve of the Great Cataclysm five years before. Looking back in the direction of the capital, Nuroc could barely make out the fringe of marshland where the two sides had traded blows. He could now picture the scenario of the previous day—how Molent and Wheas, fleeing the bloodshed in the meadows, had ridden to the boulders and sought refuge in the tunnel as Aerdan troops rode past, giving chase to more of the retreating enemy. Knowing where the tunnel led, they had undoubtedly followed it to Cothe, intent on wreaking the most damage they could manage from beneath the city. They had fared well, too, setting free the beasts beneath the coliseum and kidnapping the queen.

Nuroc stood before the opening for some time, lost in his thoughts. As General Palem had forewarned him, there were far too many tracks in the earth around the entrance for him to easily discover which set were made by the men he sought.

He finally decided on a strategy. Tethering his horse to a bent scenoak growing up between the boulders, Nuroc began to criss-cross on foot the land stretching out between the opening of the tunnel and the distant coast, scanning the ground for some sort of clue. Fortunately, much of the area he would have to search lay on higher ground, where the fog was less choking.

There were traces of conflict even this far from the main battlefield. Nuroc came across the bodies of several men who had been cut down in their retreat and left to die. One soldier had dragged himself for thirty feet across the dirt in an attempt to reach the main road before expiring from his wounds. Another lay dead next to the horse that had thrown him when it was hit by a long-range arrow. Most of these casualties were Ghetites and Shangorans, but Nuroc did stumble across an Aerdan with a split skull, lying face down in a clump of weeds. The Aerdan, like many of the other corpses, also bore the gruesome marks of predators that had picked at their flesh until they had had their fill or been chased off by others.

The sight grieved Nuroc, but he tried not to dwell on it. There was nothing to be done for these lost souls. His duty was to the living, not the dead. He kept searching for clues, but found nothing to indicate which of the many beaten trails had been traveled by Molent and Wheas. He was about to turn back when a ray of sun managed to pry through the fog and cloudcover and shed added light on the ground. Out of the corner of his eye, Nuroc saw the glint of metal from somewhere in the brush that led up from the meadows to the first roll of foothills. Intrigued, Nuroc strode back across the stretch he had just searched and climbed up into the brush. The sun fell back behind the clouds, but Nuroc still managed to find the source of the distracting sheen.

"Praise to Babyl!" Nuroc called out to the sun-god, picking up a scrap of chain mail clinging to the brush. He excitedly reached into his jupon for the piece of headgear Palem's men had found in the catacombs near the carcass of the slain crawler. The two pieces matched!

Pocketing his find, Nuroc walked past the cluster of brush and stared at the ground around him. His spirits soared even higher as he saw the tracks of two horses winding up a thin ribbon of path leading toward the Kanghat Mountains, which were obscured by the incoming fog. Nuroc was familiar enough with this area from his youth to know that if he continued in the direction the tracks were headed, he would soon come to a mountain pass that crossed the Aerdan border into Ghetite. It was a more treacherous means of reaching Ghetite than riding around the mountain range, but it was far less traveled and less apt to be vigilantly watched over by Aerdans looking to prevent a Ghetite or Shangoran from returning to their respective homelands following a rout on the battlefield.

"Molent and Wheas," Nuroc whispered to himself, crouching over the hoofprints. One set pressed more firmly into the dirt, indicating extra weight carried by that horse. The weight of a queen.

Nuroc was so engrossed with his discovery that he did not realize he was being watched until he was startled by a deep-throated growl sounding from atop a rise a few dozen feet behind him. Trying not to move too quickly, Nuroc turned his head and glanced over his shoulder.

Five kildwolves stared at him through the tendrils of fog, their mouths hung open to expose flesh-rending jaws. Their preference was for freshly-slain meat, and the bodies littering the meadows were long past that state. Nuroc would provide them with a fair meal, and he knew it.

The beasts sensed Nuroc's fear. When he slowly moved to face them and pulled forth his sword, they growled and did not retreat. There was no cover for him to run to, and any attempt to take flight would only expose his back to their pouncing charge. What little chance he had lay in keeping his eyes on the beasts and trying to anticipate their moves.

One of the wolves was larger than the others and stood to the front of them, leading the pack. Scars streaked its fur, telling of its lust for fighting. Its yellow eyes were fixed unblinkingly on Nuroc.

Nuroc stepped closer to the rise, earning another chorus of growls. He held his sword out before him, clutched in both hands, and continued to move forward. The lead kildwolf reared back on its haunches, preparing to leap forward. The others, however, did not follow suit. They stayed as they were, content to watch on.

Nuroc was only ten feet away from the beasts when the largest wolf sprang forth. Nuroc was ready for him. He met the beast's leap in midair, sweeping his sword up and into the wolf's shoulder, dodging to one side to avoid its snapping jaws.

The wolf brought Nuroc to the ground with the force of its lunge, but Nuroc rolled with the fall, concentrating on his grip on the sword. He twisted his wrists violently, jerking the blade to and fro. The wolf writhed and yelped in pain, then ceased to move.

Nuroc quickly pushed the body aside and rose to his knees, pulling his sword free and waving it at the other beasts, daring them to attack. They whined and shrank back, watching him and their leader with confusion. Finally they broke into a run and fled in separate directions, howling until they had disappeared into the fog.

Nuroc stood up shakily, rubbing blood from the scrape the kildwolf's claws had made on the side of his face. He felt the wound and was relieved that the skin had been barely broken. Sword in hand, he carefully headed back to his horse, looking around to see if the wolves might summon their courage and attempt to strike again. They didn't, and he mounted up. His horse was nervous, so Nuroc waited a few minutes before tugging the reins and riding to the site where he had found the scrap of chain mail. After another pause to sheathe his sword and secure both hands on the reins, he started up the gradual incline, his eyes on the trail that led to the mountains.

Fifteen

Nuroc's steed negotiated the last narrow, winding causeway blanketed by chilling fog and eventually emerged to a level where he could see more than a few yards before him. Half the day had been lost in the slow progress up the mountainside, and as Nuroc rested his horse before going farther, he saw the dim haze of the setting sun fade from view behind the mountaintops. Fat, languid clouds hung over the peaks, hastening the fall of darkness and posing a threat of rain.

The Aerdans had established a string of outposts along the spine of the Kanghats to guard against the invasion that had come two nights ago. Nuroc began to look in earnest for the camp overlooking this particular pass. He knew that most of the sentinels had come down from the mountains to aid in the fighting, so he did not expect to find the post manned now. What he sought was the refuge of the camp, a roof to put over his head for the night as well as a firepit he could fill with chopped wood to fend off the cold. At this altitude, the temperature was dropping with each few yards he advanced along the trail.

Unlike the more northern range of the Kanghats, where he had worked for years, prying ore from the heart of stark, barren reaches, the mountains here were lush with plantlife that benefited from the closeness to the sea and its moist air. Even under the bleakness of the dusk sky, vivid greens dotted the rock facings, showing off bright flowers like small stars. Pines rose upward haughtily wherever there was soil, and several ancient scenoaks bent their gnarly limbs as if flexing wooden muscles in the face of the taunting breeze. Small birds chirped through the brush, staying beyond sight of the majestic hawks and eagles that circled above, gliding effortlessly on rivers of wind.

A flapping louder than the beat of wings drew Nuroc's attention to an Aerdan flag flying from a pole sticking out from the top of the rock escarpment directly off to one side of the trail. On closer observation, he saw a stacked stone wall set around the crest's rim.

"Yo!" Nuroc called out on the chance men were at the post.

There was no answer. He rode up a little farther, to where a half-hidden path wound up to the camp from a less precipitous angle. As he started onto the path, he suddenly reined in his horse and stopped, pulling out his sword. He leaned out of the saddle for a closer look at the path and confirmed that the most recent tracks in the dirt led up to the camp, not down from it. More important, there were only two sets of tracks, and they looked altogether too familiar.

Swearing under his breath for having called out and made known his presence, Nuroc slipped quietly from the saddle and tied his horse to one of the pines that grew along the side of the escarpment. Then, rather than risking the trail, he sheathed his sword, exchanging it for a less wieldy dagger. He clenched the blade in his teeth and started to climb the upright cliff facing. Wind and weather had chiseled away at the stone over the years, leaving contours that provided him with the hold he needed to carry himself up closer to the walls.

Halfway up, he felt a drop of water strike his cheek, then another. It was beginning to rain. Even more disturbing, was the glimpse of smoke rising thinly from somewhere inside the camp. There could be no doubting any longer; Molent and Wheas had taken the queen to the camp. They were now probably armed and waiting for him. He was thankful at least that he had not come up the path, for surely they were waiting to ambush him there. He might yet be able to catch them by surprise.

Nuroc was aided by the first drones of thunder riding in with the approaching storm. The rumbling sounded over his clawing noises as he made his way up the escarpment. The increasing rainfall made it difficult for him to keep a solid foothold on the facing. Several times his buskins lost their grip and his feet slipped clear of the wet rock. In each instance, it was only by digging his fingers into the nearest scalloped surface for a firmer handhold that he saved himself from plummeting downward. He refused to turn back, though. Blinking the rain from his eyes, he forged on with full determination.

When he was within a few feet of the outpost walls, Nuroc managed to place one foot on a solid ledge reaching out from the cliff. He put his full weight on the foot and bent to a crouch.

Biting hard on the raw steel of his dagger, he looked up and pushed forward, propelling himself into the air. His outreached fingers closed around the limb of a scenoak extending over the camp wall. Building his momentum, he pulled himself up and swung his legs over the top. Landing on both feet inside the camp, he was ready for anything. His right hand went to his sword while his left grasped the dagger from his mouth.

Peering through the roaring downpour, he saw the smoke thickening from the dying campfire set in the middle of the outpost. Beyond the embers, a stone hut was set back from the wall, and next to it a wooden stall for horses. Near the pathway entrance a cord of split wood was stacked, ready for use. There was no trace of Molent or Wheas, their steeds, or the queen but he was certain they were near, for next to the woodpile lay three Aerdan soldiers, dead, arrows sprouting from their bodies.

Nuroc shook wet strands of light hair away from his face and ran cautiously to the bodies. Their flesh was cold and stiff, already beginning to change color. They had been dead for hours. Nuroc looked over his shoulder at the fire. The half-burned logs could not have been afire for more than an hour.

Keeping his sword and dagger out at his sides, he moved near the fire and shouted through the rain, "Show yourselves, devilspawn!" His voice boomed loudly through the camp but was not answered, save for the downhill neighing of his steed.

Between claps of thunder, Nuroc thought he heard the sound of distant hooves. He put away his dagger and used his freed hand to block the rain from his brow as he looked up toward the peaks, where he heard the sound again. There, a hundred yards away, he saw the shadowy outline of three riders astride a pair of horses, pausing on the ridgeline to look down toward the camp.

"Molent! Wheas!" Nuroc shouted. "Surrender the queen!"

Thunder rumbled across the darkening sky, followed by mocking laughter from the enemy leaders. Each raised his arms in a gesture of contempt, then they turned their horses and vanished over the other side of the mountain, with the bound queen struggling futilely on Wheas's mount.

Enraged, Nuroc bolted across the camp and down the path to his horse. He leapt into the saddle and slashed through the knot tethering the steed rather than take the time to untie it. Jerking on the shortened reins, he dug his heels into the rear flanks of his stallion and drove it charging up the slope leading to the mountain summit. His horse was a champion breed, selected personally from among the finest steeds in the royal stables. Oblivious to the torrential downpour, it pounded hooves with a furious pace at the muddied path, rapidly clearing the distance between the camp and the peak. Nuroc rode from a slight crouch to buffer the jolts as the stallion veered and swerved with uncanny finesse around the turns and rises of the uneven path. He was angry with himself for having misjudged the situation at the camp, feeling that if he had taken his horse up the path instead of assaulting the camp on foot, he might have intercepted the others before they could have fled. As it was, his only consolation was that he had seen the queen and knew she was still alive, and that he was at least close on the trail of her abductors.

Lightning began to stab through the clouds, driving on the rainy onslaught with a force that stung Nuroc's face as he rode. Fortunately, his horse was not frightened by the storm, and it galloped relentlessly until Nuroc reined it to a halt at the spot where he had last seen the others. He scanned the ground and swore a curse on the gods of weather. The rain had been sent down with so much fury that he could see no tracks in the churning mud. The far side of the mountain was even more overgrown than the slope he had just cleared, and it was impossible for him to make out any riders moving through the brush. Even if he had been able to pick up their tracks, he would not be able to follow them long before nightfall blotted out any chance of spotting them until morning. He had no choice but to seek out the nearest trail winding down toward the distant Ghetite border and hope that good fortune might smile his way.

It was not to be.

Nuroc rode down a chosen path at an unnervingly slow pace for more than an hour without encountering those he sought. By then, night had settled over the mountains and the storm still had refused to abate. He was soaked to the bone and freezing from the winds that whipped the storm along. His horse showed no signs of slackening, but Nuroc knew he would have to rest it soon. Besides, it was pointless to go on. The visibility was so poor that he could be riding within a few feet of the others and not see them. He was more apt to ride into an ambush than achieve his mission.

Also unlike the southern facing of the mountains, this range of the Kanghats did not slope down to level ground in the course of a mile. Instead, the topography was one of successive ranges that dipped occasionally into shallow valleys, where small hamlets thrived off the mountain's abundance of wild game and sturdy timber. Nuroc saw the lights of one such hamlet sparkling through the rain several miles away. It would offer the haven he had been forced to pass up at the outpost, and there was the distant possibility that Molent and Wheas had taken Queen Leindal to the same place for the same reason. Nuroc did not put it past them to raid an isolated farmhouse and slay an unarmed family if it meant securing shelter for the night.

The trail he was on grew wider the closer he came to the hamlet, and he urged his horse along at a faster pace to hasten his arrival. It proved to be another mistake on his part. Because the path was covered with puddles of rainwater, he could not foresee ruts in the trail, and in midstride his horse plunged into a gaping hole and tumbled headfirst into the rock formations that lined the path. Nuroc was pitched from the saddle and thrown over the stallion's head into the rocks.

Sixteen

The rain had let up considerably by the time Nuroc regained consciousness. The slight drizzle rinsed blood from his eyes. In addition to the scratches inflicted by the kildwolf, he now also had a large gash over his right eye from the fall. When he sat up, his skull throbbed with pain and more blood flowed from the head wound into his eyes. He wiped it away with the back of his hand and ripped off a strip of his tunic to hold over the wound. Grimacing against the pain, he staggered to his feet and looked up to the sky. There was no moon or stars to measure the time by. He had trouble seeing as far as the next bend in the trail.

His stallion was on the path watching him, and Nuroc was amazed to find the animal on its feet. When he called it over, the horse hobbled severely, favoring the leg that had rammed into the hole. It neighed with pain at each step. Nuroc stepped forward to halt it, and at the same time noticed a bruised ache in his own right thigh.

"There, there," he calmed the steed, patting the side of its head and stroking its mane. "Steady. Just stay still a minute." Nuroc leaned over and felt the mount's leg. He could not feel any definite break, although the foreleg was swollen to twice its size. The horse snorted uneasily when Nuroc touched the wound.

"It's okay," Nuroc said softly as he went to the pliant baskets strapped across the saddles. Most of the provisions within were soaked from the rain, but not the tightly-sealed clay container filled with a salve Myrania had concocted from the extract of the neotolan shrub and several other mysterious ingredients procured from the ruins of the obelisk. Nuroc knew the curative powers of the ointment, having heard of men restoring lost limbs by merely rubbing the preparation over severed stumps.

"This was meant for me in the case of dire injury," Nuroc told the horse as he opened the container and dabbed a large portion of the salve onto his fingertips. "But I think you are more in need of it now." Nuroc worked the ointment into the steed's wound, then wrapped it with a length of wet gauze taken from one of the baskets. There were still traces of the salve on his fingers, so he wiped it off on the cuts across his face. In its most potent form, the salve produced immediate results. But this was an inferior derivative, hastily made from ingredients that were not up to the standards usually demanded by sorcerers who had made the substance over the centuries. Still, Nuroc could feel the flow of blood from his cuts ebb, and the horse took a few tentative steps without appearing to be in as much pain as before the application.

"I think the hamlet will have to wait until morning," Nuroc whispered as he led the horse slowly along the path. "We'll find a place to put up for the night around here. We both need rest to let the salve take its full course."

The clouds had thinned out with the spending of the storm, and enough moonlight radiated down the mountainside for Nuroc to see the terrain around him. Looking for a likely place to camp, he noticed several bats take flight from a cave formation set back a few dozen yards from the pathway, at the base of the mountainside.

"We're in luck," he murmured, taking the reins and leading his horse carefully up off the path. The higher ground was wet and rugged, so they proceeded slowly toward the rocks until Nuroc saw the gaping entrance to a large cavern. Runoff from the mountaintops spilled over the upper lip of the orifice and splashed loudly into puddles, giving off a resonant echo that hinted at the size of the swollen cavity within.

"It sounds like there's plenty of room for us."

The horse hesitated when Nuroc first tried to lead it into the opening, but several persuasive tugs on the reins overcame its reluctance. Once within the cavern, Nuroc rejoiced at being out of the rain and wind. The relative warmth seemed more than worth the loss of light, especially as Nuroc knew he had the means by which to repel the darkness around them. He felt through the saddlebags once more for a leather pouch containing shards of flint and steel, as well as a wooden staff with its tip covered by a sheath that kept it dry. Taking the pouch and staff, Nuroc groped through the inky gloom until he found a clearing on the cavern floor. The earth there was dry, so he set down the torch and removed the sheath. He knelt over and diligently struck the flint and steel together until sparks began to leap down onto the tip of the torch, which had been soaked in a mixture of tar and the highly combustible sap of the tunar plant. The sparks clung to the torch like flecks of pollen, then spread their fire in wide, glowing circles. As soon as two of the circles touched, flames burst forth and immediately covered the entire end of the torch, throwing off a vibrant, hissing light.

The horse whinnied uncertainly and backed away as Nuroc picked up the torch and looked around at the cavern. It was even larger than he had thought. It was as if the mountaintop around it were no more than a shell. Stalactites and stalagmites pointed from the roof and floor like jagged teeth. Moisture dripped steadily from the formations poking down from the upper reaches. With a mad fluttering of wings, more bats fled from their nocturnal perches among the stalactites and vanished out into the night.

When Nuroc cast his eyes back down to the floor of the cave, he cringed. There were bones everywhere, most of them in broken fragments, all of them void of flesh and dull white under the glare of the torchlight. He knew at once that these were the bones of men. The nape hairs long his neck raised when he realized there was not a single skull among the scattered relics.

"What hellhole is this?" Nuroc wondered aloud, going for his sword. The shadows made on the cave walls by the stalagmites wavered with the movement of his torch, further unsettling him. He edged back toward his horse, at the same time noticing that the rock projections around him were all polished to a flat surface and covered with painted symbols and weird glyphs from a language he did not know, or care to. Wounded mount or not, he was not about to spend the night in this forsaken lair. Wedging the torch between two rocks, he swiftly climbed back into the saddle. Before he could turn the stallion around, there was a swift, grating sound in the cavern and he looked over his shoulder to see a row of gleaming spikes rise up from the ground at intervals of every few inches along the opening through which he had entered. Up the pointed shafts moved until they were within a few feet of the upper lip of the cave's mouth.

Nuroc was trapped within the bone-strewn confines!

Smitten with fear, Nuroc's steed held its head firm against the tugging of its reins. Nuroc finally jumped down from the saddle and rushed on foot to the spikes. Each was as thick as his arm and held rigidly in place by a sturdily constructed base of hammered metal and jaunwood. It was like a portcullis that closed upward instead of down and could not be broached by a single man.

"This must be the work of Ghetites," Nuroc remarked to himself with growing anxiety. He grabbed angrily at the bars and shook them with all his might, but they would not move. He turned to face the cave interior and shouted, "Wheas! Is this some elaborate trap you've set for me! Show yourselves. Wheas! Molent!"

His words resounded off the cave walls and came back at him, distorted and derisive. More bats battered their wings in roused unison and fled through the spikes, but there was no other response for several moments. Then, far back in the cave, there was a slight shuffling sound, followed by a strident whistle that rose in pitch until Nuroc could no longer even hear it. His horse was driven mad by the sound, however, and it neighed wildly as it rose on its hind legs. Before Nuroc could rush to its side, the steed lunged away from him and galloped past the first stalagmites into the darkness toward the rear of the cave.

"Stop!" Nuroc commanded uselessly. "Halt, curse you!"

Once the horse had run past the range of the torchlight, its hoofbeats ceased abruptly, replaced by a tortured neigh and the sounds of a struggle. Then the cave fell silent. Nuroc was about to charge after the horse, but an intuitive hunch held him back. He stood still and tensed his fingers around the hilt of his sword, staring into the darkness where his steed had vanished.

The shadows cast by the light of the torch on the stalagmites flickered along the walls of the cave, but soon Nuroc realized that not all of the dark shapes were mere umbrage. Some of the forms moved of their own accord. Limbs began to stretch out from torsos; glowing slits appeared side-by-side on rounded faces. They moved away from the walls, edging past the stalagmites, coming closer to Nuroc.

"Who are you?" Nuroc called out, well aware that it was neither Wheas or Molent or anyone of the likes he had ever seen before. He tried to force anger into the terror that ran through him, but when he spoke again his words sounded thin and empty. "Show yourselves and tell me the meaning of this!" It sounded more like a plea than a demand.

They drew nearer, coming out of the shadows until Nuroc could begin to discern details. The beings were human only in that they stood on two feet. In all other aspects, they were a grisly travesty of mankind, some mutant offspring that had evolved into a monstrously different species. They moved slowly, their broad shoulders hunched over so that their overly long arms hung down like the arms of apes, ending with brutish hands and thick, stubby fingers that bore talonlike nails. Reddish hair covered their entire bodies and framed misshapen faces, where small eyes and recessed nostrils were crowded close together above large, gaping jaws. They wore no clothing, but Nuroc knew they were no more animals than they were men. Their narrow, glowing eyes burned with the keen intelligence that had been responsible for the gate that had imprisoned him and for the intricate glyphs that adorned the stalagmites.

Nuroc had heard strange tales of horrible creatures who haunted the Kanghat ranges, but he had never given such stories much credence, as they were mostly mouthed by children or parents anxious to keep their young ones from straying into the mountains, which teemed with enough other dangers. But now he was staring into the faces of those same werebeings, and in the forefront of his mind he recalled the most terrifying part of the long-told legends—that these were creatures who lived solely on human flesh.

"Stay clear or die!" Nuroc warned the first of the abominations to step out from the shadows and move toward him on its foreshortened legs, kicking aside loose bones. The creature glared at Nuroc and drew its brownish lips back, baring the oversized teeth lining its round mouth. In a croaking voice, it muttered a few guttural words in a language that Nuroc had never before heard. He responded with the universal language of a swordswipe through the air, sending the creature back a few steps.

Other beings came forward, fanning out to form a half-circle around Nuroc. There were more than two dozen of them altogether. He watched them uneasily. He did not know if slaying one of their kind would drive off the others with the same effectiveness as the kildwolves he had encountered earlier, and he did not care to find out until it became absolutely necessary.

"You've already slain my horse," Nuroc told them. "It should give you food enough for days."

Snarling, the creatures moved closer.

Outside the cave, a single throb of thunder sounded from far off, announcing the arrival of another storm front. To Nuroc's surprise, the creatures reacted to the distant boom with looks of fear. Staring past Nuroc, their glimmering eyes focused on the skies.

Acting on his instincts, Nuroc summoned into his face the most fearsome countenance he could manage. At the same time, he straightened his free arm and flicked his wrist violently, as if he were throwing something over his shoulder and out past the bars. Turning his head slightly, he saw a jagged shaft of lightning pierce the night.

With frightened whimpers, the werebeings cowered back from the opening of the cave. Grinning like a madman, Nuroc slipped his sword back into its scabbard and used his arms to make more flicking gestures over his shoulders. Another clap of thunder rolled across the land, sounding closer and more forceful than the first blast and followed by fingers of lightning. Whimpers gave way to shrieks of alarm as the cannibals turned their backs on Nuroc and fled into the shadows.

The storm swept in and rain began to pelt the cave. Nuroc resumed his waving of arms in time to the thunder and lightning as he shouted defiantly, "Yes! Yes, I am sent by the storm gods and you have dared to imprison me!"

Although the werebeings did not comprehend Nuroc's words, they were already convinced by the supposed demonstration of his powers. As the storm brought the rains drumming down on the roof of the cavern, the barrier of spikes behind Nuroc slowly sank back into the ground. He stayed in place a few seconds more, orchestrating the tempest, then turned and ran.

The downpour whipped at him with stinging fierceness, and the clouds had snuffed all traces of the moon, leaving the way before him an opaque murk. Still he pushed on, ignoring his bruised thigh, stumbling over the slick ground in a frantic effort to leave the caves as far behind as possible. He knew he couldn't reach the hamlet in this weather, but he kept up his flight until the pain in his leg became too intense to ignore.

He had run far from the cavern, so he slowed his pace to a walk and sucked in air to replenish his tortured lungs. His leg felt as if it were resting on hot coals, and tears stung his eyes from the pain of walking on it. As his vision became accustomed to the darkness, he was able to make out the looming outline of a cliff rising up from the edge of the path close by. He straggled toward it and found that it served to deflect the brunt of the storm's fury. Even better, there was a small crevice at the base of the precipice that was untouched by the rains and large enough for him to fit into. He took up position in the opening and huddled himself into a ball, trying to stay warm. With one hand still holding onto his sword, he willed himself to concentrate on his exhaustion rather than the pain or memories of the strange beasts he had eluded. He fell asleep shivering and spent the rest of the night lost in the void of a slumber so deep that even dreams could not reach him.

Seventeen

The skies were blue and sunny when Nuroc awoke, still shivering from the chill of his soaked clothes. His limbs tingled from blocked circulation when he dragged himself from the crawlspace that had been his night's lodging. He stumbled awkwardly through the mud until he was clear of the shadow cast by the cliff. The sun's warmth was invigorating, and Nuroc shed his buskins, surcoat, and tunic to bask on a rock, wearing only a scrap of breechcloth. Still wary from his encounter the previous night, he kept his sword nearby. His thigh was swollen and mottled with blacks and blues, but the pain was almost gone. Even more promising, the facial wounds he had covered with the balm had nearly healed during his sleep. There was a slight scar in place of the deep gash that he had incurred during his fall from the horse. As the sun added the miracle of its warmth to his body, he felt alive and ready to resume his duty to the king.

Leaving the rock to breakfast on wild blueberries, Nuroc tried to get his bearings. So much of the previous night had been spent traveling in darkness, he wasn't certain where he was. With the cliff on one side of him and a rocky knoll on the other, he could not see down to the valley hamlet that had been his destination before the string of misfortunes intervened. He could see, to the west, the peaks of the next range over, rising so high that the storm had left a crown of snow instead the muddy pools that covered the lower elevations. He hoped that the task before him would not bring him to those perilous heights.

It was time for him to move on. Wherever Molent and Wheas had spent the night with the queen, they could not have been subjected to more ordeals than he had, Nuroc figured. They had probably set out from their cover at dawn, if not with the stopping of the rains. He would have to hike to the town in the valley and plead for assistance. If his luck changed, he would be given a horse and perhaps a lead in his search for those he had come so close to reaching less than half a day ago. There was still hope. He clung to that idea as he went back to the rock and gathered his clothes, binding them into a bundle to sling over his shoulder. His buskins were still damp, but he stepped into them anyway and strapped on his scabbard before setting out.

He climbed the rocky knoll in hopes of spotting the hamlet and the easiest way to it, but once he cleared the rise, Nuroc promptly dropped to a crouch and sidestepped to the cover of a boulder. He stared down the other side of the knoll, feeling as if he were facing a nightmare that had followed him into the world of the waking.

At the base of the knoll was a flattened clearing. Standing en masse around the sides of a deep pit that measured more than twenty feet wide and across, were the red-haired werebeings. Their arms swayed anxiously before them as they stared into the pit, mouthing some ritualistic oath in a series of incoherent grunts and squeals. In each of the creature's hands was a long, polelike weapon similar to the spikes that had barricaded him inside their lair the night before. He was certain that the poles were incredibly heavy, and yet the werebeings handled them as if they were made of hollowed bamboo.

The repeated utterances gradually dwindled and the beings fell quiet. One of them, who Nuroc recognized as the one who had first approached him in the cave, raised his spike over his head, holding it the way a spearfisher stands on the banks of a river in hopes of stabbing a fish. The others moved aside to give him room as he walked along the edge of the pit, all the while keeping his eyes on whatever it was that lay within. Finally, he stopped and planted his feet, then rammed the spike into the pit. Moments later, great muscles rippled along the werebeing's hulking arms as he lifted the spike back into the air.

"By the eyes of Dorban!" Nuroc uttered with shock.

Impaled at the end of the spike was a man caked with mud and writhing against the rope tied around his wrists and ankles. Even though the man was gagged, he managed a scream of tortured agony that raised Nuroc's flesh. The man squirmed a few seconds more, then fell slack on the point of the spike.

A cry went up from the other creatures as the body was lifted from the pit and swung out over the ground behind them. Their powerful jaws clacked together and the beastmen slavered as their eyes followed the corpse. The being with the pole dumped the body unceremoniously into the mud.

As the cannibals fell silent once more and another of their kind took up position at the edge of the pit, armed with his own spike, Nuroc set down his bundle and pulled out the wet, musty coat of boarskin. Jabbing his arms into the sleeves, he rushed forward and shouted down the knoll, "Stop!"

Startled, the beastmen looked up at Nuroc and immediately began to jabber fearfully. Carrying through with his bluff, Nuroc held out his arms and made as if to summon forth thunder and lightning from the cloudless sky. The werebeings responded by dropping their spikes and repeating an incomprehensible chant. From the look on their faces, Nuroc guessed that it was an oath or prayer of appeasement, if not outright worship. They came away from the edge of the pit and stood in a row before the knoll. The one who had slain the bound man went over to the corpse and plucked it up as if it were no more than a child. He carried the dead man past the others and laid it a few yards up the slope of the knoll, like an offering to Nuroc.

Nuroc slowly lowered his arms to his sides and placed his hands on his hips, mostly to stop them from trembling. It seemed to him that he was straddling the fine line between being adored and being rent limb from limb as a false god. From where he stood, he could see, in the background, the mouth of the werebeings' cave. Taking a deep breath to swell his chest, he pointed angrily toward the cave, then turned his steely eyes on the beastmen in hopes of conveying what his words could not.

The werebeings made sounds of protest and their misshapen faces seemed to be pleading, but Nuroc held firm. When they hesitated further, he resumed his pose as storm-bringer. One by one, they turned away and picked up their spikes, then loped away from the pit toward their domain, leaving Nuroc alone with the bleeding corpse. He remained atop the knoll, watching them until they had vanished in the brush.

Looking down at the body that lay in a helpless sprawl before him, Nuroc felt a burning furor at the grisly rites he had just witnessed. It was not long, however, before he realized how similar the werebeings' practices were to his own people's preference for placing men in the pit of the coliseum arena, where the claws and fangs of another kind of predator brought on deaths every bit as final and gruesome as those committed by the spike-wielding beastmen.

As he walked slowly down the hill to the body, he found himself wondering how it was that this man had ended up bound and gagged and tossed into the pit in the first place. He had little time to dwell on the possibilities, because once he took a closer look at the victim, he recoiled in shock.

The dead man was one of the young recruits from Thutchers!

Grief and bewilderment swept over Nuroc, but fast on their heels came a wave of sudden hope. Breaking into a run, he rushed past the corpse and stared into the pit. There, also bound and wriggling through the mire of mud and water, were the other missing recruits.

"Tudier!" Nuroc shouted joyously as he spotted his good friend wresting against his binds.

The muddied Thutcherian looked up at Nuroc and his eyes widened. Even through the gag, Nuroc could see that Tudier was grinning.

"Hold still and I'll help get you out. All of you!" Nuroc told them. He looked around and found a spike left behind by one of the flesheaters. He lifted it, groaning at the sheer weight and once more feeling a dreadful awe at the strength of the cave dwellers.

With some difficulty, he swung the pole around and carried it back to the edge of the pit. "Put your hands out as far away from you as you can and I'll try to cut through the rope,'' he called down to Tudier.

His friend nodded and leaned forward against the steep walls of the pit, stretching his arms out behind him. Nuroc eased the shaft down until it rested against the rim of the pit. With part of the weight absorbed by the earth, Nuroc was better able to control the pole, and he guided it farther into the pit until it wavered in the air above Tudier's wrists. Blood mixed with mud where the young recruit had attempted to work his hands free of the tightly-knotted rope. The others stopped their wriggling and watched as Nuroc carefully lowered the spike, inch by inch, until it rested on the knot.

''Okay, now brace yourself,'' Nuroc told his friend. He saw Tudier's arms tense as he pressed the knot tighter against the pointed shaft. ''Good, now pull up as hard as you can. I'll push.''

They worked in unison, both straining at the point where the spike met the rope. Finally, the pointed edge of the weapon worked through the fibers and broke the knot. With a firm jolt, Tudier pulled his wrists apart and the rope fell clear, landing with a splash in the turgid water.

Ecstatic, Tudier reached behind his head and quickly undid his gag, ripping it free and shouting gleefully, ''Praised be Dorban and all the gods!''

''Not so loud,'' Nuroc called down. ''I don't want them coming back.''

''How did you get rid of them?'' Tudier said in a lower voice as he reached down beneath the waterline to unbind his ankles. Once he was totally freed, he moved over and began untying his nearest comrade. As Tudier worked, Nuroc briefly explained his encounter with the werebeings the night before and all the events preceding. By the time he had finished, all the recruits were free and slogging through the mire, anxious to get out of the pit.

Nuroc laid on his stomach at the edge and extended his hand down to Tudier. The Thutcherian grabbed it and pulled himself up the slippery incline, then scrambled the rest of the way on his own. Tudier, in turn, offered a similar hand to the next man coming up. The procedure established, Nuroc and Tudier walked off and embraced one another heartily, slapping each other on the back, then sitting down on a dry stretch of ground nearby.

''As for us,'' Tudier explained, once he caught his breath and had wiped the mud from his face, "we gave chase to a band of fleeing Ghetites and Shangorans the night of the battle. They fled around southern slopes and then started up along the border range. We lost track of them halfway up this mountain, then made the mistake of entering the hamlet of Centinara, which is close by here."

"I saw the place last night and tried to reach it during the storm," Nuroc said.

"It's well that you didn't, or you might have wound up in the pits with the rest of us."

"How so?"

"Centinara is only a small village," Tudier said. "It's far enough from any of the trade routes that few people come or leave there, so I don't think they are well informed of the land's affairs. My guess is that the dark-skinned Ghetites hid outside the town while the Shangorans slipped into Centinara and claimed to be Aerdans and friends of their people. Whatever they told the Centinarans about us was a lie, because when we rode peacefully into their main square at dusk yesterday, asking if they'd seen any of the enemy, they fell on us by the dozens and took us all prisoners. They said they would not allow us to eat their children and make sport of their women. We protested such accusations, but their minds were made up. To them, we were criminals of the lowest order, destined for the pit. When they took us here and threw us in, I thought that our punishment was to lie there until we rotted. Then came this morning and the arrival of that clan of werespawn. Have you ever laid eyes on such monsters?"

"Not of their kind," Nuroc replied. "The people of the hamlet must make use of the pit to appease the cave dwellers and keep them from wandering into the valley."

"You saw what they did to Ulam?" Tudier said, looking over at the corpse of their slain companion.

Nuroc nodded. "Had I only known before the first spike was—"

"How could anyone have known?" Tudier interrupted, noting Nuroc's remorse.

"Still . . ."

"Still nothing. We will bury Ulam and wish him godspeed to the heavens, but what's done is done. Think of the lives you saved, Nuroc."

Nuroc nodded absently. "Yes, Yes, of course. . . ."

Tudier leaned over and grabbed his friend by the collar of his boarskin coat. "Listen to me," the mud-streaked recruit said. "We have a queen to rescue, and no doubt Molent and Wheas have already joined up with their cohorts. Enough with your self-pity! Weep for the dead and get on with the living. There are still scores to be settled."

Tudier's words struck Nuroc like blows of wisdom, chasing off the melancholy that had been brought on as much by fatigue as by the death of Ulam. Back to his normal self, he took Tudier's hands and pried them away from his coat.

"You forget that I'm a lieutenant, soldier," Nuroc said with mock gravity. "Watch how you speak to me."

The two young men faced each other. Nuroc could not keep a straight face. Together they both shared smiles.

"Yes, sir!" Tudier snickered.

"Ah, Tudier," Nuroc said. "It's good to see you again."

Tudier wiped more mud from his face and smeared it on Nuroc's coat. "Likewise, Nuroc."

Nuroc rose to his feet and called out to the others, who now stood clear of the pit. "Let's get a move on! I saw a lake near the hamlet, where you can all wash, then we'll see to arming ourselves and tracking down the enemy. When we finish with them, those Ghetite dogs will wish it was they who had been left in the pits!"

Eighteen

Weak and beleaguered, the reunited young recruits left the dirt mound marking the burial place of their comrade Ulam and trod through the muddy wastes toward the distant valley. Ulam had been a close friend to them all, the youngest of their lot and the most eager to prove himself worthy of the rank of soldier. The recruits felt as if he had taken a bit of them to the grave with him, and they were all torn by the loss. Some marched away with reddened eyes; others bit their lips and kept their emotions in check. But none were unaffected, and none would soon forget his companionship and example.

Ishra, the tallest of the Thutcherians, was bitter over the death of his best friend. When they were passing the way to the cave of the flesheaters and Nuroc pointed their lair out to the others, Ishra cried out, "I say we find a way to slay the monsters. Every last one of them!"

"I don't think that would be wise," Nuroc said over his shoulder.

"Wise or not, it must be done!" Ishra went on, verging on delirium. "Who can say how many have died at their hands? How many more will find themselves tossed to the pit in the future?"

"The hill tribes have their own ways," Tudier called back to Ishra. "It is not our place to judge them or interfere in their affairs. Our business is with the Ghetites and Shangorans."

Ishra thrust his finger in the direction of the cave, his voice rising with excitation. "And I still say our business is with the slayers of Ulam!"

Nuroc halted the column and strode back to the tall recruit, eyeing him solemnly. "Lower your voice or we will have no choice but to face them. What chance do you think we would stand, armed with nothing but mud and ready to drop from exhaustion?"

"It matters not," Ishra spat. He looked wildly around at the others. "Who sees it my way? Who will help me to avenge Ulam?"

"Nuroc is right," one of the other recruits said. "Now hold your tongue and let's be gone from here."

The others had no response, although their gazes lent their support to Nuroc.

"Then I go alone," Ishra announced, turning to break free of the group.

Nuroc stepped forward and placed a hand on the rebellious recruit's shoulder, telling him, "You will stay with us. Stop being a fool."

Ishra struck out with his fist, catching Nuroc on the side of his face. Nuroc fell back, stunned. Before Tudier could rush forward to intervene, Ishra dashed clear of the other recruits and ran off in the direction of the cave.

"Stop, Ishra!" Tudier shouted, but to no avail.

Nuroc rubbed his chin and told Tudier, "Let him go."

"But he has deserted!"

"He has followed his will," Nuroc said. "I will fault no man for that."

As he began to call out for the others to continue on their way, they were all startled by a wrenching scream. Turning back, they looked to see that one of the flesheaters had emerged from behind a rock twenty feet away and grabbed Ishra. Ishra was taller than his captor, but no match for the werebeing's strength. The recruit howled a final time before the creature lashed out with such violent fury that his brutish hand not only crushed the Thutcherian's skull, but ripped the entire head clear of the man's shoulders.

The recruits stared in numb horror as the other creatures climbed up onto the swollen boulders on either side of the trail and stared loathsomely back at them.

The recruits were surrounded!

Nuroc stepped away from his cohorts, but before he could attempt another bluff, the creature who had slain Ishra shook the body angrily and growled a torrent of werewords at Nuroc. Nuroc stared silently into the eyes of the flesheater. Behind him, the other recruits remained motionless save for their eyes, which continually scanned the rockwork around them in anticipation of the first move by the cave dwellers. The werebeings, however, did not move either. It was as if both men and creatures had turned to stone. The sun burned down on Nuroc's brow, already sweating with anxiety. He concentrated on the narrow slits of the cannibal's eyes, trying to fathom the thoughts that went through that alien mind.

At last the beast moved, slinging the body of Ishra over its shoulders and turning away, starting back toward the cave, leaving the recruit's discarded head behind. The other flesheaters held their place, however, watching the recruits and waiting.

Slowly, Nuroc moved past his men and reassumed his position at the head of the column. "Follow me," he said softly.

One by one, the men began to walk away. On either side, the flesheaters stood their ground, following the procession only with their burning eyes. The recruits focused their gazes on the muddy way before them and marched in a calm precision that belied the throbbing of their hearts against their chests and the icy grip of horror on their nerves.

It was not until they had marched as far as the first turn on the pathway that Tudier, bringing up the rear of their column, dared to cast a backward glance.

The creatures were nowhere to be seen.

"Gone," Tudier murmured. His companions looked back as well, doubting their senses.

"They've made their point," Nuroc said emptily. "I don't think we will see them again."

"I know they'll never see me again," Tudier said. "Poor Ishra. He did not understand that we do not belong here."

"And to think they dwell so close to the pass," another said feebly, and they fell back to their marching. "I wonder how many travelers have been slain through the years."

"One has to stray far from the main roads to reach these parts," Nuroc commented. "I cannot believe I became so lost in the storm."

"Take heart," a third said. "Perhaps Molent and Wheas are now in the bellies of the beasts."

"And what of the queen, then?" Nuroc asked.

The soldier had no answer. They marched on in silence.

Nineteen

"Look!"

Tudier pointed downhill, toward the shallow valley cradled between the Kanghat ranges. Thick, black smoke rose over the hamlet Centinara, and flames licked at the wet wood of homes and buildings. From where the recruits stood watching, the villagers were visible as small, frantic specks circling around the scattered blazes.

"How can it be?" one of the soldiers murmured incredulously. "After the rains, there could be no risk of fire."

"Perhaps not an accidental one," Nuroc replied. "But even drenched wood will burn if one wants it to."

"What do you mean?" the soldier asked.

"We will find out soon enough," Nuroc said. "Come, let's see if we can help."

"I will help, but only to fan the flames," another grumbled. "I've no love for these villagers after what they did to us."

"What's done is behind us," Tudier said. "Now is our chance to show them that we are not the ogres they thought us to be."

"Aye," Nuroc said, breaking into a jog. The others followed, splashing their way recklessly down the winding trail that led to the valley.

A group of townsfolk were working feverishly at the edge of a lake situated just outside the village, filling wooden buckets with water and emptying them into larger barrels set on a horse-drawn cart. They were a rugged-looking people, heavily-built with coarse faces and light hair, wearing clothes of thick wool against the cooler temperature of the valley. When they saw the recruits bounding down the hill toward them, they stopped their labor and gawked with trepidation. One of them, an older, bearded man with an oversized wool cap tilted on his head, moaned aloud, "Spirits of the dead! Are we to be punished forever?"

Nuroc shook his head as his men slowed down to catch their breath once they had reached the lake. "My men are far from dead, I assure you," he told the man. "We come to aid you if you will let us."

"It is a trick! Like that played by the others," a squat woman wailed, quickly emptying her bucket into the cart and then holding it before her defensively.

"Not so!" Tudier insisted. "Let's not waste time arguing while your village burns!"

The woman hesitated and looked to the bearded man, who gave a short nod of his head. She lowered her bucket and stepped away from the cart as Tudier grabbed up a pair of empty pails hanging from the sides of the large, half-filled barrel. Nuroc directed the other men to form a line from the cart to the bank of the lake. "Work in a chain!" he ordered, taking one of the buckets from Tudier and passing it to the man next to him. The others quickly caught on, handing the container man-to-man until the soldier closest to the lake received it and filled it with water. As he began passing the bucket back toward the cart, a second pail was already coming his way.

The villagers soon overcame their paranoia and formed a similar line next to the recruits, and the barrel on the cart began to fill at a brisk pace.

"I am Vennauld," the bearded villager called out to Nuroc, as he supervised his people. "I am head of Centinara . . . what will be left of it, at any rate. I feel we are under a curse for reasons unknown."

"How did your village start to burn?" Nuroc asked.

"After we had thrown your men into the pit," Vennauld said

in his gravelly voice, "we offered those who had warned us of your coming the shelter of our meeting hall for the night . . . to show our gratitude. Then, during the night, three more strangers arrived, drenched from the rains."

"Two men and a woman?" Nuroc asked as he emptied a bucket and passed it back to Tudier.

"Yes," the bearded man went on. "The woman was bound and gagged, and the men claimed she was a witch and consort to those men we had placed in the pits."

"That woman is our queen!" Tudier said furiously. "As for witchery, that is the way of the Ghetites and Shangorans you took under your roofs! Where are they now?"

The huge barrel was now filled, and both the villagers and the recruits paused to rest their arms as Vennauld took the reins of the lead horse and walked it forward, shifting the cart so that it faced the burning hamlet. While he worked, Vennauld said, "They are gone. When we awoke this morning, we found the meeting hall ablaze and went to investigate. While we tried to fight that fire, the outsiders stole into the homes we had just left and robbed us of food and valuables, then set our houses on fire as well! They fled to the north, and we had no choice but to let them go. It was that or give futile chase while our village succumbed to flames." He looked toward the burning buildings and added, "Even now it may be too late."

"Not if we move quickly," Nuroc said.

As a rider manned the cart and drove the horse-team, the townsfolk joined Nuroc's men in rushing ahead on foot to Centinara. To reach the town, they first had to cross a barren reach of flatland, ankle-deep with mud. Hundreds of wild goats were scattered about the soiled turf, bleating nervously as they watched the procession traipsing past them, kicking up mud as they ran and jogged.

Nuroc asked Vennauld, "Why do you leave this area unplanted? The soil looks rich enough to harvest grain, and there's plenty of water nearby for irrigation."

"Do not think we haven't tried," Vennauld said as he ran. "The goats will not allow anything to grow. If we dare to plant, they graze on the seedlings."

"You could fence off the area and keep them out."

"Fence?" Vennauld panted. "What is a fence?"

"It's a barrier to keep out certain things and to keep in

others,'' Nuroc explained, secretly amazed that so rudimentary a structure had not yet been put to use in Centinara. ''It is like the row of spikes before the cave of the flesheaters.''

''Ah, the Gungsa,'' Vennauld said with a note of dread. ''We stay clear of the cave of the Gungsa. We offer sacrifices in the pit and they leave us alone as well.''

They were close to the village now, and low-hanging smoke began to sting Nuroc's eyes. ''I was in the cave and saw only human bones,'' he told Vennauld, slowing his pace so that he would not have to breathe the smoke so deeply, ''Why do you offer up your own people to the Gungsa?''

''It is our custom,'' the villager said, also slowing down. The horse-driven cart rolled past them and up a gentle slope to the hamlet. ''Besides, it is widely known that the Gungsa live only on the flesh of men.''

''Then why is it they lured my horse into their clutches and killed it? No doubt for food.'' Nuroc countered.

''Not so!'' Vennauld said skeptically.

''I see there are far more goats in this valley than people,'' Nuroc said, looking around as they approached the town. ''Have you ever tried placing animals in the pit instead of men?''

''Why, no,'' Vennauld answered uncertainly. ''As I told you, it has always been our custom to take criminals—''

''Customs are like habits,'' Nuroc said. ''They can be bad as well as good. What will you do with your custom once you come to the day when you have no criminals to feed to the Gungsa? Will you begin to offer yourselves up? Or your children?''

Obviously troubled, the leader of the Centinarans frowned. He slowed to a halt and was about to respond to Nuroc when he changed his mind. He and Nuroc traded glances, then Vennauld finally admitted, ''Your point is valid.''

''Think on it,'' Nuroc said. ''In the meantime, let us see to saving your town.''

Centinara was in a sorry state. The meeting hall in the center of the village was already burned to the ground, reduced to a smoldering heap of blackened ash and glowing embers. The villagers' homes were fortuitously made as much from stone and mortar as wood, and the fires set in them had taken a lesser toll. Some had either already been put out or had extinguished on their own, while others were ablaze with fire gnawing at thatched roofs and timber framework. Of the hamlet's several dozen huts, half were still in various stages of burning.

Even though Nuroc and the recruits entered Centinara in the company of those residents convinced of their good intentions, those who had remained in the town viewed them with uncertainty and a hint of fear. It soon became obvious that any worry was unfounded, as the recruits rushed to the water-cart and formed a fire-fighting line reaching from the cart to the nearest threatened house. Reversing the technique used to fill the barrel, the Thutcherians began to empty it, passing water-filled buckets hand-over-hand to the front of the line, where Tudier pitched the wet load onto the flames. With an angry hiss, a section of fire was doused, spending its last fury in a billow of black smoke.

Inspired by the recruits' success, some of the villagers quickly hitched up other barreled carts and hurried them back to the lake for more water. Those who had worked with the recruits on the initial haul continued to cooperate with the effort, and between the two groups they managed to quickly put out the blaze in the first house.

While congratulations were passed about and the cart was moved over to the next home, Nuroc wiped ash from his face and told Vennauld, "We could do even more if we had tools."

Vennauld pointed across the muddied street that served as the only thoroughfare in the hamlet to a stone shed filled with farming implements. The bearded man said, "There are shovels, picks, hoes—"

"Good, good!" Nuroc exclaimed. He conferred with Tudier and a few of the others, and soon a team comprised of both recruits and townsfolk were using the tools to pitch mud and dirt onto various fires beyond range of the water wagon.

When the rest of the villagers returned with more water and more manpower, Nuroc and Vennauld organized the fire-fighting effort so that soon all the burning homes were being tended and their fires brought under control. The smoke thickened in the air around the hamlet, but the flames died proportionately until at last there was no structure beset by fire.

Men, women and children cried out cheers at the remarkable salvation of their hamlet from the brink of destruction. Much damage had been done, but nothing that could not be replaced in time. As the villagers went about inspecting their homes and snuffing random sparks that might grow into new fires, Nuroc led his men to a grassy mound situated near the outskirts of the village and they all plopped down to rest. They were exhausted, hungry, covered with mud and ash, and their eyes were red and stinging from the smoke. None of them spoke, although there were a considerable number of groans and sighs as they shifted positions on the grass in hopes of lying some way that would not bring pain.

Once they had seen to their homes, the villagers began congregating near the ruins of the meeting hall. Vennauld stood on one of the water carts and spoke at length to his fellow townsfolk, gesturing occasionally to the nearby recruits, who were out of hearing range.

"What do you think they're discussing?" one of the Thutcherians asked.

"I'm not sure," Tudier replied. "But if they come after us with lengths of rope, you can be sure I won't wait for them to tie me up for the flesheaters again."

"I doubt that will happen," Nuroc said.

At last Vennauld stepped down from the cart and started toward the recruits. The other villagers fell in place behind him. There were more than a hundred of them. Seeing them approach, the recruits looked to one another, then slowly rose to their feet, wary and weary.

"There is no need to worry," Vennauld said to them. "We come to offer our thanks and our apologies. We have learned much today." Behind their spokesman, the people of the hamlet nodded their agreement. Some were ashamed to face those they had almost put to death. Others looked to the recruits with eyes pleading for forgiveness.

"We accept," Tudier said on behalf of the recruits.

Nuroc added, "If you will allow us the use of your lake to wash ourselves, we will move on in search of our enemies."

"Your enemies are our enemies," Vennauld asserted. "Consider us your ally. And give no thought to bathing in the lakes. Come into our homes. Damaged though they be, we can still warm water on our hearths and cook all of you a meal. We will provide you with dry clothing and horses as well, and do anything else we can to repay you for what has happened."

Nuroc smiled and looked to his men. "What do you say to that?"

Before Tudier or the others could answer, one of the town elders hollered, "We'll give you weapons, too!"

"Not only weapons," a younger villager piped, taking a step

forward. "We will join you in tracking down those who betray us!"

Two dozen other young men of the hamlet cried their affirmation.

Nuroc considered the offer a moment, weighing it against his orders to seek the queen's rescue on his own. It took little thinking to place the situation in its proper perspective. It was the end—the queen's safety—that mattered most. The means should be whatever served that end best.

"Done!" Nuroc called out. "Together we will wreak our vengeance!"

Twenty

After partaking of the villagers' hospitality, Nuroc and his men rejoined forces in a musty storage shed that had been spared the plunder of the Ghetites and Shangorans, located as it was between a weed-strewn hill and a grove of leafy scenoaks. The youths of Centinara were on hand as well, in the company of Vennauld. Within the shed, sunlight poured through the wooden slats in bright streaks, illuminating a wide array of weaponry. The men outfitted themselves with swords, bucklers, daggers, and pikes—more crudely made than Aerdan arms but crafted well enough to deal death at close quarters.

"Besides the Gungsa," Vennauld informed Nuroc, "we keep arms against the whims of neighboring tribes, who may trade with us one season and raid us the next. You'll find our youths well trained in handling a sword, I'm sure."

Nuroc looked over the latest additions to his force, thick-limbed farm boys who mingled freely among the Thutcherians, exchanging words and advice regarding the village-made weapons. There seemed to be a healthy comraderie between the groups, based no doubt on familiar backgrounds. Thutchers—and Nuroc's second home of Wheshi, for that matter—were both towns of roughly the same size as the hamlet.

"They will be a great aid to us, I'm certain," Nuroc said, adjusting the woolen jupon given to him by family members at the house where he had bathed and eaten. The fit was tight against Nuroc's muscular frame, but a welcome change from the wet, ruined clothes he had worn into the village.

Once the others had chosen their weapons, Nuroc went to the shelves and looked over the arms that remained. His eyes fell at once upon a double-edged battle-ax made of polished steel wrapped around a jaunwood handle. He picked up the ax, testing its weight. It was more cumbersome than a sword, but he liked the way it balanced in his hand. He took it, along with a broad-bladed knife, then looked to his waiting charges and said, "Very well. Now let's find the men these blades were meant for."

The men filed out of the shed, and Vennauld directed them to a nearby field, where, amidst the ever-present goats, a group of several dozen spotted stallions romped through puddles and kicked up wakes of mud with playful abandon.

"I fear that your steeds were taken by the enemy," Vennauld said to Tudier. "I hope that these will compensate."

"They look like stronger horses than our own," Tudier said, admiring the graceful movement of the stallions. "But they aren't trained, are they? We hardly have time to teach them how to carry riders."

Vennauld smiled, his eyes twinkling, and the village youths chuckled among themselves. "Elmin," Vennauld called out to the oldest of the Centinarans, who was also the tallest in the entire group. "Show our new friends whether or not the stallions are trained."

Elmin stepped forth, grinning, and brought his fingers to his lips, sending a shrill whistle sounding across the field. The horses immediately slowed their gaits and turned in the direction of the shed. Elmin clapped his hands several times in quick succession and then waved to the steeds, who responded by breaking into a full run toward the assembled warriors. As Nuroc and the other Aerdans stared on with a tingling of wonder, the flecked beasts kept up their mad-paced charge until they were only a few yards from the posse, then drew to a halt in firm formation, standing shoulder to shoulder before the recruits.

"If we could train the goats as well, we would be grateful," Vennauld told Nuroc, still smiling. "As it is, we may have to build these fences you spoke of."

A second shed located closer to the village proper had lost its roof to the arson, but the riding gear kept within had been left unharmed save for the settling of ash. Dusting off saddles, reins, and bits, the farm boys and recruits carried the pieces out and readied the horses for riding. Then, taking to the saddle, they fell into two columns. Tudier headed up the Thutcherians while Elmin led the village youths. Nuroc rode between Tudier and Elmin, leading the formation over to Vennauld and the assembled villagers.

"Your men will return once we have routed the enemy," Nuroc told them. "If I do not make it this way again, my best wishes are with you in rebuilding your hamlet, and my men share the same sentiment. If we have our say, you will not have the Ghetites and Shangorans to defend yourselves against any longer."

"Again we are grateful for what you have done," Vennauld said solemnly. "We will consider your advice about appeasing the Gungsa with goats instead of our own kind. Now go, and when you free the queen, tell her that she has our loyalty and that we shall be glad to fly the Aerdan flag from our meeting hall once we have rebuilt it."

Nuroc nodded, then tugged on the reins and led his horse forward. Behind him, the other horsemen fell in line, and with a din of clattering hooves, they rode through the town, waving to the onlooking villagers. Fathers and mothers rushed forward with teary eyes to bid their sons good fortune, and children yipped with excitement, unaware of the gravity of the occasion. Once beyond the edge of Centinara, the riders picked up their speed and struck out for the road that would lead them to whatever fate the gods decreed should befall them. More than one of the youths whispered silent prayers to those gods, asking for guidance and favor.

The sun was at its noon height when the men left the village. It was halfway toward its setting before the men had traveled the the mountain pass they had to negotiate in pursuit of those horsemen responsible for the tracks that scarred the muddy course before them. If the going was rough, there was comfort in the view. The farther they made their way down the steep incline of the path, the more they could see of the verdant plain that awaited them below. Although clouds had begun to move in once more from the coast, there was enough sunlight and clear sky to lend color to the landscape. Nuroc had thought his previous views of blooming terrain were beautiful beyond belief, but the scene laid out before him now made the others pale in comparison.

"How many plains and valleys like this are there in these parts?" he asked Elmin.

"Look around," the tall youth said. "There are hundreds of peaks and dozens of ranges. Stand atop any peak and you will see another plain or valley set down between where you are and the next mountain range. You will likely find another village as well."

"Amazing," Nuroc said. "And to think of all the people dwelling here in the Kanghats, unaware of what goes on outside the mountains."

"We feel the same about you," Elmin said, though without malice. "I guess it is the way of every people to think that the world centers around them and their concerns."

"Spoken true," Nuroc said. "That is no doubt why there is always conflict, be it between countries or hamlets. There can be only one center of things, and as long as different peoples believe they are the hub around which all else should revolve, there can be no peace. It is the way of the world, I fear, the reason we are now in the saddle, seeking out our enemy."

Tudier rode forward to Nuroc's side, cracking, "Who do I hear up here, a philosopher or an officer?"

Nuroc grinned stiffly. "I fear I am parts of both."

"Well, when we clash with the Ghetites and they go for your head with a sword, I hope you don't try to defend yourself with philosophy," Tudier said. "Words make a poor shield."

"I will remember that," Nuroc answered.

"You had better," Tudier said.

The exchange left Nuroc unsettled, and the rest of the way down to the bottom of the pass he troubled over the questions he had raised. In the end, he decided it was best to avoid conflict, but when it could not be avoided, it was best to set aside all thoughts but the pursuit of victory and survival. Perhaps there might be a future age when life could be managed otherwise, but for now he saw no better way.

Twenty-One

Clouds had once again reclaimed the sky by the time the horsemen found themselves on the valley floor. A stream curled its way across the lush sward, and Nuroc motioned for the men to stop near its banks so that the horses could drink and rest. Dismounting, the troops stretched their cramped limbs and rolled the kinks from their necks and shoulders. One of the farm boys unslung his saddlebags and walked among the others, passing out rations of salted meat and dried fruit.

Nuroc nodded thanks as he took his share and began chewing at the end of the meat strip. It was goatflesh, tough to chew and bland in taste, but mixed in with bites of fruit and swallowed down with fresh, cold water from the stream, it served to appease the pangs of hunger that had begun to gnaw at him.

As Nuroc had suspected when he had first seen the stream, the enemy they sought had ridden into the shallow, flowing waters, where they could move without leaving tracks. After conversing with the farm boys, who knew the area, he decided it was most likely that the Ghetites and Shangorans had taken the stream across the width of the valley toward the pass leading down the side of the next range.

Mounting up and riding upstream, the men were silent and apprehensive. All around them, there was a quietude that seemed unnatural for a place such as this. There were few signs or sounds of wildlife other than those of fish slapping through the water to move clear of the horsemen's advance.

Nuroc suddenly turned his head toward the nearby banks, staring and listening with fierce intent.

"Yes!" he howled impassionately, coaxing his steed from the stream to land and withdrawing his ax from a leather sheath fixed to his saddle. Most men would be hard-pressed to even lift the double-edged weapon with any control, but fueled on by the enervating thrill of his discovery, he waved it over his head as if it were no heavier than a satin banner. He'd found them!

He slapped his heels on the rear flanks of his mottled stallion, causing the steed to rear majestically, kicking its front hooves at the first fall of new rainpour. The horse held Nuroc aloft in a momentary pause of deadly grandeur, then bolted forward. Behind Nuroc, the others splashed their way ashore and brought forth their weapons, shouting war cries at the top of their lungs. Their bellows and the clop of countless hooves mingled with the roll of thunder announcing the storm's arrival. The sky filled with thick swirls of gray ominous clouds that began to throw down shafts of lightning across the valley.

The marshy plain, only moments before a haven of tranquility, suddenly was rent with tumult as a hundred species took flight from the advance of Nuroc's troops. Resting antelope lurched to their feet and coursed the distance to the far edge of the valley in long, graceful bounds. A herd of elk huddled together for protection; antlered males stood proud and defiant before their mates and offspring. And, out over the small lake into which the winding stream emptied, a flock of golden herons rose from the still waters in a mad flutter of wings, falling into formation as they flew from the valley.

Nuroc ignored the scattering of wildlife. His was a hunt for a more elusive and more dangerous game. Peering through the thickening rainfall, the stern-faced horseman concentrated on what lay behind the seeming calm of a pine grove stretching from the streambank fifty yards away all the way up to the top of the mountain range they had just descended from.

The thunder overhead sounded closer, echoing loudly from one end of the valley to the other. As he neared the first row of pines, Nuroc worked free his buckler, a fine shield of boarskin drawn taut over a frame of oak and brass. Holding it in the same hand that clasped the reins, Nuroc charged his stallion into the hiding place of the enemy he knew lay waiting for him.

The buckler deflected low-hanging branches, and it also blocked the first blow of battle, a plunging dagger in the hand of a Shangoran raider who dove down on Nuroc from one of the trees. The raider was short and squat, light of skin and more agile than he was strong. He clung to the knife he had imbedded in Nuroc's shield, and with his free hand he tried to pull the horseman down to the ground. He let out a high-pitched scream and was answered by the cries of eighty fellow raiders, who dropped from the trees like ripened fruit.

Nuroc cursed this poor choice of a battleground. In the cramped quarters of the forest, a horseman was out of his element, especially when he was trying to maneuver a battle-ax around an obstinate conifer. He could not strike a decent blow at his attacker, and soon the raider had forsaken his dagger to concentrate fully on tugging at the collar of Nuroc's jerkin.

The other horsemen who charged past Nuroc to engage with the enemy met with similar hardships. Their broadswords and pikes were doing more damage to the trees than to the enemy.

Unable to lay a blade on the raider, Nuroc finally brought the butt of his ax crashing down on the shorter man's skull with so much force that the raider died with one hand still entangled in the crisscrossed strings of Nuroc's jerkin. Nuroc began to choke from the tightening of his collar as the dead man dangled like an oversized medallion on his chest.

"I'll notch my ax if I want to remember your death, Shangoran!" Nuroc snarled as he tried to untangle the dead man's hand.

"Nuroc! Behind you!"

Nuroc heeded Tudier's call in time to meet another raider's dagger with the edge of his ax. This one had not yet abandoned his perch on a low lying pine limb, so Nuroc swung the flat of his buckler into the attacker's face, knocking him to the ground, either dead or too senseless to pose a threat. Nuroc's quick turn had tightened the first raider's grip on the drawstrings of his collar, however, cutting off his breath. As Nuroc gasped for air, a wavering frame of darkness began to cloud his vision. In desperation, he choked up on the hilt of his battle-ax, gaining enough momentum in his swing to severe the dead man's hand. The Shangoran fell onto his unmoving companion in the dirt. Blood splattered freely from the still-dangling hand, staining the front of Nuroc's jupon. He had no time to dispense with his grisly souvenir, however, for he saw that his men were not having an easy time with the raiders.

The rain was coming down heavily now, dripping through the coverage of the pines and worsening the muddy, slippery surface that provided the horses with an unsure footing. Nuroc's men were spending as much time trying to stay mounted as they were fighting off the Shangorans, who surrounded the horsemen and outnumbered them two and sometimes three men to one.

"Dismount!" Nuroc cried, his deep voice piercing through the cacophony of battle. He was the first to follow his advice, jumping to the ground and slapping his steed's hindquarters to chase it away from the fracas. Two more raiders converged upon him. Off his horse, Nuroc had more room with which to flail his battle-ax, and he cut down both men with a weaving arc of steel.

A dozen of Nuroc's men had died before he had given the order to dismount, twice the fatalities incurred by the more numerous Shangorans. However, once they forsook their steeds and turned to the battle tactics of the infantry, the tide began to change in their favor. Nuroc clove through the enemy like a farmer harvesting grain, and his frenzied warring was an example taken up by his followers with gusto. Tudier began to sing merrily as he dispatched raider after raider to a bloody death, and the others found it easier to grin than scowl when their teeth were clenched in the concentration of battle. Rain mingled with their sweat, but other than an occasional loss of footing on the slick ground, neither side heeded the weather.

There were fewer than twenty Shangorans still alive when they decided to retreat, breaking from the cover of the pines and running headlong toward the stream. Some were lucky enough to mount their pursuers' abandoned steeds and race across the stream and grasslands toward the other end of the valley. Others followed but were cut down beneath the last torrent of rainfall before they could reach the horses.

By the time the carnage had ended, the bodies of more than eighty warriors littered the emerald landscape. The Aerdans and Centinarans had slain four Shangorans for each fatality they had suffered. While the farm boys cried their thanks and proclaimed victory to the heavens, Nuroc stood at the edge of the stream and looked upward, letting the thinning rain wash trickles of blood from his face. A few slashes from enemy daggers had given him cuts on his forehead and arms, but they were negligible wounds of the sort he had been receiving regularly of late without dire consequence. He squatted over the stream and splashed water on the cuts until they stopped bleeding, then gave them no further thought. The severed hand had worked itself free from his collar in the fighting, but the bloody gore on his jupon remained, and there was still a stained reminder after he washed the cloth with a few more scoops of water.

The other soldiers went about rounding up those horses that hadn't been slain or stolen by the retreating Shangorans. There were twenty-two of Nuroc's men and only sixteen horses left, but soon Tudier emerged from the cover of the pines with two other men, dragging behind them a string of eighty horses belonging to the raiders. They had been tethered uphill from the site of battle. Among the steeds were those of the Aerdans, which had been taken from Centinara earlier that morning.

"Ho! What a find, Tudier!" Nuroc called out, waving to his friend. His smile only lasted for a short time, however. Reflecting on the bloody exchange he'd just survived, he quickly realized that there had been no Ghetites among those they had faced. Even more disturbing, there had been no trace of Molent, Wheas, or the queen.

Elmin came up behind Nuroc, holding his sword on a terrified Shangoran, no older than the youngest farm boy. "A prisoner," Elmin announced proudly. "I thought you might want to talk with him before I run him through with my blade."

Nuroc thanked Elmin and looked at the enemy youth.

"Mercy!" the Shangoran begged, dropping to his knees. "I hid during the battle. I raised no sword against your men. Please show mercy!"

"Stand up," Nuroc told the youth gruffly. After the Shangoran had warily obliged, Nuroc asked him, "Where are the others?"

"They . . . they fled, as you saw," the Shangoran stammered fearfully.

"I am talking about your king and General Wheas's horde of Ghetites. Where have they gone with our queen?"

The prisoner did not reply at once, but Nuroc had only to flex his grip around the handle of his battle-ax to get the Shangoran to give him answers. "They have gone, left the valley and taken the pass down to the plains of Ghetite. They were bound for Velley. We were left behind to see that they weren't followed."

"And you spent the day waiting back in the trees for us?"

The youth shook his head. "We were camped near the stream, with guards posted up at the top of the pass you came here by way of. They saw your coming and passed word down to us so that we could take our cover and lure you into the trees, where we thought we would have our best chance."

"You planned well," Nuroc said gravely. "But you misjudged the fury behind our attack. The vengeance in our hearts made us the better warriors."

"You've had your revenge," the youth bargained. "It will do

no good to slay me, now. Besides, I can help you further if you let me live."

"We will make do without your aid," Nuroc said. "But I will spare your life for now."

The prisoner's face brightened some, but as he saw Nuroc and Elmin lean their heads together and exchange whispers, he stopped short of mouthing his gratitude.

When Nuroc and Elmin had finished speaking, the latter turned to the prisoner and said, "You will be taken back to our hamlet to answer for the deception and ruin you and your comrades visited upon us."

Ashen-faced with renewed fear, the prisoner whined, "What chance can I hope for after I face them? I am as good as dead."

"We shall see," Elmin said, leading the youth away.

Nuroc stood upon a nearby boulder and raised his voice for the others to hear. "Elmin has told me of another village, Renast, set at the far end of the valley, along the trade routes. Most of us will ride there and seek lodging for the night, as I fear another storm is yet to come. A few of you will return to your own town with prisoners and the extra horses. Only the willing and uninjured will continue on."

A few of those bearing minor wounds protested, and Nuroc relented, allowing them to stay on with his troop, which now numbered less than half the number of men who had set out from Centinara that morning.

The casualties were placed either in the saddle or over the backs of the extra horses. One of the youths from the hamlet rode to the head of this column, and, after exchanging farewells with old acquaintances and newfound friends, the party of dead and wounded began the long trek back to Centinara. Nuroc and the others watched them a while, then regrouped and turned their steed the other way, facing the rain-sparkled grasslands they would have to cross to reach the trading center of Renast.

Twenty-Two

During the years before the Great Cataclysm, when all of Dorban was under one rule, Renast had thrived as the hub of trade between territories on the northwest face of the Kanghat Mountains as well as those of the adjacent foothills. After the cataclysm, however, Ghetite emerged as a separate kingdom, and its borders cut off much of the land that had once been a part of the overland trade routes that ran through Renast, which fell under the province of Aerda. When the new kingdoms came into being, trade routes were reestablished with a mind toward the changed borders and the diplomatic ties between the various nations. Because Aerda refused to consider any association with either Ghetite or Shangora, Renast and the other stopping points along the old trade routes ceased to enjoy their strategic importance. Most of the inhabitants of these old trade centers migrated over the Kanghats and into the Aerdan heartland, seeking a share of the prosperity that was nowhere to be found on the other side of the mountain.

When Nuroc led his men into present-day Renast, they saw an empty shell of the once-grand city. Vacated stone buildings stood untended and wounded from the play of vandals and the lodging of transients and wild animals. Crawling vines and hardy weeds choked yards that had once been well groomed by teams of gardeners catering to the whims of rich merchants. The wind blew mournfully through openings no longer covered by taut hides or thick draperies.

"It is even less inviting than you forewarned us," Nuroc commented to Elmin as they rode down a rotting street pocked with squalid puddles and bits of broken wall from looted shops and deserted temples. The sound of hooves beating dully against the mud raced ahead of the horsemen like the ghosts of ragged echoes. The men looked around them uncertainly, keeping their hands close to their weapons. When a man with wild hair and tattered clothes suddenly appeared amidst the ruins, several of the recruits gasped with fright. As quickly as he had shown himself, the ragged man vanished and could be heard running off through the rubble. The horsemen looked to one another uneasily.

"At least it seems that the storm will pass us by," Elmin said, looking up at the last of the dark, plump clouds scudding overhead, bound for the mountains and a lightening of its load in the higher altitudes.

"Thanks for that," Tudier grumbled. "I'd rather sleep out in the open than seek refuge in one of these old buildings. They make my skin crawl."

"Up here will be a better place," Elmin promised. As they rounded the next corner, he pointed to a high-walled garrison made of stone blocks and lashed jaunwood. "In the days of Renast's glory, the king had the militia stationed here to prevent trading wars and raids by land pirates. Now there are few goods to watch over, and the garrison is only used by troops on their way to and from border duty down in the foothills. Still, men come often enough that the buildings are kept up. It will be a fine place to bed for the night."

Before the riding column could veer its course toward the hinged gates of the garrison, there was a sudden shifting in the breeze, and the men were assailed by the smell of roasting meat and baking breads.

Licking his lips, Tudier called out, "That smells too fresh for the ghost of a long-begone banquet, Nuroc. It's a side of ox or I'm a fool's bastard son."

Nuroc cast the Thutcherian a smirking glance, then turned to Elmin. "I smell it, too."

"Renast may be a dying town, but it still has its share of occupants." Elmin sat high in the saddle and sniffed the air, cocking his head slightly to one side. "It's coming from the old merchant's hall. Come, we may be in for a pleasant surprise."

Elmin eased his horse about and galloped off down a side street. Tudier and Nuroc exchanged looks, then shrugged their shoulders and followed, leading the other men behind them.

As Nuroc and Tudier took up positions along either side of Elmin, he told them, "In all the excitement, I almost forgot. Tomorrow marks the arrival of this season's lone trade caravan, bringing goods from the north on its way to Cothe. It is Renast's one chance to earn its living between now and the summer run. Already they are readying foodstuffs to sell the traders in the morning."

"But if what they are making is for the traders, then—"

Elmin cut Nuroc off with a wave of his hand. "Not to worry. There will be plenty for all, I am certain. I know many of the people here from previous trips during our harvest season. Provided I can vouch for you and the other men and you can promise payment from the king in the near future, I daresay Renast can accommodate the troops in ways they shan't forget."

Nuroc caught the sly glimmer in Elmin's eye and asked, "What do you mean? There is more to be had here than food and lodging?"

By the way of response, the horsemen came upon a cul-de-sac, at the end of which was a large hall, built of stone and draped with ivy. Lights shone from within the building, and, lounging about the rounded pillars supporting the portico entrance, were half a dozen women in cloaks of silk and satin, with coiffed hair and dark-lined eyes that looked out at the horsemen with expressions of allure and desire. One of them, tall and lean save for the rounded wonder of her veiled cleavage, smiled capriciously as she walked down the steps and up to the men on horseback.

"Well, now," she moaned in a husky, tantalizing voice that every man heard. She stopped before Elmin's horse and stroked the young man's leg with a single, painted finger. "What do we have here?"

"Hungry men," Elmin grinned, dismounting, "looking for food and hungry women."

The woman wove her fingers around the back of Elmin's neck and pulled his face to hers, smothering his lips with a long, forceful kiss. His hands went to her side and drew her near. Still astride their horses, Nuroc and Tudier watched on with curiosity. When the woman pulled herself away from Elmin, she let her gaze drift to the other men and take them in, one by one. Most of them smiled back sheepishly. Some looked away. Tudier bared his teeth in a grin of confidence, while Nuroc returned the woman's gaze with a polite nod.

"The merchants will be here tomorrow looking for the same thing," the woman told Elmin matter-of-factly. "They bring money with them."

"We bring the will of King Pencroft," Tudier boasted. "He will match and better your merchants' fare if we are treated well enough to go out and do his bidding with renewed spirit and drive."

The woman looked to Elmin. "He speaks the truth?"

The young man appealed to Nuroc, who thought a moment before nodding his head again.

The woman smiled and stepped away from Elmin, rejoining her fellow harlots.

"Well," she asked the others, who continued to eye the horsemen, "do you think we can put up with the company of young, lean men for an evening before we turn our attention to old, fat-bellied traders?"

One of the other women, drawing her fingers through her hair in a slow, sensual motion, looked over the riders and finally said, "How long has it been since we've had soldiers?"

"Too long," another replied, shifting her legs as she leaned against a stone column. Her cloak parted, revealing the supple outline of a half-bent leg, naked to the painted nails on her toes.

"If they are all this lovely, we may never leave," Tudier muttered, sliding from his saddle and leading his steed to the scenoak limb hammered across two poles for a hitching post.

One of the farm boys from Centinara called out from the saddle, "And to think I've passed up trips to Renast because I thought this town had nothing to offer."

The others dismounted as well and began to tether their horses before the meeting hall. Nearby, in the shadows, a ragged figure hunched over and watched. And waited.

Twenty-Three

The hall soon rang with the boisterous sounds of celebration. Wine flowed freely. Ox bones, laid bare by the ravenous hunger of the warriors, littered tables and floor alike. Under the gleam of oil lamps, Centinarans and the young men of Thutcher shared songs and stories of their countless exploits, both real and imagined. The women listened and laughed, making the visitors feel warm and welcome. And wanted. Many a soldier beamed at the soft touch of fingers stroking their legs and arms. As the night pressed on, the women took the men by the hand and lured them off to the darkened niches in the corners of the great room, where fondles were exchanged and lips pressed together in lustful abandon.

Nuroc ate and drank his fill, but admired the women from a distance. They reminded him of the girls on the whoreships that docked in the harbor of his native Wheshi. He recalled how Myrania had been held captive on such a ship by the whoremaster Sphextay, who had enslaved her with the aid of mind-twisting proffax blossoms. Watching the women made him long for the embrace of his loved one, and he found himself looking forward to the end of this quest, when he could return to Cothe and Myrania's side.

Tudier was at the same table with Nuroc, swilling from a tankard of blood-red wine as he spoke with great excitement to the women on either side of him.

"And so there we were, Nuroc and I, side by side, stroking the oars against the current of the Targoan along with the other recruits. We were bound for Cothe, to join forces with the king's militia and strike back against the threat of Ghetite and its ally Shangora." Placing his hands out before him, Tudier curled his fingers around imaginary oars and pretended he was rowing. The women snickered lightly to one another and squeezed his arms playfully.

"Wait until I finish," Tudier bade them. "Then you may distract me to your heart's desire." When they pulled their hands away, he continued, "Of course, we thought that it would be several days before we would face the enemy. Little did we know that the banks of the Targoan were teeming with Ghetites and Shangorans watching us for the moment they could spring their well-laid ambush.

"Down the river we rowed, and suddenly arrows fell upon us like a rain of death. The devilspawn had archers hiding on the north banks, horsemen hiding on the south banks, and infantry downstream, cutting down a scenoak to block the river so that we could not take the ship clear of the attack. Ghetites and Shangorans everywhere! They must have outnumbered us ten to one! Right, Nuroc?"

Nuroc finished a draw from his tankard and grinned modestly at the women. "I think the odds were closer to five to one."

"You have to count their horses!" Tudier protested. "Ten to one, five to one. What matters is that we were staring into the jaws of a massacre. All around us our officers fell like leaves in autumn, arrows in their hearts. Soon we had no leader to guide us—not so much as one man who had already taken his oath to the Shield and donned the uniform of the militia. There were only us recruits, trapped like lambs readied for the slaughter.

"It was Nuroc who rose to the situation; Nuroc who directed us to throw torches to the north banks and flush out the archers; Nuroc who sprang to his feet and filled us with courage and strength to fight back. He led us by example, lashing out at Ghetites with an oar, crushing skulls and breaking ribs, then carving Shangorans with his blade like a man possessed. Oh, what fighting! What fury! We followed his example and soon the battle was over, with ourselves the victors! There could be no doubt but that Nuroc should lead us from that point forward."

As Tudier paused to wet his dried throat, the women went back to stroking his arms, but their eyes were on Nuroc. He avoided their gazes, but could still feel himself being watched.

"Is it true?" one of them asked softly, her voice as smooth as the silk that draped her voluptuous body. Nuroc felt something touch his leg, and he jumped slightly in his seat before he realized the woman was rubbing his calves with her feet in slow, gentle strokes. Embarrassed, he clasped her feet and set them aside. She pouted slightly, then turned her attentions back to Tudier.

"Of course it's true!" Tudier insisted, raising his arms so that he could drape them over the shoulders of both women. "I'm not one to boast, but I was there beside Nuroc, fighting to the death with equal certainty.

"What I've told you is only the first of our escapades. There's still the great battle in the meadows, and also the skirmish we've just come from. I tell you, we here are the stuff of legends. Years from now, songs will be sung in our honor, and children will speak of Nuroc and Tudier and the Thutcherian recruits with the same awe now reserved for heroes like Noj-Syb and Doutat of the North!"

Nuroc chuckled to himself and shook his head, telling Tudier, "You have missed your calling, Tudier. Instead of a soldier, you should have been a poet or minstrel."

"Perhaps I will be all three!" Tudier said, refilling his goblet with an uncertain hand. The wine that had loosened his tongue was now having the same effect upon his limbs, it seemed.

"If you are all three," the shorter of the women cooed in Tudier's ear, "then how will you find the time to be a lover?" She licked his ear and let her hand stray from his arm to his leg.

Tudier took her hand and guided it to his groin, then whispered, "I have the time right now."

The woman gave Tudier a slight squeeze, then drew away and rose to her feet. "Then let us go." She looked around and raised her voice to the others, "Come, it's time we took the men to their beds at the garrison."

"At the garrison?" Tudier protested. "Why not here?"

The short woman looked at Tudier and said, "The beds there are made for two, and there's room enough for each man to find a place away from the others."

"Reason enough," Tudier said, quickly downing the last of his wine and shouting to the other men. "Onward, then; to the garrison!"

The cry was echoed by the other youths, who were equally fueled with drunken lust and a spirit of adventure. For many of them, it was their first taste of debauchery, unchecked by any awareness of the toll to be paid come morning, when heads would be apt to throb with the pain of too much drink and loins would be apt to throb with the price of too much pleasure. They cared only that they had faced death earlier that day and lived to tell of it. They were among the living and were determined to enjoy life with the same ferocity as they dealt death. They were warriors struck from the warrior's mold.

Not so Nuroc. While the others sang and chanted and left the hall with their arms around their lovers for the night, Nuroc stayed behind, staring at the goblet in his hand and sipping the wine slowly.

"Do you feel all right?"

Nuroc looked up and saw the barkeep eyeing him curiously. He was an older man, thin of build with a hawklike nose, wearing a plain tunic of coarse muslin. His eyes were dark and small.

"I am fine," Nuroc replied. "Fine."

"You should join the others," the barkeep told him.

"I will, in a moment."

"As you wish," the man mumbled before going about his business, plucking ox bones off the floor and tossing them into a small barrel set in the middle of the room. Nuroc watched with wonder as the barkeep pitched bone after bone into the barrel from different spots across the room.

"You have a good aim," Nuroc commented.

"I have much time to practice," the barkeep answered. "When the traders come, I win money off them when they bet I can't hit my mark on every toss."

"I see." Nuroc tilted back his goblet and felt the last of the wine drain warmly down his throat. He was slightly light-headed from the drink, and the sensation bothered him. Why couldn't he be like the others, who so readily gave themselves over to enjoyment? Was his grim import due solely to his loyalty to Myrania and the seriousness of his mission? Or was it something else? Had he wronged his instincts with the wine, taken himself away from the guiding hand of the fates that were said to watch over him so long as he followed the path of rightness?

He laughed at himself and rose to his feet, starting from the tavern. "Tudier was right," he scolded himself in a slurred whisper. "Enough philosophy, Nuroc."

"What's that?" the barkeep called out from across the room.

"Nothing," Nuroc said.

He moved out the door, Nuroc almost walked into the ragged man scrambling up the steps. The other man, with wide eyes amidst the smeared dirt on his face, shrank back and clung apprehensively to the ivy-laden pillar behind him.

"I saw you as we came into the village, did I not?" Nuroc asked the man, who bobbed nervously in place, wringing his hands through the folds of his garb. The strange man did not seem to understand Nuroc's words. He stayed pressed against the pillar while Nuroc walked down the steps, and went to join his compatriots at the garrison. After taking a few steps down the street, Nuroc glanced back and the man was gone.

Twenty-Four

The garrison was silent save for a rustling breeze and the laborious snores of the warriors as they droned through their sated slumber. They slept on beds of matted straw in separate rooms set side-by-side along a wooden corridor that stretched the length of one side of the garrison. Some dozed with their arms still draped over the women who had seen to their pleasure, half-dressed against the damp chill of the unheated cubicles. Others had rolled over and curled into fetal balls, smiling at secret dreams or memories of soft, warm flesh and the searching lips of the women, who also seemed to be wrapped in blankets of slumber.

Then, somewhere outside the garrison, a melodic whistle carried through the night air like the sound of a calling sparrow. But there were no sparrows in Renast, or any other of the mountain valleys in this range of the Kanghats.

One by one, the women of Renast opened their eyes in response to the whistle. One by one, they quietly rose from the sides of their lovers for the night, taking care not to disturb their sleep. After slipping back into their flimsy gowns, each of the women stole to corners or rough sawn tables, curling their slender fingers around the weapons of the men and clutching them tightly against their bosoms. For several lingering seconds, they stood over the sleeping men, looking down on them with enigmatic eyes, making certain that those who stirred did not suddenly awake. Satisfied, the women turned and left their separate rooms.

In the darkened corridor, the women fell in together and padded softly across the cold stone of the cobbled floor and out the main doorway leading to the open courtyard. Outside, under the light of the partial moon and a sprinkling of stars, the women trod the dirt leading to the gates that linked the garrison to the city. Nuroc had thrown the bolt across the gates earlier to ensure the men's privacy during the culmination of their festivities. Several of the women set down the weapons they had taken from the sleeping warriors and carefully worked the bolt free.

With equal care, the women opened the gates enough to slip through to the outside. Waiting for them was the ragged man. A leery grin split his face as he greeted the women with a hoarse-throated whisper.

"It is done?" he asked.

The head mistress nodded and behind her the other women showed the weapons they had procured from the men.

"The drugged wine worked well enough," she hissed sultrily. "They sleep like children and suspect nothing."

"Good," the man said, rubbing his soiled palms together. "At last we have our chance to strike back at Aerda for the demise of our city."

As the women made their way out of the garrison, the man in tatters turned and pursed his lips, giving off the sparrow whistle and waving to the shadows of an empty building across the deserted road. From out of the building came a stealthy procession of tall men with dark skins, carrying deadly scimitars in their closed fists.

Ghetites!

The women shrank back from the sight of the men, recalling the fierce passions with which the Ghetites had sated their lusts during that afternoon, upon their arrival in Renast. The women were no strangers to perversions and harsh love-making, but nothing had prepared them for the ravishment of the Ghetites. One did not make love to a Ghetite and then make ready for another customer moments later. But, then, the Ghetites paid well for the pleasure they took, and the women were sure they could learn to withstand the rigors of these new suitors once Renast flew the flag of Ghetite and enjoyed the prosperity of increased trade. They thought less about betraying their country than they did about their future fortunes under a new order.

As the Ghetites approached the garrison, the women rushed off silently in the other direction, making their way back to the hall where they had woven their first web of deceit. Behind them they left in the dirt those weapons they had stolen from the unsuspecting Aerdans and Centinarans.

The Ghetites filed grimly past the ragged man, who looked over the men for one in particular. When that man did not appear, the disheveled traitor motioned aside the last of the Ghetites, a dark-eyed warrior with scars from conflict blemishing his olive features.

"Where is General Wheas?" the ragged man demanded. "He was to pay me for my part in arranging your revenge on the Aerdans."

"He has left, along with King Molent and the Aerdan queen," the scar-faced Ghetite answered calmly. "They are on their way back to our capital."

"But what of my payment?" the traitor whined, raising his voice as he held out his palm. "Five ounces of silver. That was the price to be paid."

"Here is your payment," the Ghetite said, thrusting the tip of his scimitar into the other's chest. "It's not silver, but there's more than five ounces of it."

Dumbfounded, the deformed man looked down at his pierced chest. Before he could cry out or react further, the Ghetite twisted the blade and the traitor crumpled lifelessly to the ground.

Wrenching his blade free, the Ghetite fell in behind the others, and soon they were all within the garrison. There were forty of them, twice the number of men sleeping in the barracks. The quartered horses sensed the enemy and snorted nervously as they moved about in the far corner of the courtyard. The Ghetites slipped cautiously into the darkened recess of the nearest building and remained still until the horses ceased their pacing and fell silent once more. Then they broke from cover and made their way along the inner wall surrounding the garrison until they came to the barracks. One of their number crept forward and vanished inside the entry doorway. Moments later, he stuck his head out and waved the others inside.

One of the volunteers from Centinara slept in the first chamber the Ghetites came to. He lay on his back, wearing only his breechcloth as he clutched at the tunic draped over him like a blanket. An empty wine skin was set beside him on the straw, as were his buskins and empty scabbard.

Stealing up to the sleeping figure, a Ghetite crouched over and placed the cold edge of his scimitar against the throat of the Centinaran. When the youth's eyes opened and he instinctively jolted forward, the Ghetite briskly dragged the blade through his victim's neck, drawing blood from the jugular and piercing the man's windpipe. With a series of choking spasms, the farm boy died.

In the next room, Nuroc blinked and awoke from his slumber, hearing the commotion. As he started to sit up, he saw the shadowy outline of someone entering the room from the hallway. He could tell by the glint of metal and the size of his intruder that things were not as they should be.

"What goes on?" he called out, reaching across his mattress of straw for his sword. It was not there. He saw the man rushing toward him and recognized him at once as a Ghetite.

The enemy's blade sang through the air. Nuroc rolled groggily to one side and the scimitar missed him by scant inches.

"Ghetites!" Nuroc screamed as he struggled to his feet. His opponent took another swipe at him, and this time Nuroc could not dodge completely clear. He felt the glancing steel sting his thigh, and blood spurt forth from an angry gash, soaking his jupon.

Falling against the wall of his cubicle, Nuroc clung to the support of a small table, which held an extinguished oil lamp. Acting quickly, he flung the lamp at his attacker. The oil splattered out, still hot from the night's burning, and the Ghetite howled with painful rage as the searing liquid sizzled against his flesh.

Nuroc took advantage of the diversion to snatch up the table and charge the Ghetite. Before the enemy could recover from his shock and bring his blade back into play, Nuroc shattered his skull.

Another Ghetite rushed into the chamber. Nuroc took up the fallen man's scimitar and parried the first thrust of his new assailant. He countered with a riposte that sent the Ghetite reeling back defensively, blocking the doorway from entry by the other dark-skinned foes surging down the corridor.

Knowing that he faced certain death if he remained in the room, Nuroc beat the Ghetite back with a few more flourishes of the sword, then turned about and ran to the opening that faced the courtyard. He hurled himself headfirst through the window and rolled to his feet on the ground outside.

Alerted by Nuroc's cry and the injured shout of the Ghetites, the rest of his force had awakened in time to avoid the defenseless butchery that had faced the first of their men to encounter the enemy. A few were cut down before they could defend themselves, but others, including Tudier and Elmin, snatched up whatever they could get their hands on and battled their way out of the barracks. Still others had been forewarned in time to climb outside before the Ghetites had reached their rooms.

Fifteen survivors of the sneak attack gathered around Nuroc. None of them were armed, save for Tudier and Elmin, who had managed, like Nuroc, to wrest scimitars from the Ghetites they had faced and overcome. As the Ghetites poured out from the barracks, eyes blazing with wrath, Nuroc rushed to the fore of his men and shouted to them, "There are too many of them for us to fight, especially in our condition. Run to the horses and flee! I'll hold them off." When some of the others began to protest, he added, "Do as you're ordered!"

With the Ghetites almost upon him, Nuroc could not look back to see if he was obeyed, but he heard the sound of his men running across the courtyard to the horses. As he stepped forward to meet the first attacker, Tudier and Elmin came into view, following on either side of him, swords held out before them menacingly.

"You didn't think we'd let you grab all the honor, did you?" Tudier smirked at Nuroc, then brought his blade clanging sharply against the scimitar of the first Ghetite.

Nuroc and Elmin took on other foes with equal fervor. They knew that their only chance to hold the enemy back was to do the fighting of three men, and they quickly fanned out as they flashed their swords in the face of the enemy, creating a formidable barrier. Swift strokes also kept the Ghetites from closing ranks too tightly around any one of them.

Sparks showered about the threesome as blades slapped and cut against one another in a din of swordplay. Adrenalin had cut through the stupor of Nuroc, Tudier, and Elmin, but the laborious challenge of warding off three and four blades at a time took quick toll on their strength and agility. Ghetite scimitars bit closer to their marks, and finally Elmin took a slash to the swordarm that cut through nerves. Moaning, he lost hold of his sword. Tudier and Nuroc both tried to widen their offense to protect their comrade, but the task was too much, and Elmin was cut down by the scar-faced Ghetite.

"You'll die for that!" Nuroc shouted as he tried to battle his way to Elmin's murderer.

"We'll all die one day," the Ghetite chortled back. "This is your day, not mine!"

As the Ghetites moved in to finish off Nuroc and Tudier, the sound of hoofbeats drummed against the dirt of the courtyard. Nuroc shot a quick glance away from the enemy and saw his men riding toward them.

"Come, Tudier!" Nuroc shouted, wielding a shower of blows to drive back the nearest swordsmen and give him the few needed seconds to turn and break into a run toward the horses. Tudier did the same, and soon both men were racing a few feet ahead of waving blades as the Ghetites pursued them.

Falling into single file, the horsemen rode hastily through the opened gates. At the end of their retreating column were the three riderless horses meant for Nuroc, Tudier, and Elmin.

Putting on an extra burst of speed, Tudier raced alongside his steed and secured one hand on the rim of his saddle. Throwing down his sword, he used the other hand to help lift himself up onto the horse's back.

Behind him, Nuroc paced himself, taking long strides until he was running slightly in front of his horse and a few yards ahead of the pursuing Ghetites. Then, in one mind-defying flow of motion, he sprang into the air, twisting his body just enough to fling his sword back at the enemy and still be able to land atop his steed. With a triumphant roar, he grabbed hold of the reins and righted himself in the saddle. As he dared one last glance at the Ghetites, he grinned contentedly at the sight of the scar-faced swordsman lying dead in the dirt with the hurled scimitar sticking out from his chest.

Nuroc leaned over and grabbed the reins of the riderless horse, guiding it through the gates and past the body of the slain traitor.

"Elmin shall ride with us in spirit," Nuroc called out to Tudier and the others as he rode to the head of the formation. Through the brooding streets of Renast they thundered, and soon they were gone from the town that had almost been their undoing. Before them, moonlight showed them the trail that led from the valley. They rode it hard.

Twenty-Five

Without Elmin to guide them, Nuroc's men were forced to guess which of the several dirt roads would lead them to the mountain pass that led down to the foothill border between Aerda and Ghetite. As they paused their steeds at a fork branching off in four directions and consulted one another as to the best route to take, they heard the pounding hooves of Ghetite stallions taking up the chase.

Nuroc dismounted long enough to lean over the myriad tracks scoring the wet earth, then leapt back into the saddle and pointed along the road leading to the closest range of mountains.

"This route seems the most traveled," he said. "Let us hope it's the right way."

Slapping his stallion's hindquarters, Nuroc led the way down the wide roadway, which was flanked on either side by wavering grasses that rippled like green seas in the wind.

"The grasses are shoulder high," Tudier called out to Nuroc as the two men rode side-by-side. "Perhaps we should stray from the road and seek shelter there until the Ghetites have passed."

"It wouldn't work," Nuroc said. "Look at how the grass glistens with rain and dew. If we left the road, our trail would be clearly marked. No, our only chance is to outrun them and hope for the best."

Tudier spat to one side in anger. "If they were only half as many . . ."

"Aye," Nuroc said. "With better odds I'd stand up to them in a moment. But as it is, we are too few and unarmed."

They rode silently onward. The road began to bend upward. Night progressed, and the gray hues of a false dawn began to fade the nocturnal dark. Reaching a crest upon the trail, Nuroc pulled his mount to one side and waved the others on as he looked back the way they had come. He had held a secret hope that the Ghetites, in their angry haste, might have sped off on another branch of roadway in search of them. But he could clearly see that the enemy was not so easily fooled. Less than half a mile away, they rode on with determined swiftness.

"Faster!" Nuroc called out to his men as he whipped his horse past them. "They're gaining on us by the minute!"

"What were they doing in Renast anyway?" Tudier wondered aloud. "It's clearly out of their way if they were enroute to Velley."

Nuroc thought as he rode, then guessed, "Having set fire to Centinara, they must have gone to Renast for the same purpose, only to find a willing ally instead. Whatever the reason, it's clear that we will have a score to settle with those traitorous wenches that almost lured us to our deaths."

"And to think of their scheming smiles all the while we thought they were entertaining us," Tudier said. "It's a wonder they didn't slit our throats in our sleep."

"No doubt the Ghetites paid them a tidy sum to save them that pleasure." Nuroc charged his steed up the next slope, adding, "Enough talk. It slows our pace."

Tudier looked back and saw that the Ghetites were indeed gaining. If armed with bows, they would have been within range of felling Nuroc's men from their saddles. As it was, the young troops could hear the clopping hooves of their pursuers sounding like an echo behind them. They pushed the gray-spotted steeds on farther, until foam began to fleck about their champed bits.

One final rise pitched upward at a treacherous angle, and the men were forced to slow their horses or risk the steeds breaking their legs. Clearing that rise, the young horsemen found themselves on a flattened plateau bearing a single boulder that had been carved into the likeness of a perched condor.

"An altar!" one of the Centinarans gasped. "We've come to a shrine!"

As the others gaped with dismal awe, Nuroc rode forward past the stone idol to the edge of the plateau, confirming his worst fears. The plateau reached out over the rim of the last range of the Kanghats and dropped abruptly for more than several hundred feet. Down below, the bending ribbon of an angry river coursed past the base of the precipice and rolled onward through the foothills that led to the Ghetite flatlands.

"Trapped," Tudier muttered as he rode up beside Nuroc and

stared over the edge of the precipice. "This far and we're trapped."

Nuroc looked past Tudier and back at his men, who had their heads turned toward the path that had brought them here. The sound of Ghetite horsemen drew nearer.

Twenty-Six

Thirty strong, the Ghetite horsemen charged the steep incline leading to the shrine of Dorban, scimitars raised high over their heads.

"Death to the infidels!" their leader cried out.

"Death in the name of Ghetite!" screamed another.

"Off with their heads!" bellowed a third rider.

The Ghetites continued with their vengeful chants as they whipped their steeds up the slope. The path was narrow, carved through an escarpment of jagged rocks that pointed upward like earthen jaws.

As they were about to clear the rise and enter the plateau, the way before them became a scene of frenzied chaos. Riderless gray stallions neighed fiercely as they spewed forth over the rim of the plateau in a fury of flying hooves. There was no room on the trail for travel in both directions, so the gray steeds barreled headlong into the midst of the Ghetite force. Because the riderless horses were charging downhill at full gallop, theirs was a forceful momentum that the Ghetites had no way of countering. Blades were useless against the swift intensity of the colliding steeds, and within seconds both Ghetite horses and riders were being forced from the path by the driving wedge of mottled horseflesh. Men and horses alike fell roughly against the sharp surface of the escarpment, changing the cries of warfare to the groans and neighs of anguish. Ghetites wailed with pain as their legs were crushed by the weight of their falling mounts. Both Ghetite horses and Centinaran stallions filled the air with their own beastly cries as they battled for footing on the steep grade.

The snarl on the pathway dragged on for endless minutes, as fallen Ghetites struggled to their feet and limped clear of the raging horses. Only those horsemen at the end of the column had managed to remain in the saddle, but they were prevented from negotiating the path to the shrine, which was still a river of churning limbs, biting teeth, and angry hooves.

In the end, half of the Centinaran mounts had pushed through the ranks of the Ghetites and galloped off down the road that led back toward Renast. Behind them, they had left the other riderless steeds dead or crippled on the path and surrounding rock facing. The Ghetites, in turn, had suffered an even more costly toll. Twenty of their steeds had been killed or wounded in the ruckus on the slope, and the human casualties were only slightly less. Five men had died and another dozen lay wallowing in pain from falls or encounters with the teeth and hooves of maddened horses.

More time was lost in clearing the path of the dead and wounded before the surviving Ghetites finally made their way on foot to the plateau containing the stone shrine of Dorban, which now shone magnificently in the glow of the rising sun.

Aside from the idol, however, the plateau was empty. The men sought by the Ghetites were gone.

"What trickery is this?" the enraged leader of the Ghetites roared balefully. He turned to his men and waved his sword in a fanning arc. "Spread out and check over the edges of the plateau. They have to be somewhere!"

Indeed, those Ghetites who peered over the far rim of the plateau found that Nuroc and the others were halfway down the sheer facing of the precipice, clinging to clusters of brush and indentations in the stone.

"They're down here!" one of the Ghetites called back to the others while pointing over the side of the cliff.

Hearing the cries overhead, Nuroc looked up and saw the Ghetites assembling and peering down at him and his men.

"They've found us," Tudier groaned as he grappled along the cliff and inched his way down to Nuroc's side.

"A lot of good it will do them," Nuroc assured Tudier. "There's nothing up there for them to hurl down at us unless they want to toss us their swords, and if they crawl down after us they'd never get to us before we reached the gorge."

The Ghetites fumed from the top of the plateau. As Nuroc had said, they had nothing to throw down at his men but insults. Their leader shouted to the escapees, "Go ahead and climb down to the gorge! There's no way out once you're there, unless you try the river. We'll just ride down and wait for you. But first we'll arm ourselves with spears so that we can stab you in the water like helpless fish!"

Nuroc looked down and saw that there was some truth to the taunting of the Ghetite. Already he could hear the booming roar of the seething river that crashed through the steep walls of the gorge. There was only one narrow ledge of stone rising above the turbulence of the river, and it was littered with splintered driftwood and drenched weeds heaved up by the force of the foaming rapids. It was as if they were descending into a deep pit, shadowed from any light cast by the morning sun. Once they reached the bottom, their only way out would be by way of the river.

Nuroc was not the only one to notice their predicament. One of the farm boys from Centinara stopped his descent and began to tremble with fear and desperation.

"It's no use!" he whimpered as tears came to his eyes. Blood was trickling down his fingers from clawing against the rocks for a secure hold. "We're all going to die!"

"There is always a way!" Nuroc shouted out to him. "Keep going!"

"No, I can't," the youth mumbled desolately.

"You have to!" Nuroc insisted.

A few of the youth's comrades echoed Nuroc's sentiments, but the youth only shook his head and remained frozen in position on the cliffs. Nuroc and Tudier were on either side of him, and they began to crawl sideways toward him.

Looking at his bleeding fingers, the Centinaran wept, "I can't hold on!"

"You can!" Nuroc shouted, edging closer.

"No!" the youth wailed. His right hand slipped from its hold and dragged along the rock surface.

"Grab the bush!" Tudier called out. He was only a few feet away now.

Closing his eyes, the farm boy sobbed and made no attempt to secure a hold on the bush that grew out from the rock only a few inches from his right hand. His left fingers straightened out as well.

"Mother! Where are you?" the youth squealed hysterically.

"Curse you, hold on!" Nuroc ordered, to no avail.

As Nuroc and Tudier both closed in on the youth and reached

out to grab him, he gave up his grip on the stone and fell away from the cliff. Nuroc and Tudier felt a sickening chill shake their spines as they watched the Centinaran bound off the cliff facing several times before vanishing into the white waters of the river.

There was a moment's silence on the cliffs as the others all held their positions and stared down, hoping against hope that they might see the youth surface and flail his arms against the pull of the current. He never reappeared, though. The river had swallowed him in its cold, indifferent grip and swept him along like so much driftwood.

"All right," Nuroc finally said flatly. "Let's be gone from this cliff before another of us falls."

Slowly, the others resumed their precarious descent. Like their fallen compatriot, they were all bleeding from the scrape of rock against their hands and limbs. They forced themselves not to look down or up, other than to gauge their next move down the steep siding.

The river roared louder with each move they made down into the gorge. It echoed off the bald rock walls of the gorge with a bone-chilling fierceness that surpassed the strongest peal of thunder. Above that constant, unending sound, they had no way of hearing the motion far above them, where the Ghetites were leading three of their horses to the lip of the plateau.

The horses, each one of them hobbling on broken legs suffered during the altercation on the path, braced themselves against the shoves of the Ghetites and snorted their unease. When they were brought against the edge of the cliff, the steeds held their ground firmly and began to kick outward with their good legs, trying to ward off the Ghetites.

At the cry of a single order of "Now!" several of the Ghetites lashed out with their scimitars, stabbing the horses in the rear flanks and sides until they bolted with pain over the side of the precipice.

Down they plummeted, their large bodies thudding dully against the rock. Nuroc and his men looked up when bits of gravel sprayed down upon them, but they had no time to otherwise react. Two of the horses hit their marks, slamming into the screaming men who were in the way of their falls. One farm boy and one recruit crashed into the waters along with the three horses. One of the horses surfaced for a moment, then was sucked under by the current along with the others.

"Savages!" Nuroc muttered, looking from the river back up at the Ghetites who loomed above them.

"Let's get down from here before they come back with more," Tudier said.

Sacrificing caution to haste, the survivors scrambled the last few dozen feet to the cluttered ledge overlooking the roaring rapids. Spray fell on them like a constant shower of rain, but at least they were safe for the time being. Two more horses were flung down toward them, but they splashed into the river far short of striking them. This close to the river, the men could see the steeds through the churning foam, being dragged and pummeled against the stone embankments until they were swept away.

Nuroc looked up a final time to the plateau they had just descended from. The remaining Ghetites were now astride those stallions that had not been injured. They raised their scimitars in a gesture of victory, catching the light of the sun, then turned and rode from sight.

"What are we to do now?" one of the recruits asked Nuroc.

Nuroc looked at his men. Drenched and bloodied, half-naked and numbed by their ordeal, they hunched together on the crowded ledge, staring at him with hollow, uncertain eyes. Even Tudier, fearless Tudier, had been drained by the experience.

"I see only two choices," Nuroc told them gravely. "We can wait here and rest, by which time the Ghetites might ride down to the gorge to a spot where they can take aim at us with arrows while we sit like targets. Or . . ."

"Or what?" one of the others asked.

Nuroc reached down and picked up a length of driftwood from the massive heap they were huddled over. "There might be enough scraps of wood and vine to lash together a crude raft and take our chances on the river."

"But you saw how the men and horses were drawn under by the current," one of the recruits moaned.

"They fell in from a great height," Nuroc answered. "We will be lowering ourselves into the river from only a few feet above it. That's a considerable difference."

"I still say it's hopeless," the recruit said.

"Then you can stay here," Nuroc said irritably, picking up

another strip of wood and placing it alongside the other. He ripped loose a handful of weeds and lodged them in the open spaces between the pieces of wood, then wrapped a length of vine around them.

Tudier followed Nuroc's example, and soon all the men were silently reaching under them and lending a hand in the building.

"It's not apt to support us all as a raft," Nuroc said as the craft began to take shape. "But it should be buoyant enough for us to hold onto it and stay afloat. Hopefully, that will be enough."

"The faster we work, the warmer we'll stay," Tudier piped in encouragingly.

"And the faster we'll be gone from here," another added.

Rallying their spirits, the men worked diligently, ignoring the steady rumble of the passing river and its chilling spray. When there was no more vine to be used in lashing strips of wood together, they ripped at what clothing they wore for needed strips.

The sun was beginning to slant down into the gorge when the raft was finally readied. It measured the length and width of a man, and its uneven surface sagged from ill-fitting joints and the natural bend of the wood, but it held together when they lifted it into the air and shook it several times.

"What now?" Tudier said.

Nuroc looked to the water and said, "Half of us will hold onto the raft and lower ourselves as far upriver as we can. The others will wait until we swing by. If we are still afloat, jump in and grab hold as best you can."

"And what if you go under?" a Centinaran asked.

"Tudier will stay with the second group and take charge if we fail. There's enough wood here for a smaller raft, but you'd have to climb up the gorge to reach more vine."

The plan set out, Nuroc pointed to two of the Thutcherian recruits. They took hold of the raft along with him and made their way down the narrow ledge, stepping over refuse thrown up by the boiling surf. When they had gone as far as they could, Nuroc gestured for them to bend over and hold the raft out so that it hovered parallel to the surface of the river.

"Push off as flat as you can and hold on tight," Nuroc said.

The others readied themselves, then nodded to Nuroc. In

unison, the three of them shoved off from the ledge and into the river.

The raging current immediately took hold of the men and the raft, dragging it downstream but failing to pull them under. Nuroc and the other two clung to the wood and held their breath. Seconds later, they felt their comrades crash down around them and stab their fingers at the raft in hopes of securing a hold. One of them missed, and Nuroc felt fingers clutch futilely at his legs and ankles before giving way.

Down the river they were hurtled by the raw force of the current, clearing the gorge and then crashing into the stone embankment of the first bend. Nuroc felt his ribs bound off the rocks and he blew out his breath and struggled to the surface long enough to suck fresh air into his battered lungs. He saw a few heads bobbing around him, then he was pulled back down by the river and flung along.

He held on to the raft as tightly as he could and tried to kick his legs in hopes of guiding their course away from the deadly sides of the river. He could feel other legs brush against his and hear occasional gasps for air above the turbulence of the rapids. But he had no idea how many of his men were still with him, or even how much of the raft was holding up under the merciless pounding of the current.

The river rammed into another bend and there were screams from the men who struck the banks. Nuroc surfaced and managed to open his eyes long enough to see one of the farm boys heave both arms into the air and open his mouth to breathe. The river pulled the youth under and Nuroc was helpless to save him.

Once the river surged out from the rock walls that enclosed it, its course widened and the rage of its current waned slightly. Sunlight poured down on the waters and was shattered into dazzling fragments that blinded Nuroc. He was weak to the point of unconsciousness, but still he clung to the raft, sputtering for breath and straining to hear from the others. He thought he detected two other voices, but it was hard to tell.

Something hard suddenly slammed into Nuroc's knee from under the water, and seconds later he was struck in the shoulder by a similar blow. Blinking his eyes, he saw that the river was pouring its way through a bed of rocks and boulders. He grabbed harder at the raft, then heard a sharp crack as the wood was splintered against one of the boulders. Flung to one side, he lost hold of the raft and began at once to slap his arms against the pull of the current, trying to stay afloat. His limbs were numb from the cold water, however, and he had little control over his motions. The river carried him along indifferently, bounding him off the craggy riverbed and tossing him against the boulders like so much flotsam. His head finally struck an unyielding rock and the world went black.

Twenty-Seven

The void was filled with memories that flew about his mind like frantic bats, here one moment and gone the next. There he was, just shy of his teens, playing hide-and-seek in the sorcerers' garden with Myrania, carefree and giggling as he crouched under the protective cover of the neotolan bush . . . then, a few years later, tall and thin from a spurt of adolescent growth, watching over the royal sheep in the meadows outside of Cothe, sneaking off with the other shepherds to fence with stick swords as they dreamed of being great warriors . . . and then, older still, watching Myrania stroll the gardens with a young suitor from Numeria, seething with jealousy and the desolation of knowing that it was forbidden for servants to wed with sorcerers or other nobility.

Lastly, and most lingering, there was the memory of the night, five years before, when the people of Dorban stormed the sorcerer's gardens, seeking the death of Talmon-Khash, whom they blamed for the Great Cataclysm that had devastated the land on the night of the black moons. He and his parents were standing on a platform near the top of the obelisk, staring out at the riotous mob along with Talmon-Khash, who was innocent of the grievious charge laid against him. Still, the sorcerer king knew that it was hopeless for him to assert his innocence. His only choice was to protect the obelisk at any cost. That cost was to be his life. To enact the chant required to save the obelisk from harm, it would be necessary for him to exile himself to the nether world, a dimension without substance. As his one link to the living, Talmon-Khash took the ceremonial condor-sword and mingled his blood with that of Nuroc and his parents.

The final image of the memory was that of Talmon-Khash staring down at Nuroc and whispering, "You have a destiny to fulfill, and the gods will watch over you so long as you remain worthy of their cause. Remember that, always."

The image faded to the blackness of the returning void, but soon more light played about the edge of Nuroc's vision. No mere image of thought, it was his true sight that was returning to him. Nuroc's mind roused slowly, and he realized that he was alive. Alive, and once more awake to the world.

He was on his back, staring upward. Someone was leaning over him, his face a distorted blur. Nuroc blinked, and as he struggled to piece together the circumstances that had brought him to his current predicament, he felt a flash of cold fear, thinking that it was a Ghetite who glared down at him. He tried to move, but realized he was drained of energy and could only cringe from the anticipated blow of a razor-edged scimitar.

"There, there, Nuroc," came a deep, familiar voice. "Be still."

As his vision came into focus, Nuroc found himself looking up at none other than General Palem, who was outfitted in full battledress. Behind him, the sky shone a deep and brilliant blue.

Confused, Nuroc craned his neck slightly to look around him. Beside him, he saw Tudier laid out on a makeshift bed of padded grass. Beyond Tudier, there were close to a thousand Aerdan soldiers in various stages of readiness for battle. Tents were up, and the river sounded steadily in the background, past which lay the foothills and first range of the mighty Kanghats.

"We're camped along the Ghetite border," Palem said, noting Nuroc's consternation. "We arrived only this afternoon and found both you and Tudier washed up on the banks of the river, battered and near death. We've treated you both with compresses of neotolan and other ointments, but it will be a while still before you are healed enough to move."

"The others," Nuroc said weakly. "Where are the others?"

Palem shook his head slightly. "There were two bodies next to you and Tudier, but their necks had been broken. We also found bits of driftwood tied together with reeds. How was it that you were forced to use the river? How did you find Tudier? And the bodies; they are not of Aerdan stock. They look like boys from the hill tribes. How did you come to be with them?"

"I have been through much," Nuroc stated feebly.

One of the Aerdans came over with a bowl filled with steaming porridge, telling Palem, "I saw that he was up and figured he would want to eat."

Palem looked to Nuroc, who nodded his head. The soldier gave Nuroc the bowl, and Nuroc sat up while Palem propped a saddle behind his back for support. While he ate, Nuroc recounted to Palem his strange odyssey from the meadows to where he now rested. Other soldiers drifted over to listen in, and soon Tudier awoke as well and added his own tales between bites from his ration of stew. Like Nuroc, Tudier was heartsick at the news that only the two of them had survived the escape down the river.

"There were thirty of us that left Thutchers to join the militia," Tudier said sadly. "And now only I am still alive. It seems so unfair."

"The ways of war are cruel, there is no doubt," Palem told the young recruit. "Many have paid a great price in its name."

"I know a few Ghetites and Shangorans who have yet to pay their price," Tudier mumbled contemptuously.

"How is Myrania?" Nuroc asked Palem, trying to change the subject.

"Well enough," Palem said. "She wanted to ride with us, but we had to insist that she wait until she was fully recovered. A remarkable woman, she is."

"What are our plans now?" Nuroc said. "It would seem that I have failed my mission."

"The mission has neither failed nor succeeded until the fate of the queen has been ascertained," the general said. "If, as you say, she has been taken back to Velley, there is still the chance we can win her back. Our thousand men are sure to outnumber any force the Ghetites or Shangorans have managed to retain for defense. Tomorrow we will storm their capital and demand their surrender and the return of the queen."

"And if they refuse?" Nuroc asked.

Palem paused a moment. His features darkened. He said slowly, "Our orders are that the enemy is to be brought to its knees regardless of what happens to the queen. I can assure you that it was the most difficult decision King Pencroft has yet made during his reign."

A silence fell over the group, and slowly the other soldiers drifted back to their tents to complete their preparations for the next day's assault.

Palem told Nuroc, "You and Tudier will be staying in the tent just over to your right, by the scenoaks. You'd be wise to go there and rest. Give the treatment time to do its work."

"Of course," Tudier said blandly. Nuroc nodded absently, and the general rose to his feet and left to check on his men.

When they were alone, Nuroc turned to Tudier and said, "If I hadn't been so foolish, I could have saved the queen back on the other side of the Kanghats."

"There's still hope, Nuroc," Tudier said assuredly. "Besides, if you had rescued the queen back at the outpost, you would not have found us in the pit outside of Centinara and by now I'd be in the belly of a Gungsa."

"True," Nuroc admitted. "Of course, many more have died since then as we trailed—"

"Enough!" Tudier groaned impatiently. "I sweaf, Nuroc, you sometimes brood like an old crone. You have always acted in the best interests of Aerda and the men you command. You do yourself an injustice with your self-doubtings. You are already a great warrior. Trust your instincts and you will go far. Begin to second-guess yourself and you'll find yourself falling on the sharp tip of a sword before you know it. Trust me on that."

Nuroc thought on Tudier's words and finally nodded his head. "Once again you set me straight with your advice. I think you might be the philosopher among us after all."

"Pshaw!" Tudier spat, straining as he lifted himself to his feet. "Come, let's take to our tent. Another bout of sleep could only do me good. I want to be well for tomorrow's charge on Velley."

"I, too," Nuroc said, rising and following Tudier across the grounds to a large tent hung between the trunks of two ancient scenoaks. Near the tent, the army's weaponsmith worked his spinning whetstone in a fast circle and gently laid the edge of a sword at a slight angle against the curve of the stone. Sparks flew from the steel blade, and when the weaponsmith took the sword away, its sharpened edge shone fiercely in the afternoon sun.

"I trust you have an extra pair of swords for us," Tudier said to the weaponsmith.

The weaponsmith, a weathered man with thin slits for eyes and large ears sprouting out from a crop of shock-white hair, nodded and handed Tudier the sword he had just sharpened.

"With this you could slice a man at the neck and he would not know he was cut until he leaned over and his head fell off," the old man cackled with obvious glee.

Tudier took the sword and waved it through the air several times. The effort exhausted him, and his arm sagged under the weight of the blade. He looked to Nuroc and smirked, "I may have to sleep straight through until morning."

Nuroc did not bother to ask for a sword, but as he walked by the whetstone, the weaponsmith called out to him. "Now, there, lad. Would you be Nuroc?"

"Yes," Nuroc answered, pausing before the man. "Why do you ask?"

The weaponsmith held up a hand for Nuroc to wait, then turned to one side and reached into the bulging satchel lying in the grass beside him.

"The woman Myrania asked me to give you this if we found you," he said to Nuroc, handing the young man something from the satchel.

"Dorban's eyes!" Nuroc gasped, recognizing the ceremonial dagger Talmon-Khash had used to perform his ritualistic blood-mingling with Nuroc and his parents five years before. Its blade was fashioned of a unique alloy, harder than steel and yet translucent like a smoky glass. The handle was carved into the likeness of a condor's head, with inset sapphire marking the glowing eyes. The last time Nuroc had seen the blade was after he had hurled it into the breast of the giant condor god Augage had attempted to enslave in the obelisk. By piercing Dorban's chest, Nuroc had not only broken Augage's domination over the condor-god, but he had also allowed Talmon-Khash to reenter the realm of the living within the great bird itself.

"It was found in the sorcerer's gardens," the weaponsmith went on. "Myrania said that you would know the meaning, and she wanted you to have it."

As Nuroc looked down at the blade, he noticed that the knife's blade bore a faint shade of pink in addition to the hazy clearness.

"Yes," Nuroc said, thanking the man and taking the weapon back to his tent. Despite his weary condition, he could not help but feel a sense of elation. There was still a trace of Talmon-Khash's blood left in the half-sword. That slight trace might be enough to once again summon the great sorcerer back to the world of the living.

"I still say that's the finest weapon I've ever seen," Tudier said once the two men were alone inside the tent. They sat down on the edges of their cots and faced one another. Tudier added, "You still haven't told me everything about it, have you?"

Nuroc smiled slightly. "Tudier, I would tell you all in a moment if I hadn't sworn an oath of secrecy on some matters. You know that."

Tudier shrugged his shoulders. "Fair enough, Nuroc." He lay back on his cot and folded his hands behind his head as he stared up at the shadows of the oak tree thrown on the roof of the tent by the overhead sun. In moments he was asleep and snoring soundly.

Nuroc watched him, beset by his own fatigue. But he refused to lie down. He held the condor-knife aloft before him and gazed long and hard at the blade, wondering if he dared recite the chant and perform the ritual that would summon Talmon-Khash from the nether realm. He knew well enough the consequences of failure. After all, the Great Cataclysm had been brought on by a failed chant recited from the lips of the rebel sorcerer Augage. Nuroc stood little chance of invoking so drastic a result if he did not perform the act properly. He alone would pay the price of failure.

He decided he had to try. Somehow the sacred blade had fallen from the breast of the condor-god after it had destroyed the obelisk, then miraculously it had been found and guided back into Nuroc's possession. The coincidence was too great to be attributed to chance. Nuroc felt it was a sign, an omen. Talmon-Khash was calling to him. He could not ignore the call.

So determined, Nuroc turned away from his sleeping friend and secured a firm grip on the handle of the ceremonial dagger. Whispering softly, he recited the brief chant, enunciating each word with utmost care. When he was finished, he held his left wrist out and placed the blade across his pulsing arteries. Closing his eyes, he swiftly dragged the half-sword across his wrist.

When he dared to open his eyes and look down, his mouth opened in horror. Something was wrong. His blood was not seeping into the translucent blade. It spurted forth in a crimson flow. Unlike before, the wound across his wrist did not immediately heal, either. Instead, he continued to bleed with a frightening swiftness.

Already weakened from his ordeal, Nuroc felt his last reserve of energy drain from the wound. Trying to turn about, he only fell across the cot, dropping the dagger. He bobbed his lips slightly, but could not summon forth a single utterance to awaken Tudier, who remained fast asleep only a few feet away.

The blood seeped steadily from his slashed wrist, and, for the second time that day, Nuroc felt a cold curtain of blackness being pulled over him. He tried to resist the encroachment, but the curative powers of the neotolan were no match for the wound he had inflicted trying to summon forth Talmon-Khash. His eyes closed and, beat by beat, his heart slowed its pulse and his life drained from him with a chilling certainty.

Twenty-Eight

Blood fell in scarlet droplets from Nuroc's limp wrist, splattering off the dagger that lay in the dirt. Then, miraculously, one of the drops soaked into the blade. Immediately the pinkish cast of the strange alloy darkened a shade. A second, then a third drop were absorbed, and the blade turned from vague pink to a more pronounced red. The sapphires set in the eyes of the condor hilt began to glow brightly with some inner radiance, and from the partially-opened beak issued forth a ghostly emanation. It grew and wavered, like a billowing cloud, then began to take shape. Although the form remained gaseous and transparent, it gained definition and took on human features beneath a flowing cowl.

It was Talmon-Khash, caught in a state between being and nothingness, half in this world and half in another!

For several seconds, the spectral figure of the former sorcerer-king stood frozen in position, eyes closed in a look of intense concentration. When he opened his eyes, Talmon-Khash was still lingering on the threshold between substance and illusion, a ghost that seemed on the verge of disappearing from sight at any given moment.

With slow, drifting movements, Talmon-Khash reached over and placed his fingers over Nuroc's bleeding wrist. At once, the bleeding ceased. The sorcerer-king traced a finger across the deep cut made by the ceremonial knife, and the wound healed and vanished without so much as a scar.

The enactment of this feat was at the price of Talmon-Khash's further materialization. He became more of a fading specter, and seemed to be drifting back into the limbo of nonbeing more with each passing second.

Nuroc's fate seemed similar, as the color seeped from his skin and he became white with the pall of approaching death. His infrequent breaths came few and far between. The movement of his chest was barely discernible.

Talmon-Khash leaned over, whispering in Nuroc's ear, "I am not long for this world, Nuroc. Heed my words and remember. The wheels beneath the waterfall. The wheels beneath the waterfall . . ."

The words spoken, Talmon-Khash slowly knelt over the pool of blood that had drained from Nuroc's wrist onto the floor. He laid the flat of his palm against the blood as he began to lose form and drift back into a gaseous cloud. Before the transformation had run its bizarre course, however, Talmon-Khash managed to place his other hand on Nuroc's chest, directly above the heart. Even as he faded into a shapeless aura, the sorcerer-king changed in color, so that finally it was a reddish haze that hovered in the air above Nuroc's chest, then seeped in through the paling flesh.

At once the color spread through Nuroc's body and he began to breathe more freely. Death no longer held him in its icy grasp. Nuroc was alive. Deep in slumber, but alive.

Twenty-Nine

"Nuroc, wake up! They're gone!"

Tudier shook his friend again, and Nuroc finally came to, blinking his eyes with confusion. There was only a faint light outside and no trace of the sun. Nuroc wasn't sure if it was dusk or dawn. He looked at Tudier questioningly.

"We've slept through afternoon and night!" Tudier explained excitedly. "It's already dawn and Palem has ridden off with the others! I was wakened by the horses. I tried to go out and see, but there're guards posted outside the tent on Palem's orders to make sure we stay here until we've recovered. I tried to tell them I feel as fit as ever, but they wouldn't listen. Can you imagine? We're imprisoned by our own men!"

While Tudier was pacing about the tent, raising his voice so that the guards would know his discontent, Nuroc sat up on the edge of his cot and slowly came to his senses. He looked at his wrist and was amazed to see that his self-inflicted wound had disappeared and that there was no blood on the dirt around his feet. He leaned over and picked up the ceremonial dagger. Gone was the tinge of pink in the cloudy blade. He tried to think back to the afternoon before, but could remember only his failed effort to revive Talmon-Khash. And yet, lingering just beyond grasp of his conscious thought, was a feeling of another presence or encounter that had taken place. He wondered if it was a forgotten dream, or if he had been delirious and only imagined that he had attempted the chant and ritual with the condor-knife. He was certain of only one thing. Now wide awake, he felt fully revitalized from his lengthy sleep and the effects of the neotolan.

Tudier moved close to Nuroc and lowered his voice. "We can't sit by while the others tackle the Ghetites, Nuroc. I'm as strong as I ever was, and you look well enough yourself. I say we find a way past the guards and head for Velley on our own. Maybe we can catch up with Palem."

Nuroc reflected a moment, sharing Tudier's desire to lend a hand in the upcoming clash with the enemy. He looked about and could make out the outline of guards standing idly near all sides of the tent. Overhead, the swaying branches of the scenoaks also threw their spindly shadows on the roof of the tent.

"I have an idea," Nuroc said, finally. He called Tudier closer and whispered his plan. As he listened, Tudier nodded his head and smiled hopefully.

"I think it can work," the Thutcherian replied when Nuroc had finished.

They moved quickly. Nuroc carefully stood on his cot and balanced himself as he reached up and began to cut at the canvas tent's roof with his dagger. Meanwhile, Tudier tipped his cot over on one side and silently dismantled its wooden frame. He placed the slats together and then wrapped a strip of cloth around the bundle.

When Nuroc had cut a sizable flap in the roof, he poked his head out and looked around. The camp, which had been teeming with soldiers the day before, was now almost as deserted as the ghost town of Renast. Besides the guards stationed around their tent, there were only a few other soldiers standing about. Nuroc guessed that they were cooks and medics. More important, however, he saw a few horses tethered to a post on one side of their tent and, in the other direction, a field of shrubs and wild grass.

Pulling his head back inside, Nuroc looked to Tudier, who was stuffing straw into the spaces between the wooden slats. One slat stuck out from the base of the bundle like the handle of an oversized torch. Tudier took the creation over to the oil lamp that someone had left burning. He let the dying flame of the lamp catch onto the straw, then gently waved the torch in the air until the fire grew and spread to the wooden slats.

Nuroc took the torch from Tudier, cocked his arm, then threw it out through the slash in the roof.

End-over-end, the torch flew between branches of the two scenoaks and landed noisily in the field, where it broke into pieces. Although most of the foliage was wet with dew, some of the grass caught fire enough to give off smoke.

There were shouts among the guards and the other soldiers as all eyes in the camp turned to the field. At the sight of smoke, the guards left their post and rushed to investigate, drawing their weapons.

Tudier took his newly-sharpened sword to the side of the tent facing away from the fire. With one hearty swipe, he slashed through the canvas, creating a gash large enough to step through. Nuroc followed him, and they swiftly stole across the grounds to the tethered steeds. Bounding onto two of the horses, they leaned forward and untied the reins, then rode off, putting the camp behind them. Hearing the retreating horses, the guards looked up from the fire they had managed to quickly snuff. They shouted out to Nuroc and Tudier as they gave chase on foot, but when their calls went unheeded the guards stopped running.

"Anyone who wants to fight that bad deserves to," one of them muttered, watching the riders beat their way toward the open plains and the Ghetite border.

"Aye," another said, forced to grin at the resourcefulness of the escapees. "Besides, to do what they have, they must have healed faster than Palem anticipated."

"I hope so," a third said. "I don't want to face Palem's wrath otherwise."

"I think the general will have other things on his mind," the first guard said. "Come on, let's get back. Since we've lost our prisoners, we might as well fill the time with a few games of cubes."

The guards turned back to the camp, putting Nuroc and Tudier from their minds. By the time they were back to the tent they had failed to maintain vigil over, the clopping hooves of the escapee's horses could no longer be heard.

"We've done it!" Tudier howled with delight, feeling the wind against his face as he and Nuroc rode on at their hasty pace.

"I only hope we fare as well against the Ghetites and Shangorans," Nuroc shouted from his horse.

"We will, Nuroc," Tudier assured him. "We will, so long as Palem and the others leave a few for us."

Thirty

The border between Ghetite and Aerda was marked by a long-reaching wall of stone, standing shoulder-high and lined along the top with jagged rock. A fair-sized force had been retained by the Ghetites against Palem's approaching horde, and when Nuroc and Tudier reached the wall, they found the hard-packed dirt littered with corpses from both sides. Rubble lay on either side of a portion of the wall that had been broken through, and on the Ghetite side lay the abandoned battering ram that the Aerdans had used against the barrier.

Both men stopped to rest their steeds a moment and take in the ghastly sight. While no match for the toll of dead and wounded suffered in the meadows outside of Cothe, there was still enough blood and gore drenched on stone and dirt alike to have alerted the predators of the region, and the only movement Nuroc and Tudier witnessed was that of jackal packs and vultures.

"It's clear the enemy has no intention of surrender," Tudier said. "How many will have to die before their minds are changed?"

"They know the odds against them," Nuroc replied. "I think they only fight on at the orders of Molent and Wheas. If their leaders were vanquished, they would not resist us further, I'm convinced."

"By now, I bet both men are safely in the capital, surrounding themselves with as many troops as possible," Tudier mused grimly. "To get at them we will have to carve our way through entire battalions."

"Aye," Nuroc agreed. "And before we can do that, we will first have to gain access to their capital. You know where it's located. If Cothe had been situated as securely as Velley, there would have been no need for the battle in the meadows."

"No point in dwelling on that," Tudier said, backing his horse toward the Ghetite plains before them.

"Tudier! Look out!"

At Nuroc's cry, Tudier instinctively ducked. The move saved

his life, as an arrow smote through the air where his head had been only seconds before.

Behind him, a fallen Ghetite archer had struggled to his knees and fired from behind cover of the broken wall. He quickly fed another arrow into his bow, but before he could let fly with the shaft, Nuroc jerked out his condor-knife and hurled it at the Ghetite. With a dull groan, the Ghetite dropped both bow and arrow and tumbled forward over the stone rubble.

Tudier looked at the would-be assailant, then turned to Nuroc. "I owe you for that, friend. You've saved me again."

"It was nothing you have not already done for me," Nuroc said, riding over to the slain archer and dismounting long enough to retrieve his dagger. Climbing back into the saddle, he continued, "I've lost track of the times you've saved me."

"We're even, then," Tudier said, slapping his reins. "Let's move on."

Together they headed off across the Ghetite plain. Compared to the slow progress they had been forced to make back in the Kanghats, it almost seemed as if they were flying across the level wasteland. The sun rose into another day of clear, vibrant skies, lending its warmth to the men. Their steeds fell into a rhythmic gait that made the time and miles pass with fleeting swiftness.

For much of the morning, there was nothing to be seen before them but the endless plain and the line of the horizon. By noon, however, a dark tip began to appear against the horizon. The riders directed their course toward the tip, which grew in size as they approached it, gradually widening at the base until it took on the shape of a single conical peak. The summit did not end in a point, but was leveled off, marking the mouth of a long-extinct volcano.

"Velley," Tudier said, his voice edged with awe.

"I've imagined what it looked like many times," Nuroc said as they continued to ride toward the still-distant capital of Ghetite. "But it dwarfs any of the ways I envisioned it."

They lapsed back into silence, keeping their eyes on the looming mountain. There was nothing visible on the surface of the peak to betray the fact that it was the site of an entire city. Nuroc knew that Velley lay hidden within the rim of the volcano, built into the rock itself and rising just above the waterline of the great lake that had come to fill the central core over the ages. It was said that when the days were overcast, Velley was situated above the clouds, like the throne of earthbound gods. It was Augage who had seen to the construction of the city during his brief reign, using the labor of slaves to assist where his necromantic powers fell short. Spies had come back from Ghetite with conflicting stories as to the nature of the hidden city, igniting the imagination of people throughout the land. The only matter on which all could agree was that there was no place in all of Dorban that would be easier to defend and harder to assault than Velley.

Once the entire mountain was in view, Nuroc and Tudier could also see the rest of the Aerdan brigade gathered at the point where the flatlands met with the initial slope of the volcano. Sunlight winked off armor and weaponry and the calvary spread out into charging formation around the base of the mountain.

"They haven't attacked yet!" Tudier shouted happily, digging his heels into the flanks of his steed. "Come on, Nuroc! We'll make the first charge yet!"

Nuroc sped his horse behind Tudier and they made straight toward the mountain, which was still several miles away. The looming mass of the volcano began to reveal itself in detail as the two men drew closer. Narrow paths showed like brown veins between the growth of sage and other wild plantlife. Rocks and boulders protruded at irregular intervals like unpolished baubles. Close to the top of the craggy peak, there was no trace of greenery, and Nuroc could barely make out the merlons that marked the battlements of the inner city. Straining his eyes, he could see Ghetite sentinels pacing along the parapets.

They were still more than half a mile away from the other troops when a trumpet pealed a few shrill blasts through the afternoon sky. The Aerdan horsemen answered the call with raised swords and hollered war chants, then pulled on their reins and rode forward and up the slope of the mountain. From Nuroc's perspective, they looked like so many ants making their way up an anthill.

"Wait, curse you!" Tudier shouted futilely, pushing his horse on past Nuroc's.

"Take care, Tudier," Nuroc warned his friend. But the advice came too late. Tudier's steed pounded at the plains with a loping stride at the expense of sure footing. Its hooves dug into a patch of muddied soil at too sharp an angle, throwing the beast off its gait so severely that it tumbled forward. Tudier was pitched from the saddle and the horse snapped its neck under the force of its headlong landing.

Tudier was saved from the same fatal end only by virtue of his quick instincts. He rolled with the force of his collision on the plain, absorbing much of the impact. His momentum quickly brought him back to his feet, although he limped slightly from a severe bruise to the hip.

Nuroc slowed his own horse and pulled up beside Tudier, extending his hand.

"Are you all right?" he asked.

Tudier brushed himself off and took Nuroc's hand, lifting himself up onto the horse. "Yes," he said bitterly, angered with himself. "What a fool I was to try that."

"It looks as if we're attacking in waves," Nuroc said as he pulled on the reins to get his horse going again. Tudier held on behind him. "We still might be able to join the second offensive."

Palem was riding before the ranks of those men still on the level plain when he first spotted Nuroc and Tudier heading toward them. He shouted a few orders, then left his men to fall into position as he rode out to meet the latecomers.

"What is this?" he cried out angrily once he was within their hearing range. "I left you guarded to make certain you would stay put. Myrania said that it was dangerous to strain oneself so soon after treatment with the neotolan. You're lucky you didn't drop dead in the saddle on the way here!"

"As you can see, we are no worse from the wear," Nuroc said. "And we did more than mere riding to get this far. Now let us join up with the others!"

As General Palem opened his mouth to reply, he was interrupted by a thunderous sound coming from the mountainside. Tudier looked over the general's shoulder and howled, "It can't be!"

Palem and Nuroc followed Tudier's gaze, and their eyes widened with equal disbelief. Far up the side of the volcano, water was surging forth through a series of unseen openings spaced close together. The flow from the separate spouts merged into one another and cascaded down the steep slope of the mountain with forceful fury. Those riders comprising the first offensive stopped their charge up the slope, but before they could turn their horses around, the pounding wall of water swept over them. Cries and screams sounded above the descending torrent as men and horses alike were dragged down by the unleashed current and sent crashing back toward the base of the mountain.

The horsemen of the second offensive reined about and fled from the floodwaters, riding quickly toward the site where Palem had joined Nuroc and Tudier. Some of them were not fast enough to outrace the turgid waters and were brought down by its flow and collisions with those steeds and riders that had already been claimed by the Ghetite's vicious defensive.

The flow was cut off at its source far up the mountain, but in the wake of its brief onslaught, the entire facing of the mountain had changed. Gone were the floral greens and rocky grays, replaced by a slick brown sheen of mud that layered every place the floodwaters had touched. Unmoving limbs of both horses and men protruded up through the rich sediment, which extended down the volcano like a flow of molten lava and reached out into the plain to within a few dozen feet of where the remnants of the Aerdan army had managed to flee.

Stunned, Nuroc and the others watched on as figures began to emerge from the mud; men and horses who had somehow managed to survive the ravage of the flood. Mired in the slime and wounded from the force with which they had been dragged along the side of the mountain, the survivors moved eerily as they tried to work their way free.

Palem looked up to the rim of the volcano, where he could see the posted Ghetite sentinels. "I can almost hear them laughing," he muttered hostilely. "They have been waiting years, no doubt, for this chance."

"But I don't understand what happened," Tudier said.

"I do," the general replied, turning his anger on himself. "I should have expected such a ploy. Now I have lost almost half my force as a price for my stupidity."

"But by what sorcery did they—"

"It had nothing to do with sorcery," Palem interjected, cutting Tudier off. "They merely opened floodgates built around the sides of the mountain, letting the lake waters that fill the volcano rush down upon us. So they avenge their loss in the meadows."

Those horsemen who had avoided the devastation now carefully made their way into the settling mire to assist the wounded. More survivors began to appear, rising above the thick silt with dazed looks of terror. But there was no activity higher up the slope, where the force of the floodwaters had been the severest. The land there was stripped and barren.

"There's no way to negotiate the slope now, is there?" Tudier said as he followed Nuroc and Palem into the muddy wake.

Nuroc looked at the volcano and said, "They only flooded this side of the mountain. Perhaps we could circle around and try to clear another slope."

But General Palem shook his head. "I am sure they have floodgates all the way around the mountain. If we were to attempt another assault from a different direction, the results would be the same. I can't risk more troops."

"What is there to do, then?" Nuroc asked.

"I don't know," Palem said. "I don't know."

Thirty-One

Queen Leindal of Aerda was held captive in the royal palace of Velley. The day before, she had arrived in the Ghetite capital, hungry, haggard, and layered with the grime of her torturous journey from the palatial chambers of her native Cothe. Now she had been washed and fed and dressed in the finest silks to be found in all of Ghetite. Her hair was scented with aromatic perfumes, and Ghetite slaves had seen to the decorative painting of her nails. She looked like a queen and enchantress, worthy of a minstrel's song or a poet's couplet. The chamber she was in held an equal sense of grandeur and splendor, adorned with meticulous frescoes, lush divans and arrangements of exotic plants set in vases of crafted and polished stone. One might have guessed she was safely back home were it not for the bonds of hemp tied about her wrists and ankles, keeping her in place on a plush settee.

She wept at her confinement, but when she heard hands working at the bolt across her chamber door, she stayed her tears and tried to blink her eyes dry. They would not have the pleasure of seeing her wallow in her misery. She was an abducted queen, and she was determined to show a bearing of cool poise.

It was General Wheas who entered the chamber, wearing the kingly robes that had once been worn by the sorcerer Augage.

Like Leindal, he had recovered from the strain of his travels and seemed a picture of beaming health, although there was a certain sickness to his twisted smile.

"I am the same size as Augage," Wheas said as he crossed the room and stood before Leindal. "His robes look well on me, do they not?"

"Dress a pig in silk and he is still a pig," the queen said contemptuously, refusing to set her eyes on her tormentor.

Wheas laughed slightly. "Such feisty spirit! I like that in a woman."

Leindal turned her gaze on the general and said hotly, "Untie me and I'll show you feisty spirit!"

Shaking his head, Wheas paced, idling before the settee. "No, I do not think that would be wise. I think we are talking about two different types of spirit. I prefer to see my women apply it to the pursuit of pleasure."

"It would give me nothing but pleasure to slay you with my bare hands!"

Wheas laughed louder. "Such tauntings!"

"Let me loose and see!" Leindal shot back.

Wheas ignored the queen's retort and turned his back on her squirms, crossing the room to a brass censer suspended from the ceiling. He reached into his robes and withdrew a small phial. Opening it, he tapped a small amount of powder into his palm, then set it in the burner. As he went to the nearest wall and plucked a burning candle from its carved holder, he said, "I'm sure you are familiar with the powers of the proffax blossom."

Once he touched the flame of the candle to the powder in the censer, a pungent smoke curled out into the room.

"Coward!" Queen Leindal hissed. "You'll never bend my will to suit your lechery!"

General Wheas unhinged the censer and carried it over to the settee, swinging it by its chain so that the smoke swirled about Leindal.

"How long do you think you can hold your breath, Leindal?" he asked, grinning. "The blossoms will burn for some time, I assure you. Give into it. Let us share a moment's ecstasy. It will be a time unlike any you have experienced."

"I would rather die!" the queen said.

Wheas's face went dark with anger and his hand went to his belt, coming up with a dagger. He pointed its razor-sharp tip toward Leindal's face and said, "I can manage that for you as well!"

They faced off as the smoke billowed around them, then the queen looked away, the fire gone from her eyes. Wheas smiled and lowered the dagger. He breathed in deeply and rolled his head loosely about his shoulders, moaning slightly with the first wave of dreamlike joy carried by the burning proffax.

Queen Leindal also relaxed upon the settee, closing her eyes and pursing her lips slightly. As Wheas looked on, she tilted her head to one side and moved her shoulder forward, rubbing it against her chin. "Oh, yes," she sighed.

"Yes, indeed," Wheas said, setting down the knife and working at the clasps to his robe. "Do not resist the blossoms. Let them carry us away together, to where we can act as one."

She nodded slightly and moved sensuously on the settee as the sweet-smelling cloud continued to envelop them. Wheas reached out and stroked her face with the back of his hand. She turned her head and kissed his thick, calloused fingers, licking between them with her tongue.

"Yes," the general said, stroking her hair with his other hand. "That's it." He breathed more heavily of the fuming proffax, then knelt next to the settee and began to stroke that part of Leindal's leg that showed beneath the raised hem of her gown.

"So soft," he said dreamily. "All the while we were bringing you here I've longed for this moment. To touch you, to have you alone, away from that dog Molent!"

"You feel so good," Leindal whispered, swaying her head. "I want you."

Wheas leaned over and kissed Leindal on the knee, then let his lips trail up farther as he pulled her gown to one side.

Leindal brought her legs gently together and moaned, "Not here, Wheas. There's not enough room. Let's move to the divan. I want to be able to feel all of you, to take you in my arms. . . ."

The general raised his head and looked to Leindal, his face flushed with the tug of passion. "Renounce your king and say that you will be mine, then we will consecrate our love."

Leindal hesitated, but her eyes were dull from the effects of the proffax, betraying the hold of the blossoms on her mind. "We are meant to be together, Wheas," she whispered passionately. "It is the way it should be. I've come to long for you as well."

"Then say the word," he insisted. "Say that you are no longer one with Pencroft. Only then can we share ourselves fully."

"I care not for Pencroft," she answered, as if in a trance. "It's you I want. Now. Take me, Wheas, please."

A joyous grin came to Wheas. He carefully unworked the ties around the queen's ankles, then freed her hands as well. She reached out and ran her fingers through his gray-streaked hair, pulling him close. Their lips met with joined passion.

Wheas took one hand and worked it through the folds of Leindal's gown, seeking out her flesh. Feeling the warmth of her side, he gently let his fingers rove the slight ripples of her ribs and seek out the softness of her breasts. The queen leaned into his touch, at the same time reaching behind Wheas and stroking the firm muscles of his back through the material of his robe.

"We may never reach the divan after all," Wheas moaned, breaking his kiss and nuzzling his lips along Leindal's chin to the softness of her neck.

"How true," Leindal replied, a sudden coldness in her voice.

Wheas suddenly grunted and jerked away from Leindal. His face registered a look of profound shock, and his mouth hung open as he tried to speak. All that would come forth were choked gasps. He stumbled to his feet and swayed unsteadily as he reached behind him. With a pained grimace, he stiffened and pulled free the dagger Leindal had plunged into his back. He looked at the blade, red to the hilt, then back at the queen, who stared at him with icy contempt.

"You breathed the proffax too much and too soon," she told him. "Otherwise, you would not have allowed yourself to be so easily fooled."

Wheas's expression changed from drugged confusion to insolent rage. He tightened his grip on the dagger and lunged forward. Leindal leaned quickly to one side as the blade swept past her, ripping at the shoulder of her gown but missing her flesh.

General Wheas fell over the settee and dropped the knife. Leindal grabbed the weapon, but realized she would not need to use it against the general. Wheas lay face down on the cold stone floor. The blood seeping from his back was a shade darker than the crimson of his robe.

"Swine!" Leindal whispered harshly, staring at the body as she waved away the smoke of the proffax blossoms. Her thoughts were still far from clear, but she had managed to keep from breathing too much of the narcotic fumes. She rubbed at her lips with the back of her hand, repulsed at the embrace she had been forced to commit in order to slay the Ghetite.

Still holding onto the dagger, she moved across the room to the door, thinking only of flight from the chamber. Pushing the door open, she slipped out into the corridor, only to find herself face-to-face with Molent of Shangora. Startled, she had no time to react before he reached out and grabbed her wrist, holding the knife's edge away from him.

"Well, now," the short, powerful king said, smiling thinly. "What is this?"

Leindal tried to struggle, but in vain. Molent held her tightly and forced her back into the chamber, where General Wheas lay dead next to the settee.

"Very good," he murmured with obvious joy. "You have saved me a most unpleasant task, Leindal."

"Take your hands off me," Leindal said coldly.

"As you wish," Molent said, shoving the queen away once he had secured her dagger. She stumbled back, almost falling over the man she had killed. She veered awkwardly to one side, as if to regain her balance, then reached out for the fuming censer.

"Leave it be," Molent warned her, raising the dagger to a throwing position. "I am quite deadly from this range, I assure you."

Leindal moved away from the censer. With waves of the dagger, the king of Shangora directed her to stand in the center of the room. There she would find no objects she could resort to in hopes of defending herself. Molent went over to the censer and snuffed out the smoldering blossoms.

"So this is Wheas's way of seducing his women," he mused. "The fool. The slow-witted fool."

"Try to seduce me and I'll kill you any way I can," Leindal threatened.

Molent laughed lightly and faced her. "I will have you—in time and by my terms. But for today I am content with my share of victories. Wheas is no longer an obstacle to my plans for the future, thanks to you. His daughter, the princess Celeise, may prove a nuisance, but she can be easily handled. What's more, I was just on my way here to let you know that we've soundly turned back a regiment sent by your husband to retrieve you, without suffering a single casualty of our own."

"The floodgates," Leindal speculated aloud. "You unleashed the lake waters on—"

"Yes, of course," Molent interrupted glibly. It was a sight to behold, I assure you. All in all, these two accomplishments would have been more than enough to satisfy me for one day. But I have discovered even a third reason to rejoice." He reached into his cloak and withdrew Leindal's tiara, the gift from King Pencroft bearing the gem that held the Favo seed. "For the first time, I've taken a close look at this crown of yours, Leindal. It is most interesting, I have to say. Especially the large stone set in the filigree."

The queen looked into Molent's eyes and knew at once that he had guessed at the true heritage of the glistening jewel.

Molent's smile broadened and he laughed triumphantly.

Thirty-Two

The sunset was clearly visible from the Ghetite plains. Blood-red, the sun drifted into a haze of fog and threw vibrant colors against the surrounding cloud formations. Reds, flaming oranges, and deep purples—the colors shifted with the roll of the clouds and the angle of the sun until it seemingly vanished into the glittering sea. Then, like extinguished candlelight, the colors quickly faded to somber, forboding shades of black and gray.

Nuroc watched the transformation from the makeshift camp the Aerdans had pitched a few hundred yards from where the rain of mud had ended its thwarting slide down Mount Velley. The volcano was still visible to the north, crowned with dots of flame marking the torches placed along the battlements of the hidden city. He was helping a group of soldiers fashion a crude fence out of thick shrubs and uprooted saplings that had been deposited at the base of the mountain by the mudslide. A first barrier had already been erected a dozen yards farther out from the campsite. Although neither formation would serve as much of a deterrent in the event of an all-out enemy assault, the fences would hopefully prevent predators or Ghetite spies from sneaking up on the campsite unnoticed. The dead men retrieved from the slide were being buried hastily elsewhere under the light of torches.

"It looks as if we'll be finished by nightfall after all," Tudier said with encouragement.

"From the looks of those clouds, I would guess another storm is blowing in from the coast," Nuroc said, helping to secure the last length of fence into position. "Whatever this fence might keep out, it won't be the wind. I hope the men we sent back for supplies return soon."

"I agree with that," one of the other men groaned, stepping back to observe their handiwork. "When that storm comes, I want four walls around me, no matter how thin they are."

The group of men moved over to help others finish the second fence, so that finally the entire campsite was encircled by the makeshift barriers. They left a few of their number to stand guard while others returned to the camp, which at present consisted of little more than a handful of small fires and a few protective mounds made from stacked saddles. Palem sat before one of the fires with several other officers. Seeing Nuroc and Tudier, the general summoned them over.

The officers discussed at length their precarious position and the various options that lay before them. Some suggested that Palem call in reinforcements in hopes of encircling the volcano and trying to force a surrender from the enemy once they had run out of food or supplies. But Palem saw many flaws in that plan. There was no guarantee the dwindled force of Aerdans could hold off the Ghetites and Shangorans if they chose to come down from the city and fight before the requested reinforcements arrived. And even if the Aerdan forces were bolstered, it was likely that a city of Velley's rumored size would be stocked with sufficient provisions to last indefinitely.

Another suggested, "What if we brought in more troops, then circled the mountain and feigned an assault, charging up the slopes just enough to force the Ghetites to unleash the floodwaters again. We could then pull back the troops with minimal casualties and quickly wage a second attack before the water level in the lake rose back up to the floodgates."

Tudier shook his head and objected, "Who is to say there are not floodgates set lower than those used today, or that the waters of the lake would take more than a few moments to rise back up to flooding level?"

"Besides," Nuroc added, "we all saw the speed with which the water and mud rolled down the mountain. No horse is fast enough to outrace that flow. We would be risking certain death for many men for the sake of an uncertain plan."

"That leaves us with few other choices," Palem said. "We can wait for their next move and hope they will want to negotiate a peace, which seems unlikely. Or we can send a group unarmed up the mountain to bargain for the queen's release. But if I am any judge of Molent and Wheas, they will want the personal assurance of Pencroft regarding any proposed deal.

"I don't think we can wait too long to make a move, however. There are sure to be other enemy troops situated outside the capital, and if we give them the chance to mobilize, we might find ourselves waking up some morning to another bloodbath like that of the meadows, with our troops at the disadvantage."

Nuroc looked past the general at the darkening mountaintop, then said, "When you and Pencroft first sent me forth from Cothe to seek the queen's safe return, you said there are some things one man can do more effectively than an entire battalion. Perhaps if just one of us were to steal up the side of the mountain, he could reach the battlements of Velley unnoticed and see if there was some way of getting inside the walls."

"Two men would be even better," Tudier interjected. "Let Nuroc and me do what we can."

"I don't know . . ." Palem said, staring into the fire and weighing the proposal. Before he could give a definite answer, there came a shout from the other end of the camp.

"Our men come with the supplies!"

Palem rose to his feet. He told Nuroc and Tudier, "Let me think awhile on your idea. You are two of my best men. I'm not sure I want to risk you on so desperate a gambit."

The three of them strode away from the fire toward the troops arriving with supplies from the previous day's campsite. The man at the head of their column rode straight to General Palem, his face alive with excitement.

"General!" he gasped anxiously. "Only a mile back we saw a group of Ghetite horsemen stealing through the brush toward the mountain. Say the word and we will ride and apprehend them!"

"Yes!" Palem cried out. "What good fortune! We can hold them hostage and barter with their leaders. Or, better yet, we can get them to talk and tell us—"

"No," Nuroc interrupted, equally aroused. "Let them go!"

"What?" Palem said, incredulous. "Are you mad?"

"Far from it," Nuroc said quickly, calling Tudier to their side. "Listen quickly. I have a plan! . . ."

Thirty-Three

Under cover of the descending darkness, twelve Ghetite horsemen rode furtively through the dense brush that marked the edge of the plains, casting their eyes from time to time at the distant fires marking the encampment of their Aerdan foes. They were ragged and tired and in no mood to match themselves in battle against the enemy. That could come later. For now, they sought only the refuge of their capital.

They kept their steeds to a canter rather than risk betraying their position with the pummelling of fast hooves on the hardened terrain. The wind was picking up, sending clumps of harragon shrub tumbling across the plains and into the thickets around them. Each time one of the weightless shadows rolled before them, the Ghetites shook with reflexive fear and made their weapons ready to strike, thinking it might be one of the enemy attacking them on foot. Their nerves were on edge, and the chill in the breeze only made them more ill at ease and anxious to leave the plains behind them.

They circled around the mountain, passing by the dislodged earth that had been unleashed hours before by the floodwaters. Soon they had made their way halfway around Mount Velley, reaching the north facing, which bore little resemblance to its ravaged southern counterpart. Instead of being rounded, the facing was split by a deep vertical furrow that extended from a few dozen yards beneath the rim of the volcano all the way to the base of the mountain. The furrow had been formed over the course of centuries by the steady flow of water pouring forth from a natural opening in the side of the mountain. Whenever the lake water inside the extinct volcano rose to the height of the opening, it flowed down in a roaring waterfall, which became the source of a river that flowed away from the mountain to the nearby coast.

It was toward the waterfall that the Ghetites rode, unaware that they were being followed. Among the rambling shrubs of harragon being chased by the wind were two running figures stealing across the plain. Their lungs close to bursting from the strain of their stealthy pursuit, Nuroc and Tudier slowed down and collapsed behind a boulder that afforded them a view of the enemy horsemen. Sweat soaked their skin, and their feet throbbed with a pounding agony from the run. Neither was able to speak for several moments as they sucked in gasp after gasp of the crisp night air.

Then, still keeping an eye on those they followed, Tudier managed to whisper hoarsely, "I knew it! They're the same devilspawn that chased us to the shrine! I'd die for the chance to pass a sword through their ribs!"

"With any luck, we'll have a more fitting revenge," Nuroc said. He stared at the horsemen and the waterfall beyond, feeling a strange sensation. It was as if he had seen or heard about this place before, although he knew it could not be possible. He tried to shake the feeling off, but it persisted.

"It's just as I guessed," Tudier said, also looking at the waterfall and the glisten of moonlight on its cascading surface. "The lake inside the volcano is somehow fed from the ocean, no doubt through some underground connection. They can release water through the floodgates and have the level be replenished as soon as the gates are closed back up. The overflow drains off here and keeps the city forever beyond danger of flooding."

"How do the Ghetites get from here to the city?" Nuroc said. "I see no paths, and the pitch of the slope is too steep to be managed on horseback."

"Look!" Tudier hissed, pointing a finger over the top of the boulder. "They are riding under the waterfall!"

Breaking from their cover, Nuroc and Tudier made their way through wild growths of ferns and flowering shrubs before reaching the bare rock of the furrow that embraced the waterfall. There was a wide, deep pool where the cascading water foamed and swirled before trailing off down the river and back to the sea, completing its incredible cycle. The banks surrounding the pool rose perpendicular to the surface of the water, and the Ghetites were about to vanish from sight along a narrow pathway that had been chiseled from the raw stone and ran behind the waterfall.

Nuroc and Tudier proceeded cautiously along the path, pulling out their weapons and remaining alert to the first sign of danger. Although they could no longer see the Ghetites, they had no way of knowing whether the converse was true. They advanced, trying to ignore the creeping fear that the horsemen might be lying in wait behind the watery curtain before them, watching their every move.

The crashing of the waterfall was deafening, and the spray that rose from the pool was so dense that Nuroc and Tudier felt they were caught up in another tempest. The pathway was wet and slick, and it seemed a miracle that the horses had been able to travel the narrow course without slipping off into the pool.

As they came closer to the pool's end, Nuroc saw where the ledge continued behind the waterfall, although it was too dark to see more than a few feet into the narrow clearing down which the Ghetites had disappeared.

The two friends paused and looked to one another. The maddening crash of the waterfall made speech futile, but their expressions conveyed more than any words could hope to. Nodding gravely, the young men gently touched their swords together in a symbol of brotherhood, then turned back to the way before them and moved on.

It had been dark enough out in the open; behind the waterfall little moonlight pierced through the forceful veil that would crush either man to a pulp if he were to lose his balance and fall into its path. Between the blackness and the ear-numbing roar of the falls, Nuroc felt as if he were going mad. His senses scrambled by the intense overload, he was besieged by an urge to break into a run or dive off the path, anything to stop the noise and end the blackness. Instead, he concentrated on the next step before him, forcing himself to move slowly and ignore the hellish surroundings. Tudier had the flat of his blade pressed against Nuroc's side to help guide his way, and Nuroc felt an assurance in the contact. Alone, he feared he might succumb to the madness.

Five, ten, twenty feet passed and still they crept along the narrow passage, cold wet rock on their left and instant death on their right. No relief seemed in sight. Then, just ahead, Nuroc heard a different tone to the constant rumble that assaulted his ears. There was a hollow ring to the roar. Soon he reached its source, a wide opening in the face of the mountain. He ducked into it with Tudier close behind, swords at the ready.

They found themselves in a swollen archway that gave way to

a narrower tunnel. It was lit by the same eerie crystals that illuminated the catacombs beneath the sorcerer's gardens in Cothe. The tunnel extended only twenty feet before it abruptly turned, and the Ghetites had already moved around the turn. Nuroc and Tudier were alone in the archway.

After pausing to secure a firmer grip on their sanity, the two young men started down the tunnel, but stopped short of making the turn. Instead, they slowly leaned forward and peered around the corner. All that they had heretofore witnessed in no way prepared them for the sight before them.

Before them lay a subterranean cavern, thirty feet wide and twice as long. Condensation sparkled off the craggy walls and dripped from stalactites similar to those Nuroc had seen in the Gungsa cave outside of Centinara. There were torches set in sconces hammered at intervals along the walls, and their light was given off by glowcrystals with a radiance that surpassed any flame.

The horsemen were at the far end of the cavern. Half of them were guiding their horses onto a large wooden platform connected by thick ropes to an overhead frame. The frame, in turn, was attached to an even thicker series of cables that reached up through a hollowing in the roof of the cave.

Once the riders were in position on the platform, the other Ghetites climbed a stone stairway up to a ledge wide enough for them to stand on either side of a log that protruded in from the outer wall of the cave. Wooden pegs had been hammered into the log, providing a sure hold for the men as they strained in unison and pushed forward so that the log moved farther into the wall of the cave.

Tudier looked at Nuroc and whispered, "What are they doing?"

Nuroc shook his head, continuing to stare at both the platform and the group of men on the ledge. Once the Ghetites had pushed the log all the way into the wall, the platform below them suddenly jolted and began to rise! The horsemen quieted their nervous steeds as they were carried slowly upward, past the men on the stone ledge and up through the opening in the cave's roof.

"They're being carried up a shaft to the city," Nuroc surmised, keeping his voice low as he watched on with amazement. There was something unsettling about the scene before him, something beyond its unnatural wonder. The more he tried to focus on the recurring sensation, the more it continued to elude him, however.

"What should we do?" Tudier said. "There's only a handful of men now. Should we attack?"

"No, not yet," Nuroc answered. "We're safe here for the time being. Let's wait."

Wait they did, watching the men near the platform. The remaining Ghetites remained on the ledge, staring up at the opening through which the platform had vanished. Several minutes passed. Then, above the outside roar of the waterfall, the echoing blare of a horn sounded, down the vertical shaft. At once, the Ghetites rushed back to the log, securing their grips and pulling it back out from the wall. When they had done so, they scurried down the steps to their horses, unwrapping their reins from the post straddled across two stalagmites.

Presently, the platform descended to the cavern floor, empty. The Ghetites loaded their steeds onto the wooden slats as the first crew had, but only one of them stayed with the horses. The others stepped off and returned to the ledge and once more put their weight to the log. As before, the log moved closer to the outer wall, and the platform began to ascend. This time, the Ghetites hurried to the edge and, when the platform was passing them by, they clambered aboard. Seconds later, they were carried up through the opening and the chamber was soon vacated.

"I don't believe it!" Tudier said. He moved around the bend in the tunnel to enter the cavern, but Nuroc grabbed hold of his tunic and stopped him.

"The wheels beneath the waterfall!" Nuroc said excitedly.

"What?" Tudier cried out, looking at his comrade. "What are you talking about?"

Nuroc stole into the abandoned chamber long enough to grab one of the crystalline torches, then headed back toward the archway through which they had entered. Tudier followed him uncertainly, grimacing at the increasing loudness of the waterfall. He saw Nuroc put his hands to his ears and did the same.

Once he had stepped back out on the narrow causeway that ran between the rock facing and the waterfall, the torch lit up the treacherous passage, undoused by the crashing spray. Nuroc looked up. Mist drenched his face, but he blinked away the water and grinned triumphantly at what he saw.

Twenty feet up, at the same level as the ledge inside the cavern where the Ghetites had pushed the log, a massive wheel reached out into the flow of the waterfall. The wheel was made of evenly spaced iron plates that lay flat against the force of the falls. Resting on an axle supported by twin wooden beams, the wheel spun fiercely on contact with the water. Squinting hard, Nuroc could also see that cables were attached to the rim of the wheel and reaching into the opening through which the Ghetites had pushed the log. As the wheel moved, so did the cables.

Nuroc nudged Tudier and shouted in his ear, above the drone of the falls, "The wheel is part of a pulley that works the platform. I'm certain of it. The pressure of the waterfall on the wheel sets the pulley into motion. When they pull the wheel away, the platform comes back down."

"It's ingenious," Tudier exclaimed loudly. "How did you know to look for this? You spoke of the wheel before we even saw it!"

"I'm not sure," Nuroc hollered. "I think I dreamed about it last night. It's not important, though. Look, over there!" Nuroc pointed to the rock facing a few yards from them, where a series of ladderlike rungs stuck out from the stone at regular intervals. "Come, let us see if we can find some more answers!"

Nuroc took the crystalline torch and slipped it into his belt so that he could light the way and still have both hands free. He edged along the narrow walk until he reached the first rungs, then started up, with Tudier close behind.

The rungs bit coldly into their hands, and the errant spray from the falls stung them like whip lashes. They leaned as far in toward the wall as they could and slowly climbed upward.

The waterwheel continued to spin furiously as they came up beside it and stared inquisitively at its intricate construction. They could also see through the opening carved out of the rock that led to the ledge from which the Ghetites had operated the movable platform. A series of taut cables reached like webs in all directions, wrapped around strangely made wheels with tooth-like edges. As they watched, one of the turning wheels touched the edge of another and started it moving as well. Slowly, the rounded log that the Ghetites had manned began to move of its own accord, pulling the waterwheel away from the falls.

Nuroc glanced down. Tudier met his gaze with a look of astonishment. Nuroc hesitated a moment, then pointed upward. Tudier shrugged his shoulders, then nodded and they continued their ascent.

Fifty feet higher up, they came to yet another opening, where a similar waterwheel rested in a stationary position beyond range of the falls. Staring past the wheel and into the cavity behind it, Nuroc and Tudier saw a crew of six Ghetite soldiers busying themselves with a game of squarebones on either side of a pegged log like that which operated the waterwheel below.

Nuroc saw that the rungs continued to reach even farther up the side of the mountain. But he refrained from pushing on. He waved Tudier down and, as quickly as was possible under the circumstances, they returned to the passageway near the base of the waterfall. They ducked under the arch and went far enough down the tunnel so they could speak without shouting.

"That second wheel works the floodgates, right?" Tudier said, wiping water from his face and rubbing his numbed hands together.

"Only one level of them, I would guess," Nuroc said. "There are probably more wheels reaching out all the way up to the rim of the volcano. They keep guards stationed near each wheel so that they can unleash floodwaters wherever they want at a moment's notice. We could have sent all our troops up the mountainside at different times and different places and they all would have been swept up by more slides."

"What is to be done, then?" Tudier asked. "There must be some way we can take advantage of what we've learned."

"There is," Nuroc said. "It will take some doing, but it's our best chance; maybe our only chance. What you have to do is sneak back to camp and get together a group of two dozen men, then come back. In the meantime, I'll stay here. I have a few more things to check on. . . ."

Thirty-Five

Although it lacked the opulent splendor of Cothe, the Ghetite capital of Velley was no less magnificent a city. Surely it was unique in all the land, built as it was from the solid rock of Mount Velley. Unlike other towns and cities, Velley was not erected by the placement of shops and dwellings upon the ground, but rather by the intricate burrowing into the surface of the craterous rim of the extinct volcano. Seen from above, Velley consisted of honeycombed orifices and leveled terraces overlooking the deep blue lake it surrounded. The only visible structures that had been set upon the natural stone were the crenelated battlements that had been erected flush with the uppermost rim of the volcano. The battlements were made of stone blocks carved from that part of the crater hollowed out for the interiors of shops, lodges, and public buildings.

The lake itself was round and as wide as the farthest distance between the city walls of Cothe. The surrounding city was large enough to support a population of several thousand. Of that number, half were normally soldiers. Following the skirmishes with Aerda over the past few days, however, less than two hundred troops had managed to return to the sanctuary of Velley, and many of them were Shangorans. That left less than two thousand civilians, and, as the dawn sun sent up its first glimmer of light over the rim of the crater, every one of them was gathered on the broad terrace between the waters of the lake and the royal palace. Women, old men, young children—they all stood together, huddling for warmth under the cloud-streaked sky, and turned their desperate eyes toward the palace balcony framed in a riot of ivy and creeping fig.

Some were silent, but others exchanged worried murmurings, speculating as to the reason they had been summoned to appear on the terrace at so early an hour. For each ten people, there were ten separate reasons, each one asserted with looks of knowing that served little to mask the true concern that tore at hearts of the civilian Ghetites.

"I saw them bring the queen of Aerda into the palace," a grizzled peddler whispered. "Soon we will hear that the Aerdans have agreed to pay each of us the queen's weight in gold as her ransom!"

"Untrue!" gossiped the woman beside him. "They have Queen Leindal, I'll grant you that much. But she came to Ghetite willingly, having slain her husband, Pencroft of Aerda. She plans to announce that she is granting both Ghetite and Shangora portions of her former kingdom in exchange for complete rule over that part of Aerda that remains!"

A thin, audacious youth pushed his way between the peddler and the woman, insisting, "You both are mistaken. Take a look about the palace. See all the troops?" A few heads turned and confirmed that almost the entire surviving militia had gathered at strategic points surrounding the ruling house of Velley. The youth continued, "General Wheas will come forth shortly and declare a state of emergency. We will all be forced to don armor and take up weapons, then charge down the mountain to clash with the Aerdans camped out on the plain!"

Similar debates and arguments ensued among the others, filling the terrace with the steady buzz of conversation. The armed Ghetites and Shangorans about the palace watched the masses nervously. They knew the reason for the gathering and feared the possible consequences. They knew what had to be done in the best interests of both Ghetite and Shangora, but they were not as certain of the people's willingness to accept the changed circumstances. Along with their swords, they were all armed with crossbows, a more fitting weapon for striking from a distance.

Inside the main hall of the palace, Molent of Shangora peered through a slit in the velvet draperies drawn across the window overlooking the terrace. He stood frozen, with one arm outstretched, as the royal tailors finished the final alterations to the coronation robe, an affair of crushed velvet lined with the fur of the long-extinct minhur. It had been shortened to fit his compact frame, just as the imperial crown had been padded with fur lining to accommodate his smaller head.

He turned away from the window and walked back to the small, elaborately designed raft that rested on a four-wheeled cart in the center of the hall. Fashioned of the finest timber and shimmering with silver and gold plating, the raft contained chests filled with treasure, a table topped with the makings of a banquet feast, countless bouquets of brilliant flowers, and three scenoak coffins resting on a bed of kindling. The coffins were ornately carved and decorated with inset gems and filigree. One of the coffins was sealed and contained personal belongings of Augage, first king of the Ghetites. General Wheas lay in repose in a second casket, while Queen Leindal of Aerda sat upright in the third, glaring out at Molent as she struggled in vain against her bonds.

"This is your last opportunity to change your mind," Molent told Leindal calmly.

"Never," Leindal said with bitter finality.

"Better to be a living queen than a dead one," Molent said. "I can still tell them that Wheas died by another's hand. They would accept you as their own in time. You could—"

"I will never serve as your queen, just as I will never betray my country!" Leindal said hotly.

As she writhed in the coffin, trying to work her hands and legs free, Molent strode to the edge of the raft and reached over, grasping her head in his hands and forcing a kiss upon her lips.

"I could make you happy," Molent said. "With the seed of the Favo tree, we have the means to live forever, side by side—"

The queen spat in the Shangoran's dark face. "Take your kiss back, wretch!"

Enraged, Molent struck out with the back of his hand, slapping Leindal across the face. "Insolent whore!" he screamed, wiping the spit from his face.

Leindal spat again, and Molent slapped her with even more force. She wavered, then collapsed, half-falling over the side of the coffin. Molent quickly tied a gag around her mouth and eased her back into the coffin.

Clapping his hands, he summoned forth his attendants and shouted a few angry orders before storming up the spiral staircase leading to the upper level and balcony. He paused in an antechamber, pouring a dusky liquid from a onyx decanter into a matching goblet. He sniffed the drink, then quickly drained it. Licking his lips at the aftertaste, he smiled at the warm sensation radiated by the liquid as it went through his system. His anger gave way to feelings of power and confidence. He looked at his reflection in the polished surface of the mirror and liked what he saw.

With a poised swagger, Molent strode down the corridor to a room guarded by four of his most loyal officers. He nodded to them and they stepped aside, letting him into the chamber.

"Come with me to the balcony," Molent told them, "And bring your shields. I don't have to tell you why."

His cohorts nodded silently and strapped on thick bucklers of brass and jaunwood. Together, they crossed the lavishly adorned throne room and went out onto the balcony.

At first sight of Molent, the crowd fell silent with expectation. People looked to one another with wonder. The few who broke the silence with whispered mutterings all posed the same question. Where was General Wheas, natural successor to the throne of Ghetite?

When he had the attention of the masses, Molent raised his voice and cried out, "Citizens of Ghetite! There has been treachery in the halls of the palace this past night. General Wheas was slain by the hand of Queen Leindal of Aerda. Until such time as you can determine a king to take his place, I, Molent of Shangora, claim rule over Ghetite as a protectorate of my own kingdom. We must stand united against the Aerdan infidels who now hover about your capital like jackals on the scent of carrion. Let anyone who contests this decision step forward now and give his reasons."

The people were stunned. For all of their gossipmongering, few had ventured any opinion that truly reflected the circumstances before them. They were unprepared for the truth, and it took time for the revelation to sink in. Meanwhile, the troops about the palace made themselves increasingly visible, raising their bows and feeding bolts into the taut strings. The officers flanking Molent moved closer to him, holding their shields in position to quickly deflect any object hurled in Molent's direction.

If there was any opposition to Molent's proclamation, no one had the courage to step forward and voice his or her dissent. The tense silence was broken by a renewed murmuring as the citizens spoke to one another in words of shock and disbelief.

Molent raised his voice once more. "I need from you an affirmation of my interim rule. Let all those who pledge to support me as leader of Ghetite as well as Shangora signify by shouting 'aye'!"

From the balcony, Molent stared down at the people cramming the terrace. He was to be their king, whether they liked it or not. In his mind, their only choice at this moment was between willing subservience or an allegiance earned by military force.

"Aye," came the first calls, a faint ripple through the crowd.

"Aye!" others joined in, raising their voices, resigned to the inevitable.

"AYE!" The people shouted together, raising their fists above their heads for emphasis. Over and over they repeated the cry, using it to purge themselves of paranoia, fear, and hatred. *Aye,* they shouted, and in the end, they were close to believing it.

His command established, Molent beamed triumphantly at his minions. He would make them forget Augage and Wheas. He would even make them forget Ghetite; because he knew, deep in his heart, that it would not be long before there was only one kingdom along the western coast of Dorban. Ghetite would be merged with Shangora, and he would be ruler of both. Then, once they had rebuilt their strength, they would smite once more against their eastern neighbors. But, for now, he had to deal with the present.

Molent raised his arms and gestured for the masses to be quiet. After they complied, he waited a moment longer until he was sure he had their full attention. "Today there will be two burials in Velley. One will be sad, the other joyful," he boomed forth.

"As is customary with the long line of kings who ruled over Dorban before the division of the land into kingdoms, on this day we shall bury at sea your former leaders. It will be a mournful chore, to be certain, but know in your hearts that their deaths will not have been in vain. Once they have been buried, we will take to the plains and bury the Aerdans who dare to camp within our borders!"

Swept up by the force of Molent's rhetoric, the citizens of Ghetite burst forth with spontaneous cheers. Gone were their reservations about Molent. Like the militia, they saw the need for quick unity and firm resolve, and they seemed at one in their willingness to flock behind Molent, foreigner though he was.

Molent basked awhile in the adulation, then turned on the balcony and looked to the roofs overhead. He gave a signal to the guards stationed there, and the men at once set down their crossbows in favor of polished horns. Lining up side by side, they raised the horns and broke the morning air with the low notes of a mournful dirge.

Down below, the people lapsed back to a reverent quietude and submission. The gates of the main hall were opened outward, and attendants brought forth the funeral raft. Sighs rose as the citizens craned for a glimpse at the decorous vessel. The sighs turned to new whisperings once it was realized that there were not two, but three coffins on the raft. Besides the closed casket containing the belongings of Augage and the opened box that held General Wheas, there was the third coffin, wherein lay Queen Leindal of Aerda.

The raft was wheeled to the edge of the terrace, where the cool waters of the lake slapped gently against the stone. The attendants carefully lowered the raft into the water, then held it moored alongside the terrace as the trumpeters blew the final notes of their dirge.

As the final notes hung in the still air, Molent cried out, "It is the custom to have servants sent with kings to their watery graves, to assist them in their needs as they await passage to the celestial realm.

"But this is a special situation today. Downhill there are Aerdans plotting our overthrow this very minute. Were they to have their way, we would all be servants to the whims of their

King Pencroft. This being the case, what better act of defiance can there be but to send their own queen to her death and subservience to the will of our slain kings; one who died by her own deceitful hand? Do you approve?''

Again the masses cried out their approval. *''AYE!''*

"So be it!'' Molent decreed as soon as he could be heard. "That justice might be best served, Queen Leindal will be cast out on the raft while she still lives, so that she might have time to fully consider the magnitude of her crime. Attendants, ignite the raft and send it out into the lake!''

As Molent and his followers watched on, the grim-faced attendants took lighted torches and touched flame to the kindling piled high around the three coffins. Then, as the fire spread to form a blazing wreath, the attendants reached for long poles and gently pushed the raft out farther into the lake.

Because the opening through which the lake's overflow ran off was located at the far rim of the crater, there was a slight, natural current that pulled the raft toward it. Away it drifted from the terrace, moving out across the center of the lake, sending its black plumes of smoke rolling up toward the already-clouded skies. The farther out the raft flowed, the faster it moved and the more flames it fanned across its treasured belongings.

Then, as the raft was three-quarters of the way across the smooth-surfaced water and the flames were about to catch fire to the hearty wood of the caskets, a strange sound fell across the craterous city.

Silence.

Not the silence of before, which was merely the absence of human voices or the trod of footsteps across the stone pave of the terrace. This was a silence that the citizens of Velley had never known, and it took some time for them to realize the meaning of it.

Molent was among the first to see it, staring out across the lake, over the top of the burning raft. His face went livid and he stabbed a narrow finger in the direction he was looking.

"There!'' he wailed, his cool aplomb suddenly shattered. "Someone has closed off the waterfall!''

Indeed, a handful of men could be seen as small specks along the far rim of the crater, scrambling around the large slab of flattened metal they had managed to slide down across the source of the waterfall, silencing its once-steady roar.

As the gathering at the opposite end of the city watched on with stupefied awe, one of the men near the dammed opening flung himself headlong into the waters of the lake and began to swim toward the burning raft. With the waterfall blocked, there was no longer any current in the lake, and the raft slowed its drifting. Flames began to lick at the side of the three coffins.

The swimming figure stroked his arms deftly through the rippling water, clearing the distance to the raft and then splashing at the fire from all sides until it subsided and only smoke rose from the blackened offerings.

Taking care not to burn himself, the swimmer pulled himself aboard the raft, which had not burned so much that it could not support his weight.

It was Nuroc!

Rushing to the coffins, he ripped off Queen Leindal's gag and stared down at her. Her face was covered with ash but had not been burned, and yet she lay still in the charred box.

Nuroc rushed to the edge of the raft and cupped a hand into the lake. He took the water back and sprinkled it on the queen, but she still did not respond. Desperate, he leaned over her and placed his lips over hers, covering her nostrils with his fingers as he tilted her head back and lent his breath to her lungs.

It was only after he had repeated the ritual several times that he was able to pull back and see the queen begin to breathe on her own. Nuroc went to the edge of the raft for more water, spilling it over Leindal's lips until she swallowed and opened her eyes.

Having never laid eyes upon Nuroc before, she looked up at him with an expression of shock and fear. He assured her, "You are safe now, your majesty. I am sent by King Pencroft himself."

"But, I—"

"Be still for now," Nuroc told her. "Gather your strength. And trust me, all will be well now."

Far across the lake, Molent had other intentions. Vehement with rage, he shouted up to the parapets, "After them! Riddle them with arrows and put down this insurrection before it spreads!"

One of the officers standing beside Molent, a burly man called Greer, took a closer look at the men who had blocked the waterfall and told Molent soberly, "Those are not rebels, your highness. They are Aerdans!"

"Impossible!" Molent shouted, but when he looked again he realized it was so. He roared back to the other troops, "All the more reason to snuff them. Hurry!"

Making haste, Molent's troops charged away from the palace and made their way along the wide ledge of stone that wound along the lake's edge. It was not long, however, before they found that the way before them was no longer in sight.

"The lake is rising!" they shouted fearfully. "The way to the Aerdans is flooded!" They quickly loaded their bows and let fly with a volley of arrows, but it was too far a distance to their target. The shafts fell short of the funeral raft, much less the mouth of the waterfall.

The frantic warning of the troops spread terror through the residents of Velley like a plague. Their horrified gazes looked to the terrace edge where, only moments before, the funeral raft had rested on solid ground. Water now rolled across the terrace toward them, pushing them back in a state of panic. Screams and cries filled the air as Ghetites shoved against one another in the scramble to higher ground. Molent shouted down orders from the balcony, but he had lost his hold over the people. They were now ruled by fear and fear alone.

Greer now told his leader, "You must use the regal chime to get their attention and regain control. It is your only chance."

"Of course!" Molent exclaimed. Motioning to the other men around him, he quickly bade them to follow him as he retreated from the balcony and made for the stairs that led to the roof of the palace. There, untended, was the massive brass disk, mounted in a perpendicular frame. A mallet hung by a woven cord from the framework, and as Molent and the other officers put their hands to their ears, Greer took up the mallet and slammed it against the disk.

The chime sounded with a force so loud that the vibrations alone made Molent shake where he stood. Its deep, resonant tone was said to carry for miles in all directions, and it took only two more chimes before the citizens were shaken into silence as if they had been slapped in the face. Most of them had taken refuge on the battlements or the rooftops of their homes and shops.

Although he could barely hear himself above the lingering ring of the chime in his ears, Molent still shouted at the top of his lungs, "We are far from lost! Now that the chimes have alerted the men below, they will open the floodgates and the lake will recede! Perhaps the floodwaters will be strong enough to crash onto the plains and disrupt the other Aerdans, giving us time to prepare a—"

"Your time has already passed you by!" Nuroc bellowed from out on the lake, drawing attention his way. His voice carried loudly as he spoke through a megaphone he had made by breaking the bottom of a large stone urn. "Aerdans now command the waterwheels, and they will not open the floodgates unless you surrender and order your men to throw down their weapons!"

"You lie!" Molent howled back contemptuously.

Nuroc grinned from the raft and looked around him. He shouted through the urn, "Then why is it the waters of the lake continue to rise?" He turned away from Molent and appealed directly to the terrified citizens of the flooded city. "You! People of Ghetite! You have already let Molent poison your minds with his self-serving orations. Would you have him destroy your city as well, trying to hold onto a crown that is not rightfully his?"

"It is *you* who seek to destroy us!" Molent cried out to Nuroc. "Do not twist the facts about, dog!"

Nuroc ignored Molent's protests and continued to direct his remarks to the populace. "We have our queen back! Our only quarrel now is with those who still seek the overthrow of our country. Do not fool yourselves! If your troops do not surrender and your leaders do not agree to seek a peaceful settlement to our differences, Velley will sink beneath the waters and you will all be washed over the rim of the crater to face the same fate as those Aerdans who died along the mountain slopes yesterday. It is your decision, and you don't have much longer to make it!"

Even as Nuroc spoke, the lake waters began to spill into the lower levels of homes and public buildings. Wooden carts began to float eerily down the submerged streets. Children cried and women wept with desolation. Even the militia had been drained of its urge to resist.

Only Molent refused to consider Nuroc's words. He turned to the military and roared, "Find boats and rafts and take to the waters! Still that mongrel's cries and see that his fellow Aerdans taste the tips of our arrows!"

The men of the military looked up at their king, but made no move to carry out his orders.

"Treason!" Molent wailed, his voice cracking with emotion. "I'll slay you one by one with my bare hands, you cowardly vermin!"

As Molent took a step across the roof in the direction of the nearest soldiers, Greer reached out and grabbed the king by the shoulder, pulling him back. When Molent spun about and tried to draw a knife on Greer, the officer heaved his shoulders in a quick motion and sent the king falling backward over the end of the roof. Molent gave forth a surprised scream that ended abruptly as he slammed viciously onto the terrace where his ephemeral subjects had stood and offered their allegiance minutes before. Now the terrace was empty save for his corpse and the advancing floodwaters.

Greer looked out over the lake as he threw down his sword and said solemnly, "We accept your terms and surrender!"

One by one, the other members of the militia, Ghetite and Shangoran alike, dropped their weapons. The people of Velley watched on with blank faces.

Out on the raft, Nuroc heaved a great sigh and looked over his shoulder. He signaled to Tudier and Palem, who stood on the stone ledge near the sheet of metal they had placed across the drainage opening for the lake. Palem and Tudier joined the men who had already moved over to the metal sheet. Together, they pulled at the sheet until it gave way and the first torrent of overflow spewed forth through the opening, breaking the silence that marked the end of one era in Velley and the beginning of another.

Epilogue

As night folded in over the city of Velley, it was Aerdan soldiers who patrolled the parapets and streets, Aerdan soldiers who stood guard over the royal palace, where lavish feasting was in progress. The banquet hall was rich with the scent of roast mutton and boiled vegetables, the aroma of sweetbreads and fresh fruit, the heady smell of wine and ale. Serving tables had been filled with the varied offerings shortly before dusk, and now little was left but scraps and crumbs. Throughout the chamber, men sat back in hand-hewn chairs, their hungers and thirsts sated. More than a few groaned slightly from their overindulgence, stifling belches into closed fists and rubbing their swollen stomachs in hopes of appeasing the demons of indigestion.

For all the elaborateness and grandeur of the setting, however, this had not been a festive celebration. There had been no singing, no joyous banter, no mad cavorting. There might be a time for such carrying on later, but for now the men were content with the realization that there would be an end to the bloodshed that had wiped out the better part of a generation. The aura of uncertain peace hung in the air, and it was a feeling that would take some time to adjust to. Representatives from Aerda, Ghetite, and Shangora sat together like brothers, but the fraternity was brittle and tenuous. Long-sworn enemies avoided each other's eyes and wallowed in mutual uneasiness. It was a start, a first step and no more.

When the meal was completed and the servants had begun to remove the platters and trays, the Ghetites and Shangorans took their leave quietly, escorted by Aerdan guards to their chambers in the adjacent building. The Aerdan officers remained in the company of their queen. Relaxing some, they spoke more, filling the room with a buzz of light conversation until the servants had done their part and departed for the night.

"Well, then," General Palem said at last, seated beside Leindal at the head of the table where his officers had congregated. "In the morning, I shall be returning to Cothe with Queen Leindal and report to the king. This being the case, it will be necessary for someone here to assume command in my absence and see that the peace is kept."

There was silence in the room as the officers looked to Palem expectantly. Palem, in turn, looked back at only one of them.

"You are now a captain," he told Nuroc calmly.

Nuroc was stunned. "Captain?"

"That's right," Palem replied, smiling for the first time that evening. "I'm naming Tudier to your post, so it seems I have no choice but to promote you again."

To either side of Nuroc, other officers graciously offered their congratulations. Tudier nodded across the table at his friend, unable to restrain a grin of great pride and admiration. Even the queen put in a word of support for the decision. "I am sure my husband agrees with Palem's choice."

"I've hardly had time to get used to being a lieutenant," Nuroc said with a smirk.

"You won't miss it, I assure you," Palem said. "Now, do you accept or do I have to order the job upon you?"

Nuroc paused to reflect. So much had happened the past day. First, the surrender of Ghetite and Shangora, then the provisional peace accord reached with spokesmen representing the enemy countries, Greer of Shangora and Princess Celeise of Ghetite, daughter of General Wheas. Now he was being asked to assume captaincy over men he had fought beside as a mere recruit only days before. It hardly seemed possible.

"I am honored by your offer," Nuroc said finally, "but I did have hopes of returning to Cothe and seeing Myrania."

"If this Myrania is a woman like myself," Queen Leindal interjected, "she would be angry with you for passing up the opportunity before you, Nuroc."

Palem added, "She can be here in a matter of days, anyway. Surely you can manage to wait that much longer."

Nuroc's face reddened with embarrassment as the others, including the queen, chuckled to one another. Tudier came over to his friend and slapped him across the shoulder, goading, "Come now, Nuroc. You were captain once when we recruits named you our leader on the way to Cothe. You accepted the title then. Why not now?"

Nuroc shrugged his shoulders and smiled broadly. "Very well. Captain it is!"

There was a subdued but well-meant round of cheers as Tudier reached for a flagon of deep red wine and filled the others' goblets. He was about to propose a toast when the doors to the banquet hall burst inward and two guards strode fitfully to the table with troubled expressions.

"What is it?" Palem said with sudden concern. All eyes turned to the guards. The taller of them spoke.

"Princess Celeise of Ghetite has just slain two of our guards and escaped over the top of the battlements!"

"What!" Palem burst out with indignation. "Have you apprehended her?"

The tall guard shook his head grimly. "She took flight down the mudslide in some sort of sled with runners that held a course on the slick ground. I fear she is bound for the river and the open seas!"

This revelation sat heavy upon those seated around the table. Princess Celeise, who only hours before had agreed to tentative terms for peace, had already broken with those terms and fled the capital. It was an ill omen.

The shorter of the guards stepped forward and held something forth toward Queen Leindal. "We found this by the bodies of the slain guards."

Leindal gave an involuntary gasp. "The tiara!" She took it from the guard as the officers looked on with confusion. Seeing their wonder, she continued, "It was given to me by my husband on the eve of my abduction. He had chosen it from among the plunder taken from the obelisk. Molent had it in his possession last night, but Celeise must have secured it from him somehow. It is an invaluable crown!"

"Good that the princess dropped it in her flight, then," one of the officers said.

"You don't understand!" the queen said, her face pale with dread. "The value of the tiara was in the gem set in its center. Within that jewel is the seed to the Favo tree, whose fruit brings immortality."

Palem frowned, staring at the crown in the woman's hand. "But I see no such gem."

"That is what I'm trying to say!" Leindal told him excitedly. "The gem is gone! Princess Celeise has taken it with her. I am positive of it!"

"The gods help us!" an officer groaned dismally.

"Unless she is caught and stopped before she makes use of the seed," Queen Leindal forewarned, "it is she that the gods will help, for she will be like unto one of them! Immortal!"

Again cold silence befell the chamber. Almost in unison, both Palem and Nuroc lifted their gazes from the vandalized tiara and stared into each other's eyes.

"You have a new mission," Palem said gravely.

Nuroc slowly set down his goblet, as did the others.

There would be no toast tonight.

COMING SOON

DEATH STALKS THE SEA